Sandi 2-

the book -

27/10/2004 Orly Castel-Bloom

HUMAN PARTS

ORLY CASTEL-BLOOM

HUMAN PARTS

Translated from the Hebrew by Dalya Bilu

A VERBA MUNDI BOOK

DAVID R. GODINE · Publisher · Boston

First U.S. edition published in 2003 by
DAVID R. GODINE, *Publisher*
Post Office Box 450
Jaffrey, New Hampshire 03452
www.godine.com

First published in Canada by Key Porter Books Limited,
Toronto Canada 2003.

Library of Congress Cataloging-in-Publication Data

Castel-Bloom, Orly.
Castel-Bloom, Orly, 1960–
[òHalaòkim enoshiyim. English]
Human parts / by Orly Castel Bloom ;
translated from the Hebrew by Dalya Bilu.—1st ed.
p. cm.
ISBN 1-56792-256-2
I. Bilu, Dalya. II. Title.
PJ5054.C37H3513   2003
892.4'36—dc21   2003013520

FIRST U.S. EDITION
Printed in the United States of America

FOR MY CHILDREN,
OSNAT & HANOCH

PART ONE

CHAPTER ONE

IT WAS AN EXCEPTIONAL WINTER. Not at all like the brief winter the inhabitants of Israel were used to, but the kind that seems to collect leftovers from winters in other parts of the world and donate them to the Middle East: here and there a cloudburst, a shower of rain, followed by many days of pleasant but worrying sunshine, bringing a message of drought, hunger, poverty, unemployment, recession, boredom, despair and existential panic.

The winter of the year 20— arrived in this part of the world after eight years of drought, during which the Israelis were threatened with the prospect that the Sea of Galilee and the rivers leading to it and to the Mediterranean Sea would dry up forever, and the country in which the desert had not long ago been made to bloom would revert to being arid and parched.

As soon as this extraordinary winter hit, at the end of the month of Tishri, it wiped out the memory of the hard years of drought that had preceded it. It was as if the long days of heat waves and intolerable sun had never existed, and it had always been cold in Israel.

The common explanation for this deviation from the seasonal norm was that a cold weather system had descended upon the Middle East straight from the North Pole at the beginning of Tishri and settled down here for the duration of the winter. This system brought with it low temperatures for the coast of at the most five degrees Celsius during the day, and half a degree to two degrees at night.

In the mountains the temperature was almost always below zero. In the low places there was permanent frost, and ice covered the valleys at night and sometimes also during the day.

The country was drenched with every form of precipitation. The ground water gushed up from the wells and burst out, and in many areas there were floods that led to loss of life and property. Navy ships were anchored in places no one could have imagined possible before the onslaught and transformed the unimaginable into a reality. Sailboats were seen in Petah Tikva, in Or Yehuda, in Mazkeret Batya, in Kfar Saba, in Afula, in Umm al-Fahm, in almost every town and settlement flooded by the rising waters. The Sea of Galilee was stormy and its waves rose to great heights and continually washed over the many abandoned restaurants on the waterfront. Already by the end of the month of Heshvan the lake had risen above its upper red line, and even though the sluice gates to the Jordan were opened, the Tiberias shoreline advanced rapidly into the city streets, and residents living at sea-level or slightly above it hurried to evacuate their homes and move to higher and safer places.

Raindrops the size of olives fell in multitudes, and during the intervals between downpours, there was an almost constant drizzle that left the ground permanently wet.

Hailstones, sculpted in the various layers of the clouds, burst out of them in different shapes and sizes and pelted the earth, injuring the leaves, birds, shutters, cars and people in their path.

At times these hailstones were gigantic, with a circumference of over five centimeters, and sometimes they were flat and sharp, with fascinating geometrical forms.

It snowed in the hills, on the plateaus, and less frequently during this strange season, even on the coastal plains. In the high places the snow was sometimes over two and a half meters deep.

Since buildings in Israel are not designed to accommodate such quantities of snow, hail or rain, the roofs of numerous buildings collapsed on their occupants. Owing to the heavy snow drifts, trees planted by the pioneers early in the previous century fell to the ground.

Rescue teams and the Home Front Command worked overtime, and won praise for their efforts and determination, both from the nation and its spokesmen in the media. The weather forecasters, especially those appearing on television, became celebrities, and the public couldn't get enough of them. This being the case, they began to take part in commercials for heaters, umbrellas, raincoats and other accessories for the protection of Israelis taken by surprise by the cold and the moisture, and thus made a lot of money on the side, which made them all the more popular and expensive.

Every evening the nation waited for their pronouncements and hung on their every word as though they were prophets. During that strange winter the popular weather forecasters frequently took part in game shows where the first to give the correct answer won the prize. These shows were in great demand, as their high ratings attest. One forecaster won half a million shekels for the correct answer to the question, what is the life expectancy of an Asiatic lion? The next day he was fatally injured in a shooting attack when he was on his way to Ikea to buy new furniture for his home in Ariel. One week later he died of his wounds. His funeral was broadcasted on both the big national TV channels.

Yet, as if the outlandish winter wasn't enough, the period in question was also one of great danger to the existence of the State of Israel. The peace process with the Palestinians, in all its phases, collapsed like one of the houses whose roof gave way under the weight of the snow.

Many people said, at first hesitantly and then unabash-

5

edly, that the government of Israel had no partner for dialogue, and that not only was the sky falling – the ground was trembling too. "We told you so," crowed those who had always expressed the opinion that there was never any point in talking to their Arab neighbors. "At least we tried," said those hovering in the center of the political map, where shock and disbelief were gradually giving way to disillusionment and somberness. And, for those on the far left of the political map, it was business as usual with the mantra of "End the Occupation."

And so, suicide bombers took with them to the bosom of death people who had left their homes to go about their affairs. On the bus, at the railway station, at the café, at the entrance to the shopping mall, at the entrance to the nightclub, in the reception hall, in the pedestrian mall and just crossing a busy street. From ambushes on the roadsides in the West Bank and the Gaza Strip, snipers shot at people sitting in passing cars and killed them. On the main streets of the big cities, booby-trapped cars set off by remote control burst into the air and strewed death and destruction around them. People who had wrapped themselves up well against the cold before leaving home, and felt more or less protected, were blown to pieces in nearby streets, shortly after meeting someone or other and asking him some perfectly ordinary question.

Others were mortally wounded. Some of them died of their wounds in the ambulance taking them from the scene of the attack to the hospital and others died later. Many others were severely wounded, or suffered moderate, moderate to light, or light wounds.

The lightly wounded were usually those who afterwards told the media what had happened. The description of the horror almost always began with the words: "Suddenly I heard a boom."

The politicians and those who earn their bread by reporting and commenting on events were at a loss in the face of the increasing escalation. In order to make it easier for themselves and the public at large to grasp the changing reality, they invented an imaginary staircase, and dubbed every additional deterioration in the situation or every terrorist attack that was worse than the one before it as a "step up."

How the leaders of Israel pleaded with the people and asked them to show patience and restraint – until they were removed from office. Those that came after them also implored the furious Israelis to arm themselves with the stoical calm that is the ally of the greatest spiritual strength on earth, and leave it to their elected representatives and the army to deal with the complicated situation in which the country found itself.

Many heartbreaking human stories and chance events took place in those days. Horror stories about the death of entire families that had gone to have a pizza were absorbed into Israeli consciousness along with heroic stories about police officers, border guards and soldiers who prevented mass terror attacks with their bodies and their quick thinking. Life in this region of the world was filled with a great fear. The focus on the future, warmly recommended to the public as a means of coping calmly with the situation, was clouded by panic.

A profound change took place that winter in the rude, arrogant, raging, loud-mouthed Israeli archetype of the months of Av and Elul. The cold caused it, the terror attacks caused it, and the policy of restraint capped it off and numbed the feelings of the citizens. The funerals of the ter-

7

ror victims grew quieter and quieter. Many of them were hasty affairs, taking place as they did in harsh and foreign weather conditions.

The Israelis left alive became somber, expressionless, silent, reserved, closed, stunned, gloomy, complex and very unfriendly.

When Israel began to liquidate those who sent the terrorists on their missions, the Israelis woke up a little, although there was no comparison to how they had been before the outbreak of the winter and the terror attacks. It seemed as though during the months of restraint Israelis had put their feelings on hold.

Even though there were those who couldn't understand why the government didn't send a few missiles in the direction of the towns, villages and refugee camps that served as incubators for the terrorists and wipe them off the face of the earth, they were, for the meantime, an extremist minority.

CHAPTER TWO

ON THE EVENING OF THE 20TH of Tevet during this
anomalous winter the clouds were low and heavy. On the
coast there was a thunder and lightning storm, and another
barrage of hail battered the streets illuminated by the few
street lamps still working and, for a split second, by the
lightning flashes.

That evening, nature showed that she knew how to produce long, thin hail too – hail with a sting. These needles of
hail stuck like thorns in leaves, umbrellas and the coat flaps
of people caught walking the street before they could take
shelter or reach their destination.

The news broadcasts summing up the events of the day
gave details for the first time about the annual report on the
state of poverty in Israel. Its findings were described as harsh
and grave, exposing as it did the very high numbers of families living below the poverty line, far below the poverty line.
Families living from hand to mouth were seen by them as a
subject for nostalgia.

Economic and social commentators explained that these
families had, indeed, been neglected, but not without reason. It was the security situation that had drained available
social resources into caring for the many families that had
fallen victim to enemy attacks. A quick-witted anchorwoman asked the commentator if we should conclude from
this that the poor people of Israel had to be injured both by
terrorism and by poverty in order to gain the means to sur-
vive, and was told that her question was the height of cyni-
cism, even though the reply was affirmative.

Families from weak social strata, uninjured in hostile
attacks, were unable to cope with the plunging tempera-
tures. They didn't have the money to mend broken heaters,

never mind buy new ones. Many of these families did not have the appropriate equipment – heavy coats, blankets, gloves, padded boots, umbrellas, woollen hats – to cope with the new conditions imposed by the weather. The immune systems of citizens of low socio-economic status had been harmed by the exceptional cold, and due to their inability to buy fresh fruit or vitamins or other dietary supplements to strengthen the body's immune system. Accordingly, they frequently fell ill, especially the children and the elderly among them, and many of them suffered from chilblains of varying degrees of severity.

Doctors were sometimes obliged to amputate parts of the body affected by gangrene due to the cold, and one of them said to the media: "As if what the suicide bombers do to the victims that remain alive after the blast isn't enough, they have to suffer cold and neglect as well."

That doctor's appearance and hard-hitting words made a favorable impression on the producer of one of the news programs, and he was given a permanent spot at the end of every edition, after the weather forecast. On his spot, the doctor explained to the viewers how to diagnose chilblains and infections as a result of chilblains, and when to rush to the emergency room.

On the night of the 20th of Tevet, a few hours after the publication of the poverty report, the community television channel of Ramle-Lod located the Beit-Halahmi family who lived in the Ganei-Aviv neighborhood of Lod. The community channel had prepared in advance for the report, and they wanted to scoop the national channels with a touching human story of hardship – relatively refreshing in comparison to the grief and misery caused by the Arab terror.

Shortly before ten o'clock in the evening, a film crew with the necessary equipment entered the Beit-Halahmi apartment on Micah Reiser Avenue, and Kati Beit-Halahmi, the mother of the family, was asked to wake her children who had just fallen asleep. The children, four in number, twin boys and twin girls, arrived in the living room wrapped in ragged old woollen blankets, dazed with sleep and shivering with cold.

The evening edition of the local news featured a shocking story about the poverty of the family from Lod. Lod and not Lodz – as the anchorwoman on the national news mistakenly said after her channel had hurried to acquire the story from the Ramle-Lod community channel. And thus, on the midnight edition of the national news channel, the Israeli public was informed of the dire plight of the Beit-Halahmi family.

One week later, amid the continuing reports on the terrorist attacks, the victims and the government debates, there was hardly a current affairs television and radio program on which the matter of Kati Beit-Halahmi and her household was not discussed.

Again and again, Beit-Halahmi unfolded the chronicles of her family. She explained that she was named after her grandmother on her father's side, Katoon, and again and again she willingly answered the same questions. From the few years she had spent in grade school, Beit-Halahmi remembered that a full answer had to include the words that appeared in the question, and she was very careful to completely answer her questioners.

Kati was very excited by the way she was being filmed and interviewed about the difficulties of her and her family's life, and at times she cried on the air, and even though this damaged the makeup applied by professional makeup artists before she entered the studio, it didn't prevent the cameramen from taking long close-ups of her face.

With Kati's voice serving as a background to the images and interpreting them, the television showed a very depressing picture of the poverty scene in Israel. The reporters were particularly interested in the contrast between the exterior and the interior, between the neighborhood, which was relatively well maintained and new, and the harsh conditions that prevailed inside the apartment: the old and almost empty fridge, next to it the small formica table, which had one of its legs missing and replaced by a pile of little bricks standing one on top the other. In the kitchen sink, a mountain of pots and dishes that could not be washed because the liquid soap had run out. On either side of the sink, a broken marble counter, which was also slightly rotten due to a leak coming from the empty service porch. Out of the five flames on the gas stove, a match could light only two. On the bare white walls of the living room and the rest of the apartment were colorful frescoes left by the children of the former residents, who had returned to Russia, and on the three-seat sofa, which was relatively new, a muddle of clothes and newspapers.

"We bought the living-room set in Bidya on the West Bank," said Kati Beit-Halahmi, "back when you could still go there."

In the children's room, the four children slept on three thin mattresses and covered themselves with two blankets. The faces of the twins appeared blurred on the television screens, but Kati Beit-Halahmi's voice was not disguised as she informed the reporters that Adi and Topaz were ten, and Moshe and Aaron were seven, and that it had taken her ten years to get pregnant the first time with the girls.

The bathroom and toilet were dark, said Kati, because there was a short, and the electrician wanted too much money to fix it. Soon, added the mother of the family, the lightbulbs in the living room and bedrooms would give out, and they would be condemned to darkness, because who knew if they would be able to afford new ones.

The cameramen tried, almost in vain, to hunt down the father of the family, Boaz Beit-Halahmi, a short, very thin man of about forty, his sunken cheeks covered with the stubble of a week-old beard, coinciding with the date on which his razor blades had lost their effectiveness. Beit-Halahmi was photographed with an angry expression on his face only when he was cornered. On the other occasions when they tried to photograph him, he ran from room to room, limping because of a bad traffic accident from which he had been saved by a miracle, his wife explained from the TV studio.

The camera lingered too on the broken windowpane in the parents' bedroom, where they slept on a mattress that they had found on the street the summer of the previous year. On the windowpane they had stuck brown packaging tape, just like in the Gulf War, and Kati said that in spite of the packaging tape, a freezing wind penetrated through the window, day and night, and spread throughout the house, so that it made no difference how many kerosene heaters they lit. It would always be cold.

"We don't have the money for a new windowpane," she said, and was rewarded with a close-up, after which the cameras returned to the apartment and showed the television in the living room.

"It breaks down a lot." she said, "Don't think you have to hit it hard – my husband's the only one who knows where – in order to see."

13

At that moment, Boaz Beit-Halahmi's hand hit the television set, and it began to display a soap opera.

"Sometimes, when my husband's not home," added Kati Beit-Halahmi from the studio, "we don't know about the terror attacks, and we have to ask the neighbors how many are dead, how many are wounded."

Kati was convinced that by describing what went on behind the front door of her house, she would save her family from poverty, at least for the duration of the cold months. The interviewers wanted more details, more color. Directors and producers whispered instructions into their earpieces, and they questioned Kati accordingly. At first she maintained some kind of discretion, but after two or three interviews she opened up completely, and embarked on a recital of her woes from the day she met Boaz Beit-Halahmi in the emergency room of the Josephthal Hospital in Eilat, twenty-two years ago, when she was eighteen years old. In her youth, she said, she spent a lot of time in Eilat, because she never went to high school, and she worked there waitressing. She liked it a lot in Eilat. She liked the atmosphere. She even dreamed of living there. To this day she thought that if they had settled down in Eilat, they would never have sunken into such poverty.

Kati explained that she had arrived in the ER because of a cut on her foot that she got from a broken bottle on the beach. Boaz was receiving treatment there at exactly the same time after diving in the Red Sea without checking the level of oxygen in his air tanks. When she met him, he was hooked up to an oxygen machine, and despite the mask she fell for him immediately.

Afterwards they gave her a local anaesthetic, she screamed, and he took off the oxygen mask and told her jokes the whole time they were stitching her foot.

"He didn't want me to pay attention to them giving me stitches," she explained.

Only after they finished stitching, he asked her for her name, and she replied, Barazani Kati, like in school, the last name first. And he replied, as she told the viewers on one of the morning talk shows in the middle of the week, Beit-Halahmi Boaz, and that was a very beautiful moment in her life. She smiled as she spoke, because all her thoughts were on that past moment.

On Friday evening, on the talk show *At Effi's on the Porch*, Kati waited in exemplary silence on the guest sofa donated by Habitat, her legs crossed, her hands folded and resting on her lap. This was how people waited for their turn on television, she thought. From time to time she also smiled or laughed, clapped, as if she was dying to join in the fun, even though she didn't really understand what was going on.

A geologist and expert on environmental studies, who was also very charismatic, explained why he thought that the cold spell had arrived in the country.

"Yes," he said, "a wind blew in from the North Pole, but why do you think there's sulfur dioxide in the water?"

That week a large amount of the chemical sulfur dioxide had been discovered in the drinking water.

"Why?" asked Effi, who was no less charismatic himself, and Kati thought that he must earn a fortune, and in dollars too, over and under the table.

"It is my opinion, and not only mine, everyone in our institute thinks the same, that the eruption of an unknown volcano, in the locality of Mesopotamia, in other words from the Caspian Sea to the Mediterranean, is the cause of the radical change in the weather."

"A volcano erupted? Without anyone noticing?" won-

15

dered Effi, and a wave of mirth rippled through the audience. Kati giggled too.

"It's not impossible. Under the sea, or in the deeper layers of the earth, and that led to. . . ."

Here he embarked on a scientific explanation, which was interrupted as soon as it became tedious by Effi, who said, "We'll get back to you later," and turned to Kati Beit-Halahmi with the words, "Kati Beit-Halahmi."

"Yes," she said.

"So, you meet Beit-Halahmi Boaz in Eilat, and from there you return to the center of the country already married?"

"No."

"Then what happened?"

"We came back together, but then the trouble began," she said sorrowfully, without knowing if she should go into details until Effi said, "Go on, Kati, tell us about it."

"My husband's family has a large plot on a smallholders' cooperative farm not far from Lod. I don't want to say which one."

"You don't have to."

"They ostracized me and him too."

"Ostracized you? How come?" inquired Effi.

"Because of my origins. Because of my background."

For years Kati Beit-Halahmi had imagined moments at which she would shame her husband's family, but an opportunity like this – to tear the proud mask off those faces she had never seen, and in public – she had never imagined in her wildest dreams. She took a deep breath and said sadly, "Racism."

"Why racism?" inquired Effi.

"My family came here from Kurdistan with the mass immigration from Iraq, on the "Ezra and Nehemiah" operation, and were sent straight to the Ramle internment camp.

They thought I wasn't good enough for their son both because of my origins, and because of where I grew up. I told him to tell them what my parents told me to tell him, that our name comes from the city of Barazan in Kurdistan, and that we're descendants of someone who was the head of a very important yeshiva, and that my parents talk to each other in Aramaic in the form that was preserved by the Jews there from Biblical times. But my husband's parents could only think about all the jokes people told about the Kurds, and they were ashamed to have a Kurdish daughter-in-law from the Ramle internment camp, who never finished grade school.

"What jokes?" asked Effi innocently.

"Jokes, you know. The ones they tell. I don't want to go into it," she said suddenly, and noticed that she'd said something that sounded very serious, and repeated it: "I just don't want to go into it. We got married at the Ramle rabbinate. We thought that after the wedding they would get in touch with us, but instead it got worse and worse. His mother Fanya and his father Avner said, 'We had four children and now we've got three.' And then they cut him out of their will. We thought we'd be able to live on the farm, next to them, and that Boaz would get the poultry and the four dunams of woodland they promised him when he was a child. But what poultry and what woodland? They threw us to the dogs. Somehow we managed to buy a house in Ramat Eshkol. Boaz worked as a hired taxi driver. It's a pity we didn't stay in Eilat. It was a mistake."

"How disgusting," said Effi. "I myself am half Iraqi and half pure Sephardi stock, and altogether I'm a great admirer of the Ethiopian community as well. It's a scandal!" he exclaimed and was applauded by the audience.

"Yes. . . ." said Kati Beit-Halahmi. "A scandal."

17

"Society was more stratified then. We were a state in its infancy. Today everything is more open."

"Yes," said Kati, despondently. "It's a pity we're not living today. I mean to say young today. His family's cold shoulder made my husband so depressed. I would talk to him, and suddenly he wasn't there, and no matter what I said to him, he didn't hear a word. One day he picked up two fares from the airport going to Tel Aviv. On the way there was an oil spot, he slipped on it, the taxi flipped over, nothing happened to the passengers, but he was badly injured. He was in the hospital for six months, he underwent five operations, physical therapy and God knows what until he could stand on his feet again. And he still limps, and they took away his license. National Insurance gave him nineteen percent disability and we got a one time grant."

There was a break for commercials. As soon as it was over, Effi reminded the audience that they were in the middle of a fascinating interview with a poverty-stricken woman from Lod, whose heart-rending story was now being told in full for the first time.

The camera focused on her again, and she went on to say that thanks to the grant and a mortgage for young couples, and whatever they managed to get for the apartment in Ramat Eshkol, they bought an almost new apartment in Ganei Aviv. Effi interrupted to explain to the audience that when Ganei Aviv was built a lot of people from Lod and its environs thought that it was going to be the number one neighborhood in the area, but things didn't turn out that way.

"There are hardly any native Israelis there today," said Kati. "All the Israelis ran away. Russians came instead. New immigrants. Not that I've got anything against Russians, God forbid. My kids already know Russian, songs in Russian,

18

recitations, everything. I just hope they don't start eating pork as well."

"I understand you, Kati," said Effi. "And your husband Boaz? What is he doing now?"

"He's unemployed," said Kati after a short hesitation. "He won't even apply for professional rehabilitation. And it's already much more than a year since the day they decided on the degree of his disability. If he wanted to he could appeal the decision, but he doesn't want to."

"And you support the family?"

"Yes."

"What do you do?"

"At the beginning I was a seamstress for a long time, like my mother, but for the past five years I've been cleaning stairwells and a bank after the employees go home."

"A hard life," said Effi with a grave face. "And where is all this leading in your opinion?"

"I don't know," said Kati. "I can't see any future, that's the truth." She began to cry, and said in a choked voice, "We've got two sets of twins and only four gloves, I send them to school with one glove each, so that they can copy down their lessons from the blackboard, with the hand in the glove, because without gloves on they can't even hold a pencil for the cold. Their hands freeze. Can you imagine?" She fell silent. Effi said, "All this must be very hard for you."

"Very," said Kati.

Effi turned to the viewers and gave them Kati's address in Lod, which also appeared on the screen as a subtitle. He asked them to send warm clothes and, of course, gloves, and reminded them that there were two sets of twins, in other words, four children, ten and seven years old. The program came to an end. When the credits came on, and the telephone number and e-mail address for viewers' reactions,

19

Effi gave Kati a hug and said to her, off the air, "Don't worry, people will send you tons of stuff now."

On the Sunday after the program, a glazier arrived at the Beit-Halahmis' apartment and measured the windowpane in the bedroom. After him, an electrician showed up to fix the electricity in the apartment and left them about twenty 75-watt lightbulbs and ten 60-watt ones.

At ten o'clock in the morning a truck drew up next to the house in Micah Reiser Avenue loaded with warm clothes that had been collected from the end of the Sabbath and all through the night. Workers carried the boxes up to the top-floor apartment and left. Boaz yelled at his wife for shaming the family, the children, and their good name. She yelled back at him to shut his mouth, she at least was doing something to get them out of the mess they were in, apart from sitting and watching the screwed up television.

Kati opened the boxes that filled the living room. There were lots of warm clothes in them and blankets and gloves – enough for half the population of Lod. Kati took ten pairs for each child, enough for when they grew too, and clothes and coats in all sizes, up to the age of eighteen. Among the clothes were coats and warm clothes for herself and her husband too. She sorted them out and took what seemed suitable.

Between cleaning stairwells in Halalei Egoz Street and cleaning stairwells in Tzmarot Street, Kati found time to go to the slum neighborhood next to the railway tracks. She called on the inhabitants to come to her house because she had a lot of clothes to give them. She spoke to the women and they sent their children. After they had left with bursting bags, Boaz said to her:

"You're a nutcase, you're completely off your rocker. Ever

since you were on television, you've gone crazy. You're soft in the head. Lucky they didn't kill us. Who lets Arabs into their home today? Only lunatics and other Arabs."

"But they didn't kill us, right?" she said.

"Right, right," he muttered with a sneer on his face.

The quarrel between the couple could have gone on for a long time, but for the fact that it was interrupted by a telephone call from a mass circulation daily paper. They wanted to bring their readers up to date about the family's situation after the generous help given them by their compatriots. Boaz announced that he would on no account cooperate with the photographers this time, he was sick and tired of the whole thing.

A few days after the Beit-Halahmi family had broken into public awareness in Israel, the paper carried a large color photo on its back page of Kati Beit-Halahmi and her four children. All of them in gloves, scarves, hats, coats and boots. Kati and Topaz were smiling happily, but Adi, Moshe and Aaron stood staring blankly at the photographer. On the day the photograph was published, Kati emptied her wallet and bought four copies of the newspaper. She borrowed scissors from the neighbors, cut out the picture and the short piece about them, and put the four copies, folded, into plastic bags, so that the teeth of time would damage the precious newspaper as little as possible. The day would come, she thought, when she, or the children, or even Boaz, would want to remember the few days of fame they had once enjoyed, and they would be able to take the pictures out of the drawer and feast their eyes on them.

THE ATMOSPHERE, the weather forecasters repeatedly explained, was in a state of instability, due to the fact that the conditions that had created the initial cold spell, at the end of Tishri and the beginning of Heshvan, had failed to give rise to any resistance in the system. A situation like this, in which the existing system fails to resist the initial interference and turns it into a seasonal tendency, is rare, but not impossible, the population learned from the experts.

Because of the cold, the terror attacks and the prevailing mood, tourism was dealt a crushing blow. Many flights to Israel were cancelled. Foreign airlines were worried about the safety of their crews, and if they already dared to send a half-empty flight to Israel twice a week they made sure that it would leave the country before darkness descended. The air crews were afraid to sleep in Israel.

Even the town of Eilat and its surroundings, which had always attracted tourists during the winter season, turned into a ghost town. CNN, and other large television networks in its wake, showed the thin layer of ice floating on the surface of the Red Sea. Those loyal to the Israeli TV channels too were regaled with the spectacle of coral reefs covered in ice, and deserted hotels.

Due to its distance from Palestinian towns, the town of Eilat was not a target for frequent acts of terror, but the cold accomplished what the terrorists didn't, and Israel's southernmost town lost its charm. Tourists from abroad preferred remote tropical islands, even if getting there required them to spend more hours in the air than the flight to Eilat.

The situation on the shores of the Dead Sea was no better. Except for the chronically ill who were in need of its curative properties, nobody dared to go there, especially after a Finnish tourist suffering from psoriasis was killed in a shooting attack on the Jericho bypass road.

The new cold brought new viruses, unfamiliar to the population. A new strain of influenza visited Israel that winter, and was dubbed the "Saudi flu" because of the rumors that it had first appeared at the end of summer in Saudi Arabia, which was also, like the rest of the Middle East, suffering a hard winter. There were some who went so far as to claim that the Saudi flu was a form of biological warfare developed in Saudi Arabia.

Many Israelis fell ill with the Saudi flu that winter, and some died of it. The situation was so bad that almost every day or two, unless there was a big terror attack with over five dead, the people in charge of documenting the situation had new victims of both the terrorists and the Saudi flu to count. Profound gloominess reigned amongst those dwelling in Israel. Taxi drivers, who had their fingers on the pulse of the nation, told their passengers that the government policy of restraint towards the Palestinian Authority was to blame for everything. It was the policy of restraint that had led to the sharp deterioration in the population's immune systems, so that whoever didn't die of suicide bombs or car bombs died of the Saudi flu.

The flu also affected the inhabitants of the Palestinian Authority, and there, too, many people died.

Sometimes the illness and the severe cold brought fighters on both sides to their knees, and created the illusion of a cease-fire.

A rumor spread that the Saudi flu was threatening the continued existence of the State of Israel no less than the terror attacks. Top military and medical experts gave their firm opinion that the anxieties about the Saudi flu and the demise of the State of Israel were not realistic, for the time being.

A doctor from the settlement of Elkana, who had a regular program on the local radio station for the Sharon region twice a week in the afternoon, said, in an attempt to reassure his listeners, that there was no comparison between the Saudi flu and the Spanish influenza, which had slain twenty-four million people at the beginning of the twentieth century. Any such comparison was morbid and hysterical, the doctor stressed.

But the nerves of his audience were so frayed to begin with that the mere mention of that epidemic at the beginning of the previous century was enough for them to come to frightening conclusions about the similarity between the two strains of flu.

All the pleas of the doctors who joined their colleague from Elkana in stating that there was no connection between the two strains of flu, and in emphasizing the difference between them, fell on deaf ears. Once again, a furious public debate raged in all the forums of popular expression. The exhausted public came to its own imaginary conclusions. Many succumbed to the Saudi flu, and about a quarter of those infected died.

In the cemeteries they began to bury the corpses one on top of the other, and the undertakers worked day and night digging graves in the ground or building them above it. The volunteers who collected the body parts at the sites of the bomb explosions did not lack work either. The doctors and nurses stayed at the hospitals around the clock on emergency shifts and they hardly had time to rest. In the streets, in the shopping malls, in the bus terminals, people tried to act as if they were carrying on with their lives as usual, but everyone knew that the situation was intolerable. But however intolerable – that was the situation.

On the night of the 22nd of Tevet about 130 people arrived at Ichilov Hospital in Tel Aviv, seventy of them suffering from various illnesses, mainly the Saudi flu, and the rest suffering from light to moderate wounds from a suicide bombing, which took place that night at the end of the second show at the entrance to a movie theater, where they were showing an American comedy blockbuster.

The catastrophe might have been much worse, but for the alertness of a passerby, who noticed the terrorist waiting for the crowd coming out of the cinema and yelled at them: "Run! . . . Terrorist!" Many people succeeded in escaping a split second before the suicide bomber detonated the explosive belt he had brought with him from home.

At the entrance to the ER, next to the admissions desk, the efficient doctors sorted out the patients, separating those suffering from the Saudi flu and other illnesses from those wounded in the latest terror attack.

Many of the hospital wards were crowded with victims of the Saudi flu and victims of previous terror attacks, and patients were lying in the corridors. The nurses exercised all their ingenuity to invent places in which to put the beds of the new arrivals, trying as hard as they could to isolate the flu patients from the wounded in the terror attacks.

Now, too, one of the nurses hissed at her colleague as she made haste to pull on disposable gloves, "Where are we supposed to put them, on my head?"

"We'll find somewhere," her friend replied.

LIAT DUBNOV, a beautiful brunette with dark blue eyes, single on principle, thirty-nine years old, one of the victims of the Saudi flu, holder of a BA in Biblical Aramaic and a MA in Semitic languages, a fanatical collector of Hebrew calendars from the invention of the printing press on, lay in a good spot next to the window in the Internal Medicine B department and listened to the sirens of the ambulances streaming to the hospital.

Up to two days before, Dubnov had been lying in the corridor, and when a bed became available in the room next to her, next to the window, they moved her there. During the day, Liat was able to look through the window at the clouds and see whether they were cumulus or stratus, a distinction taught to her by her brother, Adir Bergson, who was two years her junior.

According to the number of ambulances and the pace of their arrival, Dubnov tried to guess the dimensions of the current terror attack. She had no television, because all the television sets available for rent at the hospital were taken, nor did she have a radio. When she arrived at the hospital twelve days ago, she thought they would discharge her immediately, and when her brother went to her apartment to fetch her clothes, she forgot to tell him to bring her laptop computer, and by now she didn't have the strength to log on to the Internet and put herself in the picture by its means.

Liat had been in bed at home for a week before she arrived at the Ichilov Hospital ER. She didn't want to burden the health system of Israel any further, and thought that she would be able to cure herself. And indeed, she tried both conventional and unconventional remedies, but nothing helped. She grew weaker by the day, she lost her appetite,

26

she ran a high fever, and in the end she called Adir and asked him to do her a favor, leave their laundromat, leave his girlfriend, whose name she kept forgetting, and come and take her to the ER.

Adir Bergson and Liat Dubnov had the same mother, Levana Kosta. She had been killed nearly three years before, during a trip to the United States. She had slipped on seaweed in one of the canyons there and fallen into the abyss. Liat had urged her to go on that organized tour, thinking that when she returned, she and her brother would have two or three months of mental respite, because their mother, who was very involved in their lives, overly involved in their opinion, would achieve a different perspective on the world.

Bergson waited with his sister in the ER until she was diagnosed with acute pneumonia in both lungs, a common complication of the Saudi flu, and he went up to the ward with her and the orderly wheeling the gurney. After that, because of his asthma, Liat told him to go home, he'd done enough, thank you very much, and he hurried off.

Liat Dubnov – pneumonia, was written on the patient's chart at the foot of her bed, together with the different medications she had received and other details such as her body temperature and the number of cubic centimeters of urine she passed.

The doctors had already changed the antibiotics they gave her three times. Now she was getting the fourth type through an intravenous drip, and if that didn't help, they told her on their rounds that day, they would add steroids as well. Liat was afraid of steroids. She didn't want to swell up and become chronically ill like her brother Bergson, with his chronic asthma, although he had not needed to take steroids lately and had become very thin. And the more he

27

shrunk, after stopping the previous treatment and starting on a new drug somebody had discovered, the more dependent he became on his girlfriend, Tasaro. He called her every half hour to find out where she was and who she was with. On his second to last visit to the hospital, Liat saw him go terribly pale after switching off his cell phone, and she asked him what was wrong. It turned out that Tasaro hadn't answered the phone, even though he was sure that she was sitting in a cafe with a girlfriend, who had immigrated to Israel with her on Operation Shlomo, as she had told him in the morning that she would be at this hour.

"She'd have to be an idiot to cheat on you, Adir. There's probably a lot of noise in the cafe from the espresso machine, and she couldn't hear the phone ring."

"As long some bomb didn't go off under a table there," said Bergson.

"We'd have heard the explosion, we'd have heard the ambulances, where would they bring the wounded if not here," Dubnov reassured her brother.

Now Liat heard the blood pounding inside her head, and she knew that she had a fever. She was afraid that while she was lying here fading away in the hospital, all her hard work at the fitness club on Ben Yehuda Street, owned by her married lover Shaul Takdim, would go down the drain. Dubnov was afraid that Takdim, after seeing her bloated with steroids, would leave her for someone else, for whom he would build a personal training program, just as he had done for her in the beginning. She burned with jealousy at the thought that he might already have somebody new, healthy, who hadn't caught the Saudi flu yet, or had caught it in a mild form. Someone married, with a great figure, maybe not as pretty as she was, but not as demanding either. Someone whose lifestyle was more suited to his than her own, who wasn't always free and eager to meet him like she was.

The nurse came in to change her infusion. She was in a big hurry and she told Liat where the ambulances were coming from and what had happened. Dubnov nodded slightly. She was too exhausted to be shocked.

"Are there any dead?" she asked.

"For the meantime, no. But you should see the catastrophes that arrived in the ER. What a mess. Full of internal injuries."

She adjusted the infusion of another patient at the other end of the room and left.

On the night of the 22nd of Tevet, Dubnov was very sad. Never mind that her brother hadn't come to visit her; she forgave him. He had a lot of things to worry about, but her boyfriend, Shaul Takdim, who in the normal course of events she saw at least twice a day – once at the health club and once not at the health club – was steadily reducing the frequency of his visits to the hospital, and their duration.

At the beginning of her hospitalization he showed up at least once a day, always for short visits because he was parked in a no-parking zone. After a few days he started coming once every two days, and said that he had double parked his car with the lights blinking, so he couldn't stay more than a minute. The last time he came, the previous day, he was distracted, and Liat saw that he had only come out of duty.

"Where's the car?" she asked him. "Did you find parking?"

"No," he said tensely. "I'm really afraid it's going to be towed. I parked at a bus stop."

"With the lights blinking?"

"Yes, sure," he said.

"Then go," she said, and he grabbed his cell phone and car keys that were lying on the nightstand by her bed, gave her a quick kiss on the forehead, and said, "Tomorrow I'll put it in the parking lot, and I'll stay a long time."

Tomorrow was the day that was already over, and Takdim hadn't come and hadn't called. She looked at her cell phone, and it seemed to her that it was ringing, and she kept picking it up and saying "Hello," and there was nothing at the other end of the line. Her fever was already very high, and she looked at her watch and saw that it wasn't yet three hours since the last time she had taken something to bring her fever down, and she didn't want to nag the medical staff, whose hands were so full anyway. Dubnov felt like a second-class patient compared to the victims of the terror attacks.

She tried to fall asleep, and in order to improve her chances of success she used her imagination as her guide. She imagined that she was in her apartment on Amos Street, which was not only her favorite street, but also her favorite prophet, sprawled out on her bed in her luxurious bedroom, with all its comforts and conveniences, taking refuge inside herself, and simply sleeping, next to the wall, hiding from the world, and not caring about anything.

This exercise didn't really help, and Dubnov began to count the real estate left to herself and her brother by their mother. The apartment on Amos Street where she lived. The apartment on Ezekiel Street where they grew up, and where Adir now lived with what's-her-name. The apartment on Joel Street where a woman who was always walking around barefoot and had very big feet lived with her family. The studio apartment on Zacharia Street that they had rented to a student, and the four-room apartment on the corner of Nahum and Nordau streets, which their mother had rented

30

years ago to a widow, who had divided the apartment in two, living in one part and using the other for a makeup school. Dubnov remembered that the school was called "Another Face" and the woman was named Angelica Gomeh. She remembered that this Angelica had grown very difficult in recent years, that her mother had told her that she'd been that way ever since her only son was killed in a helicopter disaster. The lease with Gomeh, like the rest of the family's real estate, was taken care of by an elderly lawyer Kosta insisted on retaining, because she didn't trust young lawyers.

And then, of course, there was the laundromat. Levana Kosta had bequeathed them a laundromat on Dizengoff Street, called "Clean World." The compulsory laundromat, as the sister and brother Dubnov et Bergson referred to it – because according to the terms of their mother's will, which she had brought up to date before setting off for her organized tour of America, they were not allowed to sell it until the year 2010. She also forbade them to sell the real estate she had accumulated during the course of her life until 2010. She wanted to keep it in the family.

Besides the above Dubnov also counted a few acres that had not yet been freed for construction in the area of Ramat Hasharon, and a house in Kfar Saba rented to a religious family, with whom all communication also took place through a third party.

When counting the real estate failed to put her to sleep, Dubnov tried to find gratification in thinking about her collection of rare Hebrew calendars dating from as far back as the fifteenth century, but the illness prevented her from feeling any pleasure. She hadn't told Takdim about the collection, the only one who knew about it was Adir. And now the Ethiopian probably knew about it too. But what interest could she possibly take in a collection of old calendars?

31

At lunch time Liat gave all the magazines she had received from two girlfriends, who parked in a parking zone with a parking card, to a terminal patient in the bed next to her, who was now fast asleep and snoring so loudly that Liat couldn't understand how the other patients in the room were able to sleep at all, with the racket she was making.

The terminal patient was so happy when she gave her the magazines, pouncing on them as if she had found a fortune. This seemed strange to Liat. What, thought Dubnov, she doesn't know that she's finished? Of course she knows. She had told her herself, "I'm going to die soon, and I'm trembling with fear." This being the case, wondered Dubnov, when was she going to smear on the Max Factor brown eye shadow advertised in *Vogue* magazine, the sample of which, attached to the glossy paper of the magazine, she had tried out on her eyelids? Why was she interested in the spring suit on the cover of *Woman*? In all probability the thirty days of mourning for her death would already be over by spring.

Dubnov glanced at her watch again. It was five past one in the morning. She wanted to talk to someone, specifically, to Shaul Takdim. All day she had waited for him in vain. Perhaps now he would answer her. And even if his wife answered the phone, with the voice coming out of her sick throat, she would believe her when she said, "Wrong number."

Takdim answered.

"Shaul," she said. "Where have you been? I waited for you all day."

"I was busy. I had to install new equipment in the gym today, I told you yesterday. Don't you remember? I had to make sure that everything worked properly and move the old stuff out. I had a really crazy day. I'll talk to you tomorrow. Shirli's watching a movie in the living room."

He slammed the phone down and she felt as if he was slamming her too.

His explanation was reasonable, but not sufficient. No, she thought, he should have found the time to come. A minute. Two minutes. He's got someone else. It's obvious. Again she was engulfed by a torrent of jealousy, but this time she went into cardiac arrest and died.

The last word she said was "Mother."

WHEN HIS SISTER PASSED AWAY, Adir was dozing and dreaming that he had invented a green detergent. In other words, composed of entirely natural ingredients and based on tea tree oil with its many positive properties. As a graduate of the department of atmospheric sciences, who had also worked for a few years as a weather forecaster at the meteorology station in Beit Dagan until he got sick of it, and after that for a few more years in research, at the Weizmann Institute, in the field of atmospheric chemistry, until his asthma forced him to stop, not only because of the chemicals, but also because of the stress – Bergson was well up in chemistry and biology and as he mixed the components in his dream he muttered to himself from time to time, "Just not phosphate."

One of the things that triggered his asthma attacks was the phosphate in laundry detergent, and he would sense it in the air, erupting from the laundromat a few meters before he entered it, and fill with anxiety, even though he had never had a serious asthma attack that resulted from the air coming from the laundromat. His two most severe recent attacks had come about for other reasons entirely. The last was due to psychological stress, and the one before last happened during a fit of laughter while watching a rerun of an episode of *Fawlty Towers* two years ago, at the end of his affair with Iris Ventura. Ventura was a divorcee and mother of three, who had left her husband the architect Othniel Grossman and their beautiful home on Dor Dor v'Dorshav Street in Jerusalem, and returned with her children to north Tel Aviv, to the area of the ancient prophets, not far from the avenue where she had grown up. In her new situation Ventura could only afford a moldy apartment at the end of Jeremiah Street, on the fourth floor and without an elevator.

In recent weeks, without his sister Liat at his side at the laundromat to share the burden of the supervision, maintenance and collection of the coins from the washing machines at the end of the day, Bergson was exhausted and he slept like a baby. The two gigantic new washing machines and the two dryers that Liat had gone to Italy to acquire half a year before, while considerably increasing the profits of Clean World, also meant that he and his sister had to work a lot harder. Not only dealing with the laundry powder and the filters of the dryers – jobs Bergson did with a handkerchief over his face – dealing with the many coins in the new machines was a stupefying task, and Bergson sometimes simply chose to drop the ten shekel coins into his pocket, rather than embarking on the Sisyphean task of filling in the boring invoices and receipts. Dubnov et Bergson had even invested in closed-circuit television and turned "Clean World" into a self-service laundromat, with prominent signs in red and white warning the public that the place was equipped with the most up-to-date surveillance systems, and that the owners bore no responsibility for losses. This was how the two of them preferred to run the business, not like their mother, who was there all day, supervising, working like a slave. On the whole it was clear to Adir why Liat had been so insistent at the time that their mother take that trip to America.

She wanted her to see a free and efficient economy at its best. That things had worked out otherwise – that was life.

On the night in question, Adir and Tasaro went to bed late because they heard the explosion at the cinema in the city center, and they remained glued to the television screen for a while, until Tasaro said, "Enough, I have to get up early tomorrow," and Adir switched off the twenty-one inch set they kept in the bedroom.

For the past week Tasaro had been busy with a shoot, and she would leave the apartment on Ezekiel Street at four-thirty in the morning. In order to be fresh for the camera, she took care to go to bed early, and Adir didn't mind falling asleep with her curled up on his chest.

Tasaro Tasama and Julia Nasimov, a new immigrant from Russia, were modeling for the new catalog of a well-known swimsuit designer. The concept of the swimsuit designer and his advertising agency was a synthesis of the human and the formal.

"The human contrast between the colors of the two models – one black and one white – continues the strong contrast between the colors of this year's swimsuits, which are also exclusively black and white," the designer wrote in the introduction to the catalog.

Two elements, added the designer, unite the two models who are so different to each other: the swimsuits on the one hand, and Judaism on the other.

Tasaro fell asleep at once. Bergson lay awake a little longer and looked in the darkness at a street lamp next to the building catching the drizzle in its light, and tried to think for himself, out of his own knowledge, what the meaning of this winter was. But before he tackled the question in depth, he recalled the mystical interpretations he had heard that day on the radio, on the army channel or the Voice of Israel, that the many terror attacks and the European winter fore-told the coming of the Messiah, and that the people of Israel had to unite both against the enemy and the elements.

Adir wondered how they could unite. People weren't

36

molecules. Bergson had never understood this unification that took place between people in times of trouble. He suspected it of being shallow and external. He thought that evolution was actually producing people now who were not at all interested in uniting, like himself, and he was rather contemptuous of all this togetherness, both among the Jews and among the Palestinians.

He didn't have a solution of his own to the conflict and therefore he didn't interfere, he didn't even make any comments when he heard of a terror attack. Not that he was indifferent, he just thought that it would take years until this conflict was resolved. Maybe even a thousand. When he thought about it seriously, and he often thought about it seriously, he asked himself why the State of Israel didn't move itself to some deserted plain where there weren't any enemies, like one of the poles. It was only a question of adaptation. It was true that it could take hundreds of years to adapt to such extreme weather conditions, but here too, the conflict might be somehow or other solved on paper, but the hatred would go on existing for many generations to come. The North (or South) Pole, on the other hand, with all the millions of tons of ice around it, constituted a vast area of separation and protection from the rest of the world, and it would be a lot more efficient than the thin "seam line" that everybody was talking about now.

Besides that, he knew, the air at the poles was fresh and pure, and his chances of survival there were higher. He also knew that all this was nothing but a fantasy before falling asleep. All their real estate was here, and without it they would have nothing to live on, whereas now they could whistle all the way to the bank and back.

⸙ ⸙ ⸙

"Just not phosphate, maybe zoolite. . ." he muttered again in his sleep. Tasaro woke up and looked at her thin blond boyfriend. She couldn't understand what he was saying and she shook him lightly.

"Wake up, you're having a bad dream," she said to him.

"It isn't a bad dream, go back to sleep," he said and they turned their backs on each other and fell fast asleep until six-thirty in the morning.

At six thirty in the morning Adir and Taraso were woken up by the ringing of the telephone. Tasaro answered it and she was very upset because she was late for the shoot and she was afraid that she would be fired.

"It's for you. . ." she said to Adir, handed him the telephone and quickly snatched up her clothes. On the other hand, she thought, they haven't got anyone else, she just had to ask her agency if coming late this one time would mean that she would get less work after they finished shooting the swimsuit catalog.

"Who is it at this hour?" asked Adir, half asleep.

"I don't know," said Tasaro, "I'm late, they're going to kill me." And she ran to the bathroom.

Adir picked up the telephone and said hello. It was the nurse, Nira, on the line. She asked him to come at once.

Adir asked, "Why? Is my sister's life in danger?"

"No, no," said Nira. "Her life's not in danger."

"Then why at once?"

"She's dead, Mr. Bergson, I'm sorry to inform you," said Nira.

"What? Thank you," he mumbled, put the phone down, and went on sitting there, frozen.

He was still sitting there when his girlfriend came out of the shower, refreshed and wet-haired.

"What happened?" she asked when she saw him like that.

"Liat's dead," he said.

"What?" said Tasaro and sat down on the edge of the bed.

"You heard me," said Adir. "I have to go there. You don't have to come with me. Go to your shoot and I'll let you know what's happening. Oh God. Where are my car keys?"

"How should. . ." said Tasaro and fell silent, and she looked for the keys to the Golf until she found them.

At the hospital he was greeted by two downcast doctors who hadn't slept for seventy or perhaps eighty hours, and could hardly stand on their feet. One of them had red eyes. He spoke to Adir and the second doctor touched his shoulder lightly, or perhaps he was leaning on him so that he wouldn't fall over.

Now Bergson asked for more details. They told him that she died in her sleep and didn't feel a thing. Adir asked, but how is it possible, such a young girl, she'd never been so sick in her life, and the last time he visited her – he couldn't remember when it was – she was fine.

"Fine?" said the doctor with the red eyes, "No no. Please be accurate. We admitted her with a severe case of pneumonia that developed as a result of the Saudi flu. If you wish we'll ask for an autopsy."

"Autopsy?" repeated Adir. Up to now he had never in his life had the opportunity to say or hear himself saying this word, but had only heard it or read it.

"Yes, but I don't recommend it. It would be a pity to cut her up now. I can tell you right away that she died of heart failure. All the signs. . . ."

Adir checked the state of his breathing, and it was actually okay. It was his stomach that hurt so badly.

"Do you want to see her?" asked the doctor. "I can take you to see her."

"No, I would prefer not to," said Bergson, and walked out of the ward, went down in the elevator, left the old building, and entered the various wings of the Suoraski Medical Center. He became increasingly lost in the long corridors of this labyrinthine hospital, to which more and more wings had been added over the years, above ground and below ground, some of them finished and others still being built. Reality suddenly seemed so abstract that he felt as if he had lost his balance. How was he going to take life minus Liat? How could he live without her?

Now he realized how dependent he was on her opinions, and that it was Liat who always kept him from doing stupid things. For example, she was the one who advised him to leave Iris, a childhood friend of hers with whom she had recently cut off relations, because what would he get out of it, apart from a load of trouble. Three children. And with those heavy names too, Osher and Oz for the boys, and Herut for the little girl. Not that she had anything against the children, she told him in one of their heart-to-hearts. But the very fact that she had given those names to her children – Happiness, Strength and Freedom – showed how heavy Iris was, he'd better believe it, she knew him and she knew her. Ever since they were children everyone knew that Iris Ventura was a very heavy load, she pronounced. And he allowed himself to be persuaded, quite easily to tell the truth, because he really was sick and tired of hearing her complain about her ex-husband, Othniel Grossman, all the time, and how he had cheated her over the alimony and robbed her, simply robbed her blind of everything she had invested in their home in Jerusalem, and now go talk to the trees and the stones – he was completely absorbed in his new life with his girlfriend, without giving a thought to the fact that his children didn't even have a computer, and that they were living in a rented apartment, where the kitchen ceiling was black with mold.

Liat also had something to say about his relationship with Tasaro. She said unequivocally: Adir was a free-thinking man and so on, and she could actually understand what he saw in her, but the problem was that Israeli society wasn't ready for their type of coupling yet. He should think carefully. About himself, and about his asthma, and about the children they would give birth to. Think carefully, she repeated whenever she felt that her brother was about to do something of which she did not approve.

Now all these opinions were dead along with the woman who had given them. Her watchful eyes were closed, he thought, as he continued to wander into all kinds of wards and departments, from observation to hospitalization, from in-patients to outpatients, from Wing 3 to Wing 2. At last he asked a nurse who walked past him how to get to the parking lot, and she stopped and gave him directions. He wasn't listening and asked her to repeat herself. She repeated the directions and he more or less understood them, and thanked her.

In the parking lot he forgot if he was parked on lower level two or lower level three. He went almost went out of his mind until he found a blue Golf like his. But when he released the alarm to unlock the door, this Golf did not respond, and he continued his search, still feeling weightless as if he were on the moon.

He found his car at the entrance to lower level four and started the engine. With the starting of the engine came a certain relief that he was still among the living.

He began driving and thought about what was in store.

About the funeral, how was he going to eulogize her in front of everybody, what was he going to say? He would say that she was head and shoulders above the common run, a woman of valor, a light unto the gentiles, without explanations, or with explanations, he would tell the mourners that she loved Aramaic, really loved it, so much so that she even recorded the message on her answering machine in Aramaic. The mourners would just think that she was weird. Better not to eulogize her at all, he decided. Better simply to say Kaddish and have a matter-of-fact funeral without any frills, in any case nobody could share the hole gaping inside him because of her death. It was his hole. He was responsible for its maintenance.

He switched on the radio and heard a helicopter report on the morning's traffic jams, and a news flash about two people who had died of their wounds from yesterday's terror attack. He let out a bitter sigh: his Liat was gone and the world hadn't stopped. People died and were born, understood something and grew confused again, and then – clarity once more. The light turned green. He charged forward and entered Hamedina Square.

You have to keep going, he said to himself as he emerged from the square on the other side of Weizmann Street. A girl whose father had died this morning of the wounds he had received yesterday in a shooting attack in the West Bank was talking on the radio. Adir remembered hearing that one of the victims had been very badly wounded. His fifteen-year-old daughter asked how much longer, and the radio announcer said he hoped she would know no more sorrow.

Suddenly Adir found himself regretting that his sister had only died of the Saudi flu and not in a terror attack. Now he wouldn't be able to write anything dramatic in the death notice, such as May the Lord Avenge Her Blood. He began composing the death notice in his head, and hesitated as to whether to write "the family" or his name, since "the family" in fact consisted only of him.

A tear formed in the corner of his right eye, but it was so small that it didn't fall, but stayed there until it evaporated.

Bergson was sure that Tasaro would be waiting for him at home, but she only called from time to time to ask if he needed her, and told him that she was doing everything in her power to get away from the shoot early. But because of her lateness this morning there were a couple of shots they still had to finish. Actually everybody was very sympathetic. She had told them that her boyfriend's sister had died. Adir told her not to worry, in any case the funeral was only tomorrow. Tasaro said she would get back as soon as she could.

"Take your time," said Adir. "All I'm doing now is taking care of the arrangements."

"Are you alright?" she asked.

"As alright as possible," he replied and hung up.

Again he thought about the death notice and what to say in it. He had always amused himself with the composition of the announcement of his own death, because of the asthma. It had never occurred to him that he would have to worry about composing a death notice for Liat, who was such a permanent fixture, rooted in Amos Street with all her dictionaries from ancient Aramaic to spoken Hebrew, from the Aramaic dialect of the Jews of Kurdistan to spoken Hebrew, from Akkadian to biblical Aramaic, and from Aramaic to Sumerian, and the mythologies of all the nations of the region. Once she sang him a song of the alphabet in the dialect of Aramaic spoken by the Kurdish mountain Jews, and he laughed like anything. He was especially pleased by a few of the letters that he recognized, and he also admired her studying something that was becoming extinct, whereas he himself had studied the atmosphere, which was more eternal than any civilization.

"My Liat is no more," sounded too intimate to him. The whole world didn't have to know how attached he had been to his elder sister. On the other hand, *I regret to announce the untimely death of,* new line, *my sister,* new line, *Liat Dubnov,* new line, *Adir Bergson.* New line, *The funeral will take place. . .* sounded fine to him. He smiled, remembering how she had told him, only a month ago, what she had said when they asked her at the health club what she did in life. "I stay," she replied, and how right that was.

Liat Dubnov stayed specifically on Amos Street, she never set foot outside her apartment except to go to her therapist and to the health club owned by that fox Takdim. The rest of the time she stayed with her books, her dictionaries, and her crumbling calendars, which she kept in a special little room, where the light was always dim.

Adir knew that Tasaro would be a little offended that he hadn't included her in the announcement, next to him, but with all his love for her, she wasn't a member of the family and she hadn't been at all close with Liat. On the contrary, the two of them couldn't stand each other. The long and the short of it was that Liat disapproved of Tasaro much more than she disapproved of Ventura, perhaps because she was afraid that Adir would be stuck with Tasaro for many more years to come.

The summer before that crazy winter, one Friday afternoon, the three of them, Adir, Liat and Tasaro, were sitting on Liat's porch, and trying to have a spontaneous conversation, which was in fact forced, about the political situation as reported in the weekend papers. The conversation was so artificial that Adir stood up, said that he couldn't breathe, that he was dying of hunger, that he was going to pick up some take-out, and he turned to his sister and asked her where he should go for it, what exactly he should bring, and about how much it would cost. Dubnov was the queen of take-out. All the delivery boys and all the restaurants in town that made deliveries knew her.

She told him exactly where to go and what to bring and how much it should cost. He said he would have to go to the ATM.

"Then go," said Liat. "Tasaro and I will set the table. We'll eat inside, in the air-conditioning."

Levana Kosta's children had been brought up never to use checks or credit cards. Only cash. "That's the only way you can feel the money coming and going," their mother taught them.

In Adir's absence, Liat cross-examined Tasaro. After the cross-examination they were both silent. Tasaro was ashamed of the details she had given about herself, and Liat didn't say anything like, never mind, we all have our traumas, but kept quiet and set the table by herself. When Tasaro wanted to help, Liat said that in any case she didn't know where the tableware was kept. When Adir returned with the ready-to-eat food in semi-transparent plastic containers, he immediately sensed the tension in the air, and realized that he had been wrong to leave the two women alone together.

They all ate quickly, in any case the food was terrible, Liat said, and Adir agreed with her, he had thrown away

45

shekels for nothing. In the end he got up and signalled to his girlfriend that they were leaving. Tasaro wanted to help clean up, but Liat, who was dying for them to go and leave her by herself, said, "No, no, never mind, I'll do it."

"Okay," her brother quickly agreed. "Anyway I have to go use my inhaler."

Downstairs, on the long street named after the prophet Amos, Adir's Golf was parked on the sidewalk and behind it was Liat's old white Lark, which had been Levana's when it was new. As soon as the two of them got into Adir's car, and the air-conditioner was working and restoring their spirits, Adir asked Tasaro what had happened up there while he was at the Indian restaurant.

Tasaro said, "Nothing."

Adir said that he wanted to know, that he had a right to know, and she burst into tears, and Adir understood that Liat had gotten everything out of her.

On the one hand Adir was angry with his sister, and on the other hand he felt relieved, that the information he had concealed about Tasaro's shady past at the Central Bus Station, had finally reached his sister's ears – straight from the horse's mouth – and he no longer had to tell her anything. She had the whole weekend to digest it.

SOMETIMES VENTURA, Adir's ex-girlfriend, would give Liat a call, and sometimes it was Dubnov who would call Iris. When they were children they would do their homework together every day and talk about everything. As adults they spoke to each other, carefully, about once every six months. The Saturday after that miserable visit, Dubnov called Ventura and told her what she had discovered about her brother's current girlfriend. She wanted to console Iris with Tasaro's life story – but instead she achieved the complete opposite. Ventura understood that Tasaro, as opposed to herself, was an exotic bombshell, and she didn't have the ghost of a chance that Adir would leave Tasaro and come back to her. Never, Ventura decided after the conversation with Dubnov, never would Adir leave Tasaro, because Tasaro had a good story, with a national, social and personal plot, and he also needed her, because of his asthma and other things. With her, for example, he could afford to pamper himself, because she didn't have to divide her attention. She didn't have any children from a previous marriage. She was his, net.

Tasaro stole the show from Ventura. Two months in the desert. Where did she have two months in the desert? A father who was carried on a stretcher, until he died. Israeli Air Force planes flying her and family here in a clandestine operation secretly planned for months.

Adir met Tasaro at a support group for asthma sufferers. She came to the group's meeting place to see her ex-boyfriend, Dido, when they were still an item. Dido owned a candy store in the new Central Bus Station, and he too suffered from asthma, and attended the weekly meetings on Rhines Street.

Four years before Dido had taken the young girl under his wing, when she was hanging around the Central Bus Station with a group of Ethiopian youngsters who had come to Israel like her, on Operation Shlomo, and helped her prepare to take her matriculation equivalency exams.

A spark went off between Adir and Tasaro the moment they set eyes on each other, and almost immediately Tasaro left her boyfriend, who took in another girl in her place, called Dananash. The day she went to remove the last of her belongings from Dido's apartment in Yad Eliyahu, while Adir waited downstairs with his car engine running, she had the chutzpah to go straight from there to the last of her matriculation exams, three units of math, and to get a grade of eight out of ten – Liat told Ventura during the same phone conversation that broke her heart.

Ventura herself had received nine out of ten in math, not on the equivalency, on the five-section exam, but what did that help her against someone so young and good-natured and with such a terrific figure and on top of that from the Beita Yisrael Jewish community of Ethiopia who was fluent in Amharic? Iris, by contrast, was a boring, banal native-born Israeli, and she even absolved Adir for leaving her for Tasaro. When all was said and done, how much patience could a person have to hear over and over again about her ex-husband, Othniel Grossman, with whom she had lived in wealth and reasonable contentment for more than ten years on Dor Dor v'Dorshav Street in Jerusalem, until he fell in love with a new immigrant from Russia, whom he met at a friend's forty-fifth birthday party? The Russian girl came with somebody else and left with somebody else – Othniel. Iris didn't go to that birthday party, because Herut, who was very little at the time, had reacted badly to some immunization shot she had received that morning at the Well

Baby clinic, and she hadn't wanted to leave her with a babysitter.

The lengthy process of the divorce had worn Iris out and ground her down. One day, terrified at the prospect of bringing up three children by herself, without much money, she got so depressed that she couldn't get out of bed in the apartment on Jeremiah Street. After two weeks during which she barely functioned and looked ghastly, she forced herself to get out of bed and went to the HMO clinic, where the doctor wrote her a prescription for a popular drug against depression and anxiety.

In her dire straits, Ventura pinned her hopes on Adir. He listened to her, or at least so it seemed to her, and that helped her a lot. For a little over a year they were together, until this glamour girl came along – and usurped her place.

Ventura said to him: "You can't do this to me."

"You can't do this to me," is what she said to her husband too when he told her about his new girlfriend.

Ventura said to herself that her life history included two abandonments – both of them because of new immigrants. In other words, someone in the state had to pay the price of the immigration to Israel, whether it was the massive wave that came from Russia because of the fall of the Iron Curtain, or whether it was the result of dramatic Zionist operations, such as Operation Shlomo. Nobody in the higher echelons of power thought about her when they approved the operation, and she certainly didn't enter the heads of the people who had dismantled the Soviet Union.

Nobody at the Jewish Agency thought of her either, or maybe they did. They thought that Israeli men and women were ready, tempered, made of stone. They had to absorb the new arrivals, whatever the price.

Like a ghost, Iris walked the streets of northwest Tel Aviv

after the breakup with Adir. For two and a half hours she walked back and forth in all the streets named after the minor and major prophets, and when she tried to calm herself by repeating the phrase "Whatever doesn't kill me makes me stronger," she was overcome by even greater bitterness. She had heard this piece of wisdom from a lot of people when she broke down during the divorce proceedings, but only she knew the truth. And the truth was: that she had not been strengthened in the least by the parting from Othniel, and after Adir threw her away for Tasaro – she was totally destroyed.

On Sunday the 12th of Tevet Iris's washing machine, the one she had brought with her from Jerusalem, gave up the ghost. Iris was in the living room watching the Hallmark channel while the children's laundry dried on the radiator. Two days previously she had been fired from the advertising firm of Kazakov and Co., where she worked as a freelance graphic artist, and with the addition of the minimal alimony she received from the father of her children succeeded in surviving. Danny Kazakov handed her the letter of dismissal and said that he was sorry, there was a terrible slump in the market, his business was in poor shape altogether.

It was a little before midday when the drum of the washing machine began to make excessively loud noises during the spin cycle, as if something inside had gone out of control. Iris took her eyes off the television screen, quickly finished turning the drying garments of eleven-year-old Osher, nine-year-old Oz, and five-year-old Herut onto their other, damp side, and strode anxiously toward the bathroom.

She stopped the washing machine, which was full of wet laundry. She opened the door on the front of the machine, and a stream of water poured out. She quickly closed the door and called the technician whose name and phone number were on a magnet on her fridge.

The technician informed her over the phone that he took a hundred and fifty shekels for an estimate, and if she agreed, he took fifty percent off the overall sum of the estimate.

The next day, in the morning, he came, opened the door of the washing machine, asked for some rags, threw the laundry, which was already beginning to smell bad, into the bathtub, poked about inside for quite a long time, and informed her that the washing machine had had its day, and the only thing she could do with it was bury it. He left Ventura with thirty-four shekels, floor rags no longer capable of absorbing anything, stinking water all over the apartment – and went on his way.

While she was sweeping the water into the drainage hole in the floor of the cold porch, Iris wondered what she should do now. The main drawback was that she had no money at all to buy a new washing machine. After ten of her checks had bounced, the bank had begun to restrict her overdraft. For nearly a year now she had had no credit card, and they had taken back her ATM card too. Her income this month consisted of the alimony Othniel transferred to her account at the beginning of every month, and the severance pay the Kazakovs had given her when they fired her.

The only advantage in the new situation, Iris concluded, was that now at least she would be able to do her laundry at the Clean World, and run into Bergson.

In the coming days Ventura went down to the Clean World to wash and dry the family laundry, and she did so at the times when she knew that Adir or Liat came to collect the coins and to check the level of the laundry detergent.

She didn't see Liat, because the first time she went there with her laundry, she saw Adir. He told her that Liat had caught the Saudi flu, and that she was in Ichilov Hospital. Iris asked him what ward she was in, and made up her mind to go to visit her sick childhood friend, but she didn't get around to it.

Instead, she went almost every day to the laundromat, hoping to meet Adir there. And indeed, sometimes she ran into him and sometimes she didn't. And when he wasn't there, she would walk a few more meters to the White and Bright laundry down the street, because they didn't have self-service there yet, although she had heard that soon everything would be strictly coin-operated at White and Bright too. In the meantime, but only in the meantime, the owners allowed her to get her laundry done on credit.

On the morning of the 23rd of Tevet, Iris went down to Clean World with two big yellow plastic bags full of bedsheets. That morning she broke her usual habit of doing her laundry in the evenings, after the children went to bed, because they had announced over the radio that a big storm would start in the afternoon. Since she knew that Adir wouldn't be there at this hour she took no trouble about her appearance and didn't even comb her hair, just wrapped herself in a coat and made for Clean World with her dirty laundry.

There was a cold, strong wind blowing from the sea. Iris was missing buttons on her coat, which blew open. Since all she was wearing under it were the sweats she used as pajamas, she thought she was going to freeze. With the last of her strength she battled against the wind until she reached Clean World.

The death notice was already posted on the laundry door. Iris read in astonishment:

52

My Sister
Liat Dubnov
Has suddenly passed away
Adir Bergson

And below the time of the funeral, *today at 2 P.M. at the Yarkon Cemetery. Shiva will be held at the apartment of the deceased, on Amos Street. . . .*

It isn't always possible to get to the bottom of things, in fact most of the time it's impossible. At such moments the world seemed to Iris as flat as the death notice. As obscure and inconsiderate as its contents.

Liat had died of the Saudi flu! Who would have believed that she would end up like this! Ventura put the two heavy yellow bags of laundry down in the puddle that had collected in front of the laundromat, took hold of the two flaps of her coat, closed it, and read the notice again and again. She didn't notice the puddle, or the fact that one of the bags had a hole in it, and muddy water seeped into it and dirtied the sheets even more.

Almost immediately the severe toothache from which she had been suffering for the past six months disappeared. It was the three pregnancies that had ruined her teeth. Iris knew that it was a question of several thousand shekels at least, and that dental treatment was something she could only dream about.

"Ach," sighed Ventura. If only she had a close friend, to whom she would have been able to tell the litany of all her recent troubles: the early death of her childhood friend, her dismissal from the advertising firm, her loneliness, her increasing poverty, her toothache, and the fact that she didn't want to spend money on painkillers, because she kept every penny she could scrape together in case the children asked her for a few shekels for school. Ventura hated having to say to say to them, "I haven't got it."

Instead she bought the cheapest pills for her toothache, and only when she really couldn't bear it any longer. When it hurt her she sat up in the living room all night long, holding ice packs to her cheek, staring at the idiotic movies they only dared to show in the middle of the night.

At her last meeting with Adir, two days before, he told her that Liat was feeling so-so, and he also asked her, by the way, when she intended to buy a new washing machine. Iris smiled and said:

"What a contradiction, Adir! Surely you shouldn't want me to buy a new washing machine. That's the aim, no, for there to be as few people as possible with washing machines, so that they'll all come to Clean World and help you make it to the end of the month...."

"You know very well that I don't have any problems making it to the end of the month," Adir said to her on that last meeting, and asked her to please hurry up.

Iris read the short death notice again. She looked for her cell phone in her coat pockets and called Adir, to ask him how it had happened, how such a thing had come about, but the cell phone was at home, and besides, she had a lousy one that operated on cards that cost eighty shekels, and she didn't have eighty shekels, and whenever she forgot her situation and tried to make a call, she heard a female voice saying, "Your credit has dropped to below three shekels." For the time being, Ventura could only receive calls on her cell phone.

The funeral, thought Ventura in alarm, the Yarkon Cemetery, how was she going to get there? She had to go to the funeral. That was clear. She had grown up with Liat and

Adir, she had been the girlfriend of Adir, Liat's only living relative.

Ventura walked away from Clean World towards White and Bright, trying to remember how much gas there was in her yellow Justy. Was there enough to get there and back, she asked herself, or only there, or maybe only halfway there. This thought was banished from her mind when she entered White and Bright and realized that it too had turned overnight into a self-service laundromat, with new machines and closed-circuit television. There was a notice written in red on pale green pasteboard: At long last we've become coin-operated. Customers with debts are asked to pay them ASAP. . . .

Iris owed them two-hundred-something shekels. "They can wait," she thought, and put the bed linen into their enormous new washing machine. Only now she noticed the new, muddy stains on the linen, added double the amount of detergent, and raised the temperature. In any case the colors are faded, she thought, so let them fade a bit more, the main thing is for the sheets to come out clean.

Not having any desire to live, but not having any alternative either, Iris stared at the laundry going round and round. The finality of Liat's situation made her feel dizzy, Liat who had always seemed to her so much more solid and strong than she was herself, perhaps due to Liat's narcissism and snobbishness. The half-brother and sister had developed a sense of superiority over the rest of their peers, both because of the family fortune and because their mother had drummed it into their heads that she was the first single mother in Israel, as if this gave them some kind of special status. In any case, once they had written her up in a women's magazine and crowned her as the first or the second single

55

mother in the country. In Iris's opinion, Kosta was a hard woman who was too self-centered. She had even taught her children to be proud of the fact that they had cut off all connections with their fathers.

"My mother was a free spirit," Liat once said to her. "She had a baby with every man she loved. And she only loved two."

Ventura sat down on an olive-green plastic chair, which reminded her of the color of the cover of Dubnow's *Jewish History*, which Liat Dubnov had at her house. When they were children they would sit for hours doing their Jewish history homework with the help of that book. Iris would complain to her friend that it was impossible to find what they needed in her Dubnow, that it was too complicated, but Liat insisted that they work from it. Iris well remembered the division of labor between them: she would look in the index, and Liat would find the right page and place the open volume between them. Afterwards, they would argue about the answer, and sometimes call Shifra, to give them the bottom line. Shifra's father had a doctorate in Jewish history, and Shifra did her homework according to the book her father wrote.

One day, Liat boasted to Iris that they had received Dubnow's history for nothing. Iris said to her, "Even if you got it for nothing, that doesn't mean that Dubnow was connected to your father."

"It doesn't mean that he was," said Liat, "and it doesn't mean that he wasn't."

This was during a period when Ventura caught Liat lying a lot, and for the most part she didn't know when she was telling the truth and when she was lying. Later on this period came to a close. People said that Dubnov's mother sent her daughter to a psychologist, privately.

When Ventura heard that Dubnov, after travelling the length and breadth of the United States for a year, had returned to Israel and registered at the University of Tel Aviv to study Aramaic, she envied her for specializing in a subject she loved, while she herself had compromised and gone to study graphic art at the Bezalel Art School, because she was told it was more practical. But it didn't really interest her. She wanted to teach history; not just the history of the Jews, but of all the nations in the world.

VENTURA MOVED TO JERUSALEM soon after the death of her parents, when she was twenty-one. They died one after the other, during the same year, just after she had finished her army service. Her father committed suicide on Yom Kippur, and her mother died two months later, of cardiac arrest, while taking a shower.

With what was left of their savings, their daughter paid for her graphic art course at Bezalel, and with the rent she received for her parents' apartment in Tel Aviv, she paid her rent in Jerusalem.

At the beginning of little Iris's life it seemed that she was all set for the nice life of a pretty, diligent, obedient, nice little girl in a nice part of north Tel Aviv. As a child, she lived with her parents and her sister Nava on Nordau Boulevard, and went to kindergarten on Amos Street, the same kindergarten to which she sent Herut today, but in her day there was an old Yemenite woman living nearby, who was said to be a relative of the famous singer Shoshana Damari. This old woman kept yelling at the children to shut up, and they shut up because they were afraid of her, especially after they heard that she was related to Shoshana Damari, as if Shoshana Damari would do them some harm.

Once she crossed Amos Street without first looking both ways. A cyclist knocked her down. Nothing happened to her, and he went on riding and looking back at her sitting on the asphalt. She was so frightened that she peed in her pants, but nobody noticed.

Two weeks after that the Ventura family drove down to the beach in Michmoret with all kinds of friends of theirs who had emigrated to Israel with them in '48. On the beach they knew so well, the old friends put up a tent, and forced the children to eat before they went into the water, like they always did. Everything was fun and games, until the moment when they couldn't find Nava, her little sister who was one year younger than she was.

Neither her mother nor her father had told Iris to watch over Nava and not to take her eyes off her, but it was she who they blamed for Nava's drowning. And so Ventura's life story includes the death of a sister by drowning on Michmoret Beach and the feelings of guilt that wreaked havoc on her self-esteem and personal development.

Quite soon after Nava's death and her funeral – Ventura would never forget Nava's funeral, she was suffering from an eye infection at the time and she could hardly open her eyes – her parents sank into a life of survival and nothing more. Back and forth from home to work. And the friends who had immigrated with them stopped coming to the house. After the shiva they simply disappeared. Iris didn't dare ask where they had disappeared to.

Iris married Othniel, who came to Bezalel to give a series of three lectures. She thought that with him she would have the normal family life she had always wanted. Shortly after their marriage, she graduated from art school, and from then on she devoted all of her attention to her family.

Three years after marrying an architect, Ventura Grossman made a grave real-estate mistake. She sold the apartment in north Tel Aviv to an orthopedist who turned it into a clinic. Iris wanted a dream home, and with the money from the sale of the apartment, the couple renovated the house on Dor Dor v'Dorshav Street in Jerusalem according to her husband's designs and transformed it into a palace, with a patio that had a little waterfall in the center. Everyone who entered the house said, "It's a palace!" and marvelled at the beauty of the patio.

With the money left over they paid for two parties to celebrate the circumcision first of Osher, and then of Oz who came after him. To both ceremonies, which were held in the palace itself, Iris invited her Tel-Aviv friends – for she had no family – among them Liat Dubnov, Adir Bergson, and their mother who was still alive at the time. It was very important to Iris for people in the big city to know that she was making such a success of her life.

After she caught Grossman cheating on her, she wanted a divorce. Grossman wanted a reconciliation, but the wounded Ventura refused, and demanded a division of property. Only then did she discover that the deed to the house in Jerusalem was in the name of Othniel's parents, who were both alive and kicking. After an exhausting legal battle Ventura gave up all her rights, all she wanted was to get out, and she returned to Jeremiah Street in Tel Aviv almost destitute.

In her first year back in Tel Aviv, at least four days a week, she would drive past the house where she had lived with her parents in the yellow Justy Othniel had bought her for her thirtieth birthday, and eat her heart out.

Ventura had a backup plan, that if she was stuck without a penny, she would become orthodox.

Her idea was that if she became orthodox, the religious institutions in the country, all kinds of nonprofit organizations run by the "Sephardi Guardians of the Torah" party, in other words, Shas, would help her to live and educate her children.

In the evenings, after the children fell asleep and she remained sitting alone opposite the television thinking about what was to be done, her thoughts would wander to this possibility, and she would imagine herself wearing a head-scarf and wrapped in long skirts and long-sleeved blouses in the middle of summer, and Osher and Oz with earlocks and yarmulkes running around in the yard of a school in the religious suburb of Bnei Brak, and Herut getting married to some other orthodox penitent and having ten children with him, and as she had once heard, dragging out their breast-feeding as long as possible, in order to put off getting pregnant again. During the long nights, while lying awake with her toothache, she would ask herself what religious organization would pay for her dental reconstruction, if and when. She supposed that there must be a special nonprofit organization that would help her finally get rid of her advanced dental decay, and that the same charitable hand would also put implants in those places where she no longer had any teeth left. Luckily she only needed implants to replace her wisdom teeth. As chance would have it Ventura's incisors had remained as perfect as they were before the birth of her children. Now, sitting in White and Bright and waiting for her load to finish, she felt the familiar pain again, but not with the same degree of intensity as at night. Since she didn't have the money to buy painkillers, and the ice was so cold at this time of year, she recalled that alcohol helped, by anaesthetizing the painful place, and decided to save up for a bottle of cheap vodka, but as soon as the pain subsided she forgot about it.

Outside it began to rain and the customers in the laundromat said that the storm had arrived ahead of schedule. Iris looked at the slanting lines a moment before they shattered on the ground. The funeral would take place in the pouring rain, not like her sister's funeral, which had taken place in the middle of the summer in the blazing sun.

How it had burnt her skin to wear black then! Not only had she been burnt by the sun at Michmoret Beach on that terrible Saturday, but also at the funeral itself, where the rays of the sun had penetrated the black clothes they had made her wear on top of her sunburn. People around her were drinking water out of soda bottles, because it was back before the country had begun to import mineral water. People drank tap water back then. It was a completely different time. Her aunt had brought ice water to the funeral in a family-sized orangeade bottle. She handed the bottle to Iris. Iris said that she wasn't thirsty.

The washing machine stopped running, and Iris transferred the damp laundry to the dryer. She inserted the coins, shekels and half shekels, which she had scraped together from every corner of the house. Three times she had counted her change before she set out on her expedition to the laundromat, and she knew that she had the exact amount, but suddenly, in the field, she counted – and she found herself one shekel short. She pushed her hands deep into the pockets of her raincoat, perhaps it had fallen out of her purse or was hiding between the folds, but at the bottom of her pockets she only found disintegrating bits of paper from previous winters.

Helplessly she looked around, looking for the owner, so that he would lend her a shekel, or do something to the machine to make it work, in any case she owed them money, what was one more shekel. But the only people in the place were Tel Avivians, men and women, who didn't look as if they were native Tel Avivians at all, and Ventura felt superior to them, any way she looked at it. She was a native of Tel Aviv, she had been born in this city, while they, however hard they tried, and even if they lived here for the rest of their lives from now on, would always have something in their mentality that would pop up to prove that they had been born and bred in Ra'anana, for example. Iris, who had no reason to feel superior to them in any respect detectable to the naked eye, saw them as immigrants to the big city, provincials.

One of these immigrants opened his wallet. Iris took a peek. So many credit cards! And the guy wasn't even twenty-five years old. His wallet was full of coins. In an instant she filled with bitterness. It was already a reflex with her.

I'll bet he's the son of diamond dealers from an exclusive suburb like Kfar Shmaryahu or Herzlia Pituach, she thought. She was just about to press the coin-return button, when her eye was drawn to a glittering shekel lying on a chair on top of a wet newspaper from the day before, with big head-lines about the terror attacks from the previous day, or the day before that. Since then there had been another two, calculated Ventura, and she got up and sat down with an absent-minded air on the wet newspaper, on the shekel. And then with a demonstration of discomfort, ostensibly because of the wetness of the newspaper, she made a face, raised herself up a little, and pulled the paper and the shekel out from under her. On her face she wore a stern expression, which she called up from the distant past, when she drilled new recruits at Training Base 12, before she applied for a transfer to another base. She put the shekel into the dryer's coin slot, and as she was about to sit down again, she found the wet newspaper on her chair, this time on its other side, with a black-and-white picture of Kati Beit-Halahmi from one of her confessional interviews, before she had received the consignment of warm clothes from all over the country.

Iris recognized the poor, unfortunate, ostracized woman from Lod looking up at her from the wet newspaper, and she felt a general, abstract pity for Beit-Halahmi and her family.

In spite of everything, she thought, there's no comparison between my situation and hers – she's been deep in the shit since childhood, and I have no intention of remaining in the gutter. I'm not used to this poverty. It's something completely different.

Through the laundromat window she saw Tusi, Adir's mongrel dog, crossing Dizengoff Street in the rain by itself, and she was flooded by a more tangible form of pity, both for the dog and for its owner Adir. She thought that if she was still his girlfriend, she would now be holding the dog's leash, concerning herself with Adir's welfare, maybe making him some herb tea, and she definitely wouldn't be here, short of a shekel, in this laundromat, with all these recently immigrated snobs and their piercings.

What a shame that everything was over between her and Adir! How much he needed her now, and he didn't even know it! How tragic! Ventura shook her head at length.

If the dog was outside alone, she reflected when her previous train of thought came to an end, it meant that Adir was home alone, because – was it yesterday, or the day before – she had seen Tasaro running with the dog in the rain, holding a carton of calcium-enriched milk?

"If I was Adir's girlfriend I would buy him soy milk or ferret milk," she had thought when she saw Tasaro running. She had read, or heard, or seen somewhere that ferret milk was good for the chronically ill.

That Tasaro . . . what a character. She was a number and

64

no mistake … thinking of Adir, but always putting herself first, as if she were innocent, even though she was really a devil, Ventura concluded to herself. … Buying him calcium-enriched milk and thinking that she'd done her duty, instead of giving him what he really needed now: Love. Warmth. The silly little cow. Neglect, decided Ventura. Pure and simple neglect. And he was head over heels in love with the silly bitch!

Angrily, she threw the newspaper onto the empty chair next to her. She had already read it the day before, and she knew all about the Beit-Halahmi family from the special feature pages, and the horrifying terror attack that had taken place in Netanya had been covered at length on the first few pages. Iris had already seen the harsh pictures of that event, described as one of the worst in the history of Netanya, on television: a terrorist had gunned down people at the Central Bus Station, fifteen dead, sixty wounded, three of them mortally – and, therefore, she felt a kind of revulsion for the outdated newspaper.

The newspaper, for its part, succeeded in clinging to the edge of the chair next to Iris for a moment, after which it slipped and fell onto the muddy floor.

Iris felt bad, empty, as a result of the out-of-date newspaper's fall. She took its fall personally, and stretched her body, almost falling flat on her face, in an attempt to pick the paper up, but she couldn't reach it and was obliged to stand up, bend down, pick it up and put it on the chair directly across from her seat.

When she finally returned to her seat – she made up her mind: she would have to find a ride to the funeral. When all was said and done, times were hard. But, when all was said and done, she didn't have the gas, or the means to get it. A

severe, stabbing toothache, made her decide, once it subsided a little, to turn to Liat's dentist, Dr. Yoram Danziger,
who had whitened Liat's teeth six months before, and Iris
had envied her acutely at the time, for being at the stage of
worrying about whitening, but now, what good were white
teeth to Liat? Iris sighed out loud. Life was so unpredictable.
Only two months ago, when it began to be clear that this
winter was impossible but true – she had met her walking
down Gordon Street, and asked her, how her teeth could be
so white when she was a smoker.

Liat replied, "Yoram Danziger. The ultimate dentist. His
face got burnt in Lebanon." She laughed suddenly, and Ventura couldn't understand what was so funny until Liat went
on to say: "You can see that every plastic surgeon who tried
to fix his face started in a certain direction and gave up, and
then another plastic surgeon tried another direction and
gave up, and now, I'm sure, his face looks even worse than
it did in the beginning. All kinds of different beginnings,
get it?"

"Yes," said Iris.

"But his hands are gold, Iris. Believe me. If you ever need
a fantastic dentist, go to him. He's a wizard, I'm telling you,
one of a kind. If the way his face looks makes you feel
uncomfortable – close your eyes during the treatment."

"I always close them anyway," said Iris.

Back at home, at about ten in the morning, she looked up
Danziger's number in the phone book, not wanting to call
information, which cost the same as three local calls. Danziger, who lived on Bavly, and whose clinic was in David
Yellin Street, didn't even know that Liat was dead, and Iris
was the one who had to break the news to him. No, he had
no problem with picking her up, he said. Nor did he have

a problem with bringing her back, and Ventura thought that on the way back from the cemetery to Tel Aviv, maybe she would mention something about her toothache, and it wasn't impossible that out of some kind of kindred feeling – since they had both known Liat – he would give her a discount. It all depended on the atmosphere that would exist between them in the car. With his aesthetic situation, it was likely that he didn't have any clients at all, and he would jump at the chance.

ON TRANS-SAMARIA ROAD, from the direction of Samaria, two processions drove towards each other. The one going from west to east was taking Dubnov to her eternal rest, and the other, going from east to west, was taking Ziv Barami to his eternal rest. Both processions were heading for the Yarkon Cemetery. It was late afternoon, but the sky was dark and dripping.

At the head of the funeral procession going from east to west was the Burial Society's black van. After it came two dark security cars, with blinking blue lights on their roofs, but without their sirens on, only the lights flickering in the rain. After them came an old white Subaru, occupied by the chief mourners, and after that, the long dark VIP limousine. In it was a driver, and in the back seat – Reuven Tekoa.

Little more than a year had passed since Tekoa had been elected by a crushing majority in the Knesset to serve as the President of the State of Israel for the next five years, and for more than half of the time that had passed since he had declared from the Knesset podium, "I pledge allegiance to the State of Israel and promise to uphold its laws and to faithfully perform my role as the President of the State" – he had been rushing from funeral to funeral, from one condolence call to another, and from there to visit the wounded at the hospital, and so on and so forth.

Now Tekoa was on his way to the funeral of Ziv, a seventeen-year-old boy from Alfei Menashe, whose parents and two sisters were sitting in the Subaru. For a week Ziv Barami had been listed as missing, and yesterday his body had been found in a cave next to an Arab village. It turned out that he had been stoned to death on the day of his disappearance, when he went for a walk with his dog, and strayed into the

68

vicinity of the Arab village. The stoners killed the dog as well. The stoning of boy was one of a series of grave incidents that took place on the same day, one more of those "days of rage" declared from time to time by the Palestinians. Tekoa had already been to five funerals that week, and his crowded schedule included the addresses of houses where mourners were sitting shiva, as well as the addresses of other houses he had to visit in the course of performing his duties.

Tekoa yawned, and he was glad that there was nobody with him in the car, apart from the driver, who, by now, he considered part of the limousine, since he was such a silent, submissive man.

The necessity for the policy of restraint, to which the government still adhered, was becoming less and less apparent to the President, and he found it difficult to overcome his powerful desire for revenge. Like many during those terrible days, Tekoa ran various scenarios of total war through his exhausted mind, a war in which he could envisage no other possible outcome but the victory of Israel and the defeat of the other side.

Most of the scenarios imagined by the President were stymied by the entity known as world public opinion, and thus Tekoa retreated again to the recognition that it was better for Israel to restrain itself, for even if the Israelis won a total war against the Arabs, the victory would only bring them greater troubles than before, as had the ecstatic victory of the Six-Day War.

In the Six-Day War, Tekoa served as a senior officer in the Shin Bet security service, and already then he had heard his superiors and peers in the service predict the disastrous consequences that the sweeping victory would bring in its wake. And so, he was robbed of the joy of victory. After the war, he served for a few years as the head of the National Security College, and in the end he retired from public service and turned to affairs of an unclear nature. Some said he dealt arms and even uranium, and others that he was involved in nothing but textiles.

About a year before the Yom Kippur War, he reemerged into the public eye when he published an article in the "Opinion" section of a big newspaper, in which he warned of an upcoming war, which would continue "for many years to come, in different forms and on different fronts." After the furious reactions he received, especially from the government, for harming national morale, he decided to abandon his business affairs for a while in order to write a serious and detailed book about the difficulties in which Israel found itself as a result of the Six-Day War.

In 568 pages, Tekoa set forth his position, which he sometimes argued for and sometimes simply stated, as if it was a fact as plain as day. The book was coldly received by the military, but this did not prevent it from becoming a bestseller, since it came out soon after the outbreak of the War for Peace in Galilee, and the Israelis wanted to read and know more about their country's security situation.

After the war he served for many years as Israel's ambassador to Belgium. During those years he acquired a working knowledge of French, and his English became excellent. At the beginning of the '90s he returned to Israel and local politics. He reached the exalted position of President owning to the fact that he was well liked in high places. It was thought that in addition to the advantages of his appealing appearance and fine taste in clothes, he possessed a sufficiently profound knowledge of Israel's complex situation, an excellent command of three languages, an innate composure, and a relatively high intelligence. To these the many people who favored his candidacy for the presidency added the fact that his roots were deeply planted in Jerusalem. The legend that had been handed down from generation to generation in his family, and found an honored place in his public image, which was zealously built up in the media, said that the Tekoa family was one of the few families in the country that had left the land for Babylon for only a short time after the destruction of the First Temple, taking the first opportunity to return to Zion in the days of Ezra, and ignoring the advice of the prophet Jeremiah, an outspoken advocate of Jewish settlement in Babylon.

Tekoa was therefore above and beyond any communal classification along the lines of the Sephardi/Ashkenazi distinction, and this fact was made much of in the days preceding his election by the Knesset to the foremost office in the state. He and his people continually stressed his background, and Reuven Tekoa easily defeated his opponent, who had emigrated to Israel from the United States with the establishment of the state.

The President's limousine was, naturally, bulletproof and reinforced to protect against stones. His bodyguards rode both in front of him and behind him, they too in stone and bulletproof automobiles. The Subaru in which the family of the deceased was riding was protected against stones, but not bulletproof. During the trip to the cemetery an argument even broke out between the occupants of the car, whether to invest thousands of dollars in bulletproofing it, or whether to leave the settlement. This argument continued until Ziv's mother screamed: "Stop it, aren't you ashamed? Let me bury my child!"

, , ,

71

The funeral procession of the deceased Dubnov was also led by a black van belonging to the biggest burial society in Israel, the "Chevra Kadisha." After it came Adir's blue Golf. Next to him sat Tasaro. She had not had time to undo all ninety plaited braids they had done to her hair for the swimsuit catalog photo-shoot. She had only managed to remove the layers of makeup they had put on her face before the morning shoot, when Adir, who was standing on the balcony and waiting for telephone instructions from the undertakers, said to her, "Come on, we're leaving."

During the ride Tasaro busied herself with undoing her braids. Shortly after the Kfar Hayarok junction Adir said to her, "Enough already. Tie it back the way it is and leave it."

She did as he said.

Dr. Danziger's white Volvo too advanced eastward. Next to the dentist Iris Ventura sat shrinking in her seat, unable to look him in his scarred face and say a single word either about the deceased or about the security situation. Silence suited them both. The interior of the car was given over entirely to the radio. Danziger had the army channel on at full volume, and Iris asked herself if his hearing had also been damaged in the mountains of Lebanon, or if he too was to be included among those who became one with the security-political situation. On the radio they were speaking about the atrocity committed by an Arab mob against the boy Ziv Barami from Alfei Menashe, whose funeral procession was at that moment advancing from east to west towards the Yarkon Cemetery.

Afterwards, the Israeli radio station interviewed people from the other side of the conflict, and they poured their pain into the microphone. The station saw it fit to interview an Arab Knesset member, who presented his point of view. The MK had hardly opened his mouth, addressing the broadcaster by his first name, when Danziger shut him up. He thundered, "I don't understand the Israeli media, believe me, Dorit."

"Iris," whispered Iris.

"Why do they have to interview them at all? Why give them a chance to open their mouths? I don't understand how they can be so stupid. They're a useless bunch, the lot of them, I'm telling you."

"I personally agree with you," said Iris. "But on the other hand I understand them too."

"What do you mean you understand *them*? What's there to understand? Obviously they're in a bad way. But it's war, my dear, war."

Iris wanted to reach out to him and she said, "You're one hundred percent right."

"Because what do they want? Huh? What do they want? They want everything. *Every*thing."

"You're absolutely right," said Iris.

He was silent. The radio played a song, and Danziger switched to Channel 2, where they were describing the special security arrangements for the upcoming Snow Festival at Mount Hermon, the first of its kind.

"Revolting," exclaimed Danziger, and Iris couldn't tell if he was referring to the Snow Festival, or the bad security situation.

"I don't understand," said Danziger. "Kill me, but I don't understand."

"In the end, all in all, you're right," said Iris to be on the safe side. "The problem is that they're our enemy, and peace is made with enemies. There's no other option. At some stage or other we'll have to sit down with them. Not with the Chinese or the Swedes. With them."

"Revolting," repeated Danziger.

Iris hoped that Liat's funeral would soften him, and she would be able to tell him about her teeth, and in the meantime to begin to have them treated on credit. She looked at his profile, just for a minute.

"I don't like people looking at me, Dorit," he said.

"Sorry. My name's Iris."

"Iris, Shmiris. Don't look at me too much. It makes me nervous."

"Sorry."

Driving behind them, alone in his wife's little Peugeot, was Shaul Takdim, the married boyfriend of the deceased. His radio was switched off, and he was steeped in melancholy because of the death of the woman who had recently been his. His melancholy was expressed externally by a cloud of inaccessibility, and internally by self-flagellation. Takdim felt very guilty for having hung up on her and slammed the phone down on the night of her death. He was consumed by remorse for letting her die with the feeling that he had abandoned her, when the truth was that he simply couldn't talk, his wife might have heard, and he couldn't take the risk. In any case she had already caught him cheating on her with various women who worked out at the gym when he first established his health club, and he, even though it was something he couldn't control, had promised to stop. Takdim had established his health club with capital belonging to his wife's family, and he was therefore very afraid of her.

Adir had informed him of her death that morning, and the first thing he did, because he couldn't bear the news on his own, was tell all the regular clients of the club, who knew Liat. To his wife he said that one of their most serious exercisers had passed away from the Saudi flu. She said that she would have accompanied him to the funeral but she had to go to an important meeting. His wife was about to open a gourmet restaurant and she was interviewing various chefs, and it drove Takdim crazy to think that she might outstrip his achievements. Almost all the regular exercisers at the gym said that they would come and, in fact, most of them were now driving behind the director of their health club, with their lights on, the rain beating on the roofs of their cars, and their wipers swishing back and forth.

Adir too was busy checking attendance. He glanced into the mirror to see if the funeral procession was long, but it was actually too short to satisfy him, no more than fifteen or twenty cars whose occupants he recognized. And this turnout after he had given people more than twenty-four hours to get themselves organized. Adir knew that there wouldn't be many more waiting for him at the cemetery gates. At most, another ten. In light of it all, he thought, there had been a big contradiction in his sister's life: on the one hand, she had made a big hullabaloo about the mere fact of her existence, holding extravagant birthday parties for herself with guests from all walks of life. Adir had no idea where she found them. Tasaro told him that they couldn't be sure she didn't pick them up off the street, like collecting people for a minyan. Tasaro was sure that Liat was crazy, that she was a woman with a lot of problems. On the other hand, Dubnov lived like a recluse, for days on end she didn't answer the phone, and above all she liked being alone, with her books, in the apartment on Amos Street, which she had renovated immediately after their mother died.

Adir had notified everyone he knew she knew, and he had also made sure to have the death notices posted all over the area. He hadn't had the time to go through her address book and make another hundred calls, and say over and over again, "Hello, this is Adir, Liat's brother. I'm sorry to have to tell you. . . ."

He believed that the rumor of her death would spread, and people would turn up for the shiva.

Among the cars, Bergson noticed a taxi occupied by women his mother had played bridge with. Bringing up the rear of the procession, he guessed, there would be a handful of friends of his, mainly people who had studied atmospheric science with him. The rain began pouring down in big drops; he turned the wipers up to their top speed and thought: If worst comes to worst, it'll be a quiet, intimate funeral.

CHAPTER NINE

AT THE SAME LATE AFTERNOON HOUR, the Beit-Halahmi household in Ganei-Aviv was a hive of activity. Kati and Boaz Beit-Halahmi had already known for over twenty-four hours that the President of Israel, Reuven Tekoa, was going to pay them a visit in the very near future, and they had even heard it on the 8 A.M. news. At first they had been notified that the President and his entourage would come in the morning, but later they were told that he would only arrive in the afternoon, because he was escorting the boy Ziv Barami to his eternal rest.

Kati sent the children to school, and quickly cleaned the stairwells she had to clean that morning on Alei Koteret and Tzamarot streets. She was in a state. She didn't know what was the right impression for them to make on the President: poor and pleasant, poor and embittered, or poor and cheerful, relaxed and full of hope for the future.

Kati Beit-Halahmi, who had made the journey into and out of public awareness all on her own, and who had fed the media with the story of her life, wanted to prove to the President that they were in dire straits so that he would do something about it, but, on the other hand, because of her pride, she also wanted to honor the President and buy all kinds of refreshments for him with all the money she had, even though in that case he would surely say to himself, what's all the fuss about, they don't seem short of anything to me ... and perhaps he would even think that they had just been telling stories for the cameras.

She cleaned and tidied the apartment, and dusted places that she had never reached before. Boaz watched her stand on a chair and clean cobwebs.

At least let the place be clean and tidy, she thought, and

turned to her husband to ask him whether in his opinion they should emphasize their poverty or whether it would be better to try to conceal it. Boaz replied that the President's visit was of no interest to him whatsoever, in any case he had no intention of being at home when he arrived.

"But the President!" cried Kati getting off the chair and wiping her footprints off it. "The President is coming! How many more times in your life will you see the President of the State of Israel coming to visit you in your home?"

"Never," said Boaz, and he pulled his coat off the hook next to the front door and left.

Kati wiped the living-room couches with a damp, scented cloth, and took a deep breath, to smell the fresh smell. The telephone, on which they could only receive calls, rang. On the line – the President's office. A secretary informed her that the President was at this moment attending the funeral of the Barami boy, after which he still had to pay five condolence calls at the homes of terror attack victims, and this being the case, his visit to the Beit-Halahmis would have to be postponed to a later date.

"When?" asked Kati.

"We'll be in touch," said the secretary.

"Sure," said Kati, disappointed.

"Madam, madam," cried the secretary. "Believe me, the President wants very much to come. The President regards the social issue as a matter of the highest importance, but due to the all the casualties and the funerals, his priorities have had to change."

"I understand."

"The minute there's a cease-fire, I promise I'll get back to you," said the secretary.

"No problem," said Kati and hung up. She was almost crying, and for a few seconds she automatically went on

78

dusting the television, until she stopped and asked herself why she was bothering.

Kati sat down on the sofa, feeling very hurt. The telephone rang again and she was sure that it was the President's office calling to inform her that the President insisted on coming in spite of everything, but it was Micah, the acting producer of the program *At Effi's on the Porch*. A miracle had occurred. She was invited to take part in the program this coming Friday; someone else had cancelled, and they very much wanted her instead. The show was being recorded today, a taxi would come to fetch her that afternoon and take her to the studio in Jerusalem.

Kati gave the acting producer directions to her neighborhood and to her apartment, and when she finished the phone call, she went and stood in front of the mirror and thought that in another world, another fate, with another husband, another life, she could have been a very, very famous woman. And perhaps that other world was beginning to take over this world, starting tomorrow, on Effi's television program.

She washed her face and put on a bit of makeup, just to see herself looking a little better, even though she knew that at the television studio they would go to work on her face and bring out all its beauty.

It had been a long time since Kati had used the few cosmetics she possessed, and most of them were already dried-up and useless. Nevertheless, she felt that a change was about to take place in her life, a change that was incompatible with the facts of her regular life. This contradiction made her restless, and she went to the kitchen, to heat up the children's dinner, so they would have something to eat when they came home from the long school day, in case the cafeteria food had not been enough to satiate them.

Every morning Boaz would wake up early, and make the children's sandwiches for their ten-o'clock break. Two or three times a week, after they left, Boaz would prepare hot dishes according to his mother's recipes. All Kati had to do was heat them up. She didn't like him taking over her kitchen, but she let him do it, because during the course of their married life she had noticed that it calmed him down, and that if he didn't have a few hours alone in the kitchen during the week, he was in danger of having a meltdown and taking out all his disappointments in life on her. No, he didn't hit her, but he smashed things, trashed the house, and she had to clean it up.

If the President had come, as they had promised her, perhaps she would have whispered in his ear, explained to him why their house looked like such a mess, as if they were in the middle of renovations, but in the end he didn't come.

A split second after Beit-Halahmi muttered to herself, "He isn't going to come" about the President of Israel, the rain that had started falling earlier began coming down even harder, showing no consideration at all for the funerals of either Barami nor Dubnov. In less than a minute the open grave filled with water. Bergson looked at what was happening with shock on his face. He wondered if the water would seep down into the ground, if the gravediggers would order him to interrupt the proceedings and wait for this to happen, or else they would have to drown his sister's body. As he looked hopefully at Liat's open grave, wishing that the rain would stop and that the water would be absorbed by the deeper layers of the earth, Ventura's cell phone began to ring. Iris had set her ringer to the tune of the song "Diva" that had represented Israel in the Eurovision song contest, and Adir wanted to kill her and throw her body into the grave. How could she have left her cell phone on?!

Ventura was horribly embarrassed. Her fingers dug deep into her bag to find her Nokia and silence it. Her umbrella fell, and the rain fell straight on her, but she didn't bend down to pick it up, she feverishly went on looking for her cell phone. But instead of finding the rounded little antenna or the body of the Nokia phone, in order to pull it out and silence it – her fingers encountered unpaid bills, police reports, once for talking on the phone without a hands-free unit while she was driving, and once for exceeding the speed limit of 75 kph within the city limits, traffic tickets from the Jerusalem municipality, from the Tel Aviv municipality, for parking her Justy in a no-parking zone, a wallet with no money, but crammed full of various warning notices and advertisements for solar heating, which she wanted to show her landlord before summer began so that he would install it for her, reminders to pay various school bills, rolls of film she had taken of the children at a Hanukkah party and on other occasions, and which she didn't have the money to develop, batteries that had died and a package of new batteries that she had lifted from the supermarket a month before right under the eyes of the checkout clerk who had turned a blind eye for a minute, and which she had forgotten about completely. Everything except for the damned cell phone.

The mourners looked at her, Adir with flashing eyes. She was already soaked through to the marrow of her bones. She was cold. Her teeth were chattering. She looked at the mourners under their umbrellas. They all looked so holy to her with the skullcaps on their heads, some of them made of cardboard.

She left the scene, running through the cemetery with the tune that had won Israel first place in the Eurovision contest ringing in the depths of her bag, until she was far enough away. She stopped next to the grave of one Shaltiel, "our beloved," found the cell phone, and silenced it. She managed to catch that the call came from Jerusalem, and wondered what Othniel wanted from her now.

She wanted to return to Liat's funeral, which was what she had come here for, but her eye was caught by the funeral of Ziv Barami. "So many people," she thought, "it must be somebody important," and she drew closer, with her hand deep in her bag and her fingers holding the cell phone, in case it rebelled and rang again even though she had turned it off.

A security guard detached himself from the mourners and hurried towards her. His hand was on the pistol on his belt. He ordered her to halt. She stopped. He drew his gun, aimed it at her, and called out: "Hands up, don't move."

Iris was wounded to the quick. These were difficult times, but to suspect her?

"Can I put my bag down?" she asked in a panic.

"Do it fast. Empty the contents onto the ground."

She did as he told her, and raised her hands, mumbling to herself, "Trying times, Iris, trying times." She prayed that Adir and the rest of the mourners at Liat's funeral couldn't see what was happening to her. She couldn't see them, because she had her back to them.

"Do you suspect me?" she asked.

"Two steps back, please," said the security guard. "Take off your coat too, and put it on the ground."

Iris took off her coat and threw it onto the wet ground, and raised her hands in the air again, grateful that it had stopped raining at least.

The security guard rummaged among the contents of her bag, and in the pockets of her coat. Then he returned his pistol to its holster, and took out a metal detector. He passed it over her body, round her head and between her legs.

"Are we done?" asked Iris, terrified.

"Okay, put your hands down. You can get dressed. Identity card please."

"It's in my bag," said Iris, pale with fright. "Are we done? Can I. . . ."

"Yes, yes. Pick up your belongings."

Iris bent down again, took the blue card out of her wallet and gave it to him. He glanced at it and gave it back to her.

"What are you doing here?"

"What am I doing here? I'll tell you what I'm doing here. I came to the funeral of a very good friend of mine, and suddenly my cell phone rang and I ran over here to switch it off." She pointed to Liat's funeral. Some of the mourners were staring in fascination at her and the security guard.

"I understand. Next time don't walk around with your hand in your bag. This is a high security area here."

"I didn't know. I'm sorry."

Some of the people at Barami's funeral were also looking at her curiously. Only at her. There were television cameras there, and microphones hanging from long rods over Tekoa, who was eulogizing the dead boy. He was speaking in a loud voice, or into one of the microphones. She heard him say, "We won't allow murderers in cold blood. . . ." It's the President, she said to herself, and she blushed. She had never been so humiliated in public before. She was ashamed to return to Liat's funeral. The rain that had stopped threatened to start again, and a few seconds later a light rain began to fall. Her coat was wet and muddy. She was shivering with cold and embarrassment. It was clear that she would have to have the coat dry-cleaned, and it wouldn't do her any

83

harm either to stand in front of a heater for an hour and dry herself. She slung the coat over her shoulders, plucked up her courage and returned to the funeral. On the way, she recovered her umbrella from where she had let it fall to the ground and went and stood next to Danziger, who was standing a little way off from the grave, his hands folded behind his back and a cardboard skullcap on his head. Iris noticed that there were raindrops on the skullcap that had not yet been absorbed by the cardboard, and then turned her attention to the funeral proceedings. The grave was already covered with flowers. Danziger whispered to her, "Don't ask, they put her into a completely wet grave and covered her with mud."

"It doesn't matter," said Iris, and thought, what difference does it make, she's dead. Dead people don't have that kind of problem anymore.

It started to rain hard. The umbrellas were not much help. People got wet from the rain pouring down their neighbors' umbrellas, and waited patiently for Adir to finish reading the short eulogy that he had decided to deliver after all, about the uniqueness of his sister, her love of beauty, of the Aramaic language, of ancient languages in general, and of their dead mother, who was now gathering her to herself. As he was speaking he choked on the words. Tasaro stood next to him, her face expressionless and her hand resting on his shoulder. Adir said that he was left alone in the world and burst into tears, and for a couple of seconds Iris, too, allowed her tears to flow. Danziger put his arm around her.

"What a wonderful person she was. . . ." she mumbled. "Pure gold."

"She was, she was," said Danziger, rocking Ventura to comfort her.

"Open your umbrella," Danziger requested, and she

opened it and he bent down and huddled up against her. Iris noticed that his skullcap was completely wet and had lost its shape. She was glad that she wasn't the only one who looked ridiculous, and she felt consoled.

On the way back from the cemetery, each of the cars went its own way. The Barami family returned to sit shiva in the settlement of Alfei Menashe. President Reuven Tekoa was driven to Ra'anana to pay a condolence call to a family who had been very offended by the failure of anyone in an official position to pay their respects up to then. His secretary called to inform him that she had cancelled Lod, but not to forget that at the end of the day he had a meeting with various experts and consultants, regarding the question of whether to declare that the State of Israel was in a state of emergency. The King of Jordan had already declared that the Kingdom of Jordan was in a state of emergency. The President of Egypt was considering the matter, and the head of the Palestinian Authority was only prevented from declaring a state of emergency in the territories because of its unclear political status, his secretary reminded him. Tekoa thanked her and concluded the conversation. He was tired and he yawned, uttering a long "Ahhhhhh...." as he did so.

"Did you say something, Mr. President?" asked his driver.

"I was just yawning. I've got that meeting about whether to declare that the State of Israel is in a state of emergency," said the President.

"Do it, Mr. President. Do it, and get it over with."

"There's terrible pressure on me from the government, do you know how much money we'll have to give the farmers? Maybe the Americans will be pleased with us for giving money to the farmers instead of buying more weapons...." Tekoa chuckled and stared at the vehicles his driver was passing on the road. He always drove too fast, and the President had already pointed this out to him.

One of the cars passed by the President's driver was that of Danziger, next to whom sat Ventura. A moment later, the President's car overtook Adir's car too, with Tasaro sitting next to him. The rain was coming down in floods again.

"What a downpour," remarked Tekoa as he looked out of the window.

Danziger's car overtook Adir's car. Danziger was concentrating on his driving, which was made difficult by the pouring rain. Ventura noticed, since Adir was always in her thoughts, his car being overtaken by Danziger's car. Adir too was concentrating on his driving, although it was evident that he was very agitated and upset. He talked and talked and waved his hands in the air. At first, Iris thought that he was speaking on a hands-free car phone, however, when Adir drove past in the right lane, overtaking Danziger whose car was stuck behind a truck in the left lane, she saw Tasaro answering him, leaning towards him as she did so.

Iris said to herself that she was experiencing the feeling of jealousy. Distancing things in this way made her jealousy seem smaller and less monstrous than if she had identified heart and soul with this extreme emotion and given herself over to it. On the science channel, she had once seen someone, a spiritual person, who had explained the difference between feeling a certain emotion and experiencing yourself feeling this emotion. He said that experiencing yourself feeling a certain emotion was a higher level of consciousness. Iris wanted to be on a higher level of consciousness.

At the Kfar Hayarok junction Adir turned left, while Danziger went on driving straight ahead.

"Why didn't you turn left?" asked Iris.

"I can't stand that road," said Danziger. "I prefer taking

86

the Ayalon freeway, or turning left on the Haifa highway. Do you have a problem with that?"

"Not really," said Iris.

"Because if you're unhappy about it, just say so, and I'll make a U-turn on the spot," said Danziger and laughed. Iris laughed too. Her laughter was appropriate, even if inauthentic from her point of view. She experienced the experience of the artificial laughter, and felt revulsion toward herself. She thought that Adir, if he had been sitting there in place of the dentist whose services she required, on credit, would have sensed that her laughter was phony. On more than one occasion, when they were seeing each other, he had said, "You should only laugh when you find something really funny."

She stopped laughing and said, "I heard that you are an excellent dentist."

"Thank you very much. Who did you hear it from?"

"From Liat. I met her in the street after she'd finished having her teeth whitened by you. She was very pleased."

"Ah, Liat. She drove me crazy. She wanted them whiter than snow. In the end I said to her, what, do you want me to paint them with Wite-Out?"

Again they both chuckled.

"I myself am in desperate need of dental treatment."

"Then go for it."

"My teeth were ruined by my pregnancies. Three pregnancies. The children took all my calcium. I'm divorced. My ex-husband isn't even prepared to help me pay for the dentist. What a maniac."

"Oh come on, who says he has to? My ex-wife also comes up with all kinds of crazy stuff about things she claims happened to her because of me. She wants me to go half-and-half with her for the psychotherapy that she's having. She was a mess when I married her. Let her ask her parents to pay."

"That's not right," Iris pronounced. "But I'm not talking to you about psychotherapy. That's really going too far."

"Why? It's exactly the same thing. She says that she can't take care of our children properly without the psychotherapy, and you can say that you lost calcium, or that you can't eat properly so that you'll have enough strength to take care of the children. There's no end to it."

"There's no end to it," said Iris blankly.

Danziger turned right out of Rokach Avenue. On the other side of the road, in the direction of the fair center, there was a big traffic jam.

He switched on the radio. They listened to the news. Danziger listened attentively; Iris listened without taking anything in. When the news was over, she wanted to turn to the dentist and suggest that he take care of her teeth, that they come to an arrangement about the money. She said, "The truth is that I really –"

Her cell phone rang again. She couldn't remember when she had switched it on again. She took it out of her bag and peeked at the display. It was Adir. He was one of the first people to get a cell phone. He got a 050 number and he still had the same number.

When they were a couple and she saw his number on the display, her face would light up. Now that their romance lay in ruins, she almost had a heart attack when she saw his number, because she knew – it wasn't that he wanted her back, he simply wanted to ask her something trivial . . . like that time when they changed the sign of the laundromat, and he wanted her advice as a graphic artist. Adir's call wiped everything else from her mind, where she was, any other presence except for his, and as far as she was concerned at that moment, Danziger might as well have been a taxi driver.

"Hello," she answered the phone. "Straight ahead here," she said to Danziger, even though she knew that he knew.

"Iris, I have a proposition for you," said Adir.

"Just a second, Adir, I'll be with you in a second ... Yoram," she turned to Danziger, moving the cell phone from her face, "stop here for me, please, I'll be in touch. I have your number."

She got out of his car without paying any further attention to him.

"What's the proposition?" she said into the phone, walking along the street in no specific direction.

"It's about the shiva."

"What about the shiva?"

"I had a terrible fight with Tasaro."

"Really? Why?"

"She wanted to prepare Ethiopian food. I understand her – she's so sweet – she wanted to contribute her share. But it's not appropriate now."

"Absolutely not."

"You don't know how we argued all the way in the car."

"I don't know what to say to you."

"Never mind, it will pass. She left in tears."

"What do you say!"

"She'll be back."

"Of course she will."

She stopped in front of a display window with dresses that were so expensive they didn't even have the price in the window. Iris quickly calculated the price of one of the dresses, which would have looked great on her, if she had the money, and if she were ten kilos thinner. "What I propose, Iris," continued Adir on the other end of the line, "is

89

for you to come to the shiva, and be there all seven days, as long as people come to pay their respects. Tasaro has work to do. I don't want her to miss out, you understand? It's important to me for her to be financially independent. She knows how important it is."

"It's very important," said Iris who was beginning to lose her patience. "How can I help you?"

"I thought of one thousand dollars," said Adir. "For cleaning, catering and everything. That's one thousand clean and under the table. It's worth your while. I want you to prepare cooked food. Like Liat made for my mother's shiva, you remember what she made?"

"She made . . . yes . . . I remember . . . like Jewish food?"

"Tasteless Jewish food, you remember?"

"Yes."

"You know how to make that stuff, I remember."

"You remember?"

"Yes. Every Friday, and also the pots you used to bring in the middle of the week. Remember?"

"It was tasteless?"

"Not tasteless in the sense of not tasty. Tasteless in the sense of homey, warm. Maternal."

"The soup, the schnitzel and the mashed potatoes?"

"Yes. I think we should go for the same menu every day. So we don't have to rack our brains, and also out of respect for the occasion. The same food, but plenty of it, because a lot of people who didn't make it to the funeral will probably come by. I put up notices all over the neighborhood. The news will spread. People will come to the shiva. My idea is a bit like in the army. You did kitchen duty in the army, right?"

"It's not a problem for me. Absolutely not. I can whip it

up in a jiffy. I'm used to it. You want cooked food in the morning? Why not just crackers, borekas and rugelach?"

"Look, Ventura, I don't intend for people to eat schnitzels in the morning. For the mornings, cookies and so on. I don't want to exaggerate and say hot cereal. Even though that's what Liat ate every morning. A decent bowl of hot cereal with everything the body requires. I got the whole concept from my mother's shiva, but if you don't want to. . . ."

"I want to, I want to, what do you mean if I don't want to? Of course I want to. You know, I actually like the idea a lot, tasteless Jewish food and the same menu every day. Very traditional. Nice, very nice."

"You think so?"

"Yes. Today what with food getting so gourmet, people don't touch mashed potatoes anymore, unless they've got truffles and butter from Normandy on them. It's not the way it used to be."

"I want it to be kosher too. Just for the shiva."

"Are you going to sit shiva at your place or Liat's?"

"Liat's. She was a vegetarian, so her house is kosher anyway. I'm going to go past the ATM now, take out a thousand shekels for you to buy the ingredients, and put it in your mailbox. Don't forget to go down and get it. In about twenty minutes the money will be there in your mailbox."

"Okay, but hang on a minute," said Iris. "Is it a thousand dollars including ingredients?"

"No, it's a thousand dollars just for the work. Alright? Tasaro and I will sleep at my place, so you can come early in the morning and fix the food fresh. I'll come later, and she'll go off on her affairs. I don't want to force Tasaro to come to the shiva after all the horrors she went through on the way to Sudan. Her father died on the journey. She herself was terribly sick. And all that to get to Israel. Can you understand it? Going through all that just to come here of all places?"

"She would probably be better off there than here," said Ventura. "I mean, the opposite."

"There are things she tells me, what they do to them here. It's a rotten country, I'm telling you, a rotten country, with all the terrorism and the shit."

Iris was silent. She didn't like it when people insulted Israel, in spite of everything.

"All right," said Adir, "so we have a deal?"

"No problem," said Iris, and stopped in front of a shop selling cosmetics with promises of a smooth skin. She started to think about what to do with the thousand dollars. She went on thinking about what she would do with the thousand dollars after they finished talking too. A washing machine first, never mind the brand. Second, with what was left, and there would definitely be some left, Ventura planned simply to be able to breathe a bit, to pay the thousand she owed the minimarket, so they would stop looking at her like a criminal, to fill the tank of her car with gasoline, and oil for the engine and the brakes, and to splash a few hundred at the cut-price market, to buy enough to last for a month. Maybe this month she would find a steady job, and make enough for herself and her children to live a normal life.

In the evening, after buying the food for the shiva, Iris sat in front of the television, and made calculations. In the background was the news. The reporters showed the casualties of that day's shooting attacks, their cars full of bullet holes, and explained to the viewers where the terrorists had ambushed them, where they had come from, and where they had escaped to. After that they showed the winter, more houses flooded, streets turned into rivers, fallen trees, among them a big palm tree lying across a main road, with water raging in and out of its fronds. More disgruntled citizens left without a roof over their heads, and mayors and local councilors who were doing everything to provide every citizen with a place to sleep and hot soup to eat.

How small man was in the face of nature, thought Iris, lucky she lived on the fourth floor, and in North Tel Aviv. When she returned to the city of her birth she had hesitated as to whether to rent an apartment in the south, and save some money; now she was glad she was in the north. The drainage in northwest Tel Aviv had always been better than in other places in the city.

She was very pleased that she had accepted the offer from Adir, in spite of all her memories. Iris considered whether she should ask him for an advance. It was quite logical really. Half at the beginning and half at the end. Not that she imagined he would try to cheat her – of course not – he had always been fair. Maybe she would ask for an advance, maybe not. However it worked out. The President of Israel appeared on the screen. Iris watched him delivering a speech to the nation:

"People of Israel, children of Israel, new and old immigrants, citizens of long standing and returning emigrants ... difficult days have come upon us both in the political and economic spheres and in the sphere of nature. We are only mortal, and as such all we can do is adjust to what nature delivers. As for the security situation, I can only repeat that we have a strong army, we have a good government, we must stand strong and united. . . ."

Subtitles ran past at the bottom of the screen: "President Tekoa declares the State of Israel in a state of emergency, President Tekoa declares the State of Israel in a state of emergency. President Tekoa declares the State of Israel in. . . ."

Iris switched off the television and sighed out loud.

"What, Mommy?" yelled Osher from the children's room.

"Nothing," she said.

"Did you call me?" He appeared in the living room in his pajamas, reminding her of when he was a baby.

"No, sweetie," she smiled at him and kissed him. "Go to sleep. It's late. There's school tomorrow."

PART TWO

ADIR SAT SHIVA until the 29th of Tevet. To his distress only a few dozen people came to Liat's apartment to pay their respects rather than the hundreds he was expecting. And even those who did take the trouble to come he didn't know. Some of them got on his nerves by saying, "Be strong," "Hang in there," or, "Tomorrow is another day." Adir would have preferred them to shake his hand and say, "Sorry for your loss."

Some of the condolence callers were men and women who worked out at the health club. Adir recognized them by their trim figures, which struck the eye as soon as they removed their coats. Among them were people who said, "Be strong," and there was one who, after telling him that she was sorry for his loss, went on a tour of the apartment and then came back to him and said that there were too many sharp corners there, and this was a bad thing according to feng shui. Someone else told him that the mezuzah on the doorpost wasn't kosher, and he had a friend who knew about these things, who would be happy to come and change it for nothing. Adir wrote down the friend's phone number, just to get the man off his back.

On the third day of the shiva Shaul Takdim, Liat's lover, showed up, tanned and trim. Adir received him with a sour face. Takdim asked him all kinds of annoying questions about Liat's last moments: who knew about them, what she had said, and about her collection of antique calendars. Adir said that he was sure she hadn't murmured Takdim's name, and was surprised that he knew about the collection at all. He asked him if he was interested in buying it, and said it would cost him a million dollars. Takdim snickered and said that he had to get back to the gym, he was expecting a container of new equipment. "Be strong," he said to Adir, and took off.

From time to time Bergson wondered why so few people had showed up at the shiva. The explanation he found most convincing was the most impenetrable:

People were fed up with death.

Iris Ventura threw a lot of Jewish food into the trash cans along Amos Street that week. Some of it she took home with her in the evenings, in semi-transparent plastic Tupperware, added flavoring, mainly crushed garlic, a lot of salt and a bit of pepper, and for herself also Tabasco or horseradish left over from Passover. The less fresh food she gave to the cats on Amos Street, who quickly came to know her and gathered around whenever she came downstairs with the garbage bags.

On the fourth day of the shiva, Ventura noticed a group of foreign workers watching her as she threw out the trash, and she began to leave the bags outside the cans, in spite of the rain, thinking to herself, what's rain? Mineral water, that will add its own flavors.

The week of fame enjoyed by the Beit-Halahmi family – the parents Kati and Boaz, and the children, Adi, Topaz, Aaron and Moshe – began on the night of the 20th of Tevet, when, as will be remembered, the report on poverty in the State of Israel was released, in the wake of which the local television station of Ramle-Lod sent a camera crew to pay them a visit. The media circus around the family ended with a small still voice on the 27th of Tevet.

On that Monday, the presenter of the morning show to which Kati had been invited, as the popular representative of poverty in Israel, announced that poverty was no longer the hot news it had been the week before, and that the most important item on the agenda was now the frequency of the terror attacks and the question of Israel's response to them. This being the case, he informed his colleagues, he wasn't going to give the lady from Lod more than a minute and half's interview, and in fact he cut her short and went on to ask the viewers to call in their replies to the question: What, in your opinion, should be Israel's response to Palestinian aggression?

Kati, a media has-been, was thrown straight from the studio into a taxi waiting to take her home to Lod. Outside, a light snow was falling and the temperature was two or three degrees below zero. Kati looked at the snow drifts and it all seemed to her like a dream. The taxi drove very fast, as if to remove her as quickly as possible from the sphere of public interest, where everybody was already sick and tired of her.

She felt a heavy weight pressing on her chest, and she was afraid to peep into the future. She knew only too well what it looked like: work, Boaz, home, rissoles, yelling, floor-rags, bleach, detergent, stairwells, copybooks for school, six shekels each – and one great weariness.

Not for nothing had public interest been diverted from poverty and its victims. The week had opened with two large-scale terror strikes in big cities, each of them taking the lives of twenty people and leaving scores of wounded. These attacks immediately diverted public interest from anything else, including the mystery surrounding the freak weather conditions. And following hot on the heels of these two strikes, for the first time in the history of the State of Israel, a bombing outrage in the Golan Heights: a large pipe-bomb hidden under a snow drift at the entrance to the new shopping mall in Katzrin went off and caused scores of deaths.

President Tekoa had his work cut out for him. Weather conditions did not always permit his helicopter to take off, and sometimes he was obliged to make his way to the many funerals and to the hospitals in his limousine, driving for hours on end and taking naps between one funeral and the next. When he missed the funeral itself due to the condition of the roads, he instructed his driver to go straight to the home of the mourners.

On the 28th of Tevet, the President underwent an echo cardiogram, at rest and under stress, because of a high pulse rate. The results showed that he was healthy, a little tense, nothing more, and that he could continue to perform his duties, but at a slower pace. But when he entered the Rambam Hospital in Haifa to visit the victims injured by a bomb that went off at the check-post junction, the President collapsed and lost consciousness.

The picture of the President lying in a faint at the hospital entrance was on the front page of all the big newspapers, with his bodyguards, looking at a loss for words, bending over him. Later they said that at first they didn't know if the President had been shot by a sniper or collapsed from exhaustion.

In the newspapers and on the television and radio current affairs programs, profiles of the President were hastily prepared, in case he passed on. But Tekoa did not pass on, nor did he have Saudi flu, as the state television channel reported. He was suffering from exhaustion, and this being the case, the profiles were printed and broadcast and screened, but without the bitter end. Much was also made of the fact that he asked that his stay in the hospital be as short as possible, "in order to free up the bed." Someone leaked to the cable channel of Haifa and the North, that the President had 10.4 hemoglobin, and that he was being given iron. An enterprising reporter from the state commercial channel got hold of the President's crowded schedule in the days preceding his collapse, and concluded his report by saying that it was doubtful if an athlete of thirty would have been able to carry on under such pressure.

For three days Tekoa rested. One and a half days in the hospital, and one and a half days in his bed in the President's residence. On the fourth day he recovered his strength, and was able to set out once more on his somber journeys from funeral to funeral, from hospital to condolence call, and so on without end.

During the same week the "kitchen cabinet" met three times, each time in the wee hours of the night. In spite of the escalation of the popular uprising of the Palestinian Arabs in the territories, and sometimes also in Israel itself, the kitchen cabinet decided to continue its policy of restraint, to exhaust its diplomatic options, and on no account to be dragged into a total war.

"The government's hands are tied. America gives the orders. Otherwise we'll be paying fifty shekels for a pint of milk here," said Boaz Beit-Halahmi to his children Aaron and Topaz, when they were sitting together and watching the news. The three of them were sitting on the loveseat, part of the same set that Boaz had bought in Bidya before the trouble began.

"America's got the kitchen cabinet by the balls. Otherwise we'd stick it to the Arabs good and proper and show them what's what...."

The television screen showed weeping families emerging from the institute of forensic pathology at Abu Kabir.

"Poor things," said Boaz. "They have to identify their relatives by pieces. Teeth, hands, shoes, rings. From blasts like that you don't come out in one piece. A person's torn to bits."

"Why are you telling the children those things?" Kati yelled from the sink where she was washing the dishes. "Why do they have to know such things?"

"Why shouldn't they know?" yelled Beit-Halahmi. "Let them know where they're living. Let them know."

"Sometimes," Boaz Beit-Halahmi went on explaining to his children, "there's nothing left to bury, and they put in stones, or pieces of wood, so that the families will think they're burying something."

On the small screen there appeared, one after the other, pictures of the victims of the pipe-bomb at Katzrin with information about the time and place of their funerals. Here and there the announcer stumbled over the pronunciation of the complicated family names of the victims, but the times of the funerals and the ages of the victims were always accurate.

Three kilos of brown sugar, a packet of saccharin, two jars of regular Taster's Choice freeze-dried coffee, two decaffeinated, and ten liters of low-fat milk were consumed by the condolence callers during the course of Liat's shiva. In the Beit-Halahmi's small apartment the sugar consumption of the camera crews and the interviewers stood at about six kilos of white sugar and one kilo of brown. The people responsible for keeping the public informed did not use artificial sweeteners at all, and the coffee they drank was Turkish and black. The budget for all of the foregoing was off-the-cuff – in complete contrast to the budget of Iris Ventura, which was strictly anchored in the accounts she did every evening in case her employer wanted to see an up-to-date picture of his expenses.

Every day, after the last of the condolence callers had departed, Ventura cleaned Liat's apartment, and she didn't leave until the kitchen counter shone. Responsibility for keeping the apartment on Micah Reiser Avenue clean rested with Kati, since she was a cleaning woman anyway, and in any case it was hard for Boaz to bend down after his accident. Something had happened to Kati in the course of the media festival that surrounded her and her family. She hardly turned up for work in the stairwells and the bank at all, because she was "busy being photographed." At home, too, she didn't invest too much energy, because she said to herself that after they were all gone she would do a thorough job of cleaning up. And at the same time she also stopped following events on her favorite soap opera *Because of a Kiss*, and hanging on the words and exploits of its heroine, whom she adored, Claudia Helena.

Boaz, who noticed the changes in his wife's behavior, grew more and more sour, and whenever someone from the media left he would spray behind him with an air-purifier and say to Kati, "How many times have I told you to tell them not to smoke here."

First Boaz noticed the change that had taken place in his wife; he examined her and studied her new, unfamiliar behavior. Then he tried to interest her in something cute Adi had said to Moshe one morning, but she wasn't impressed, and Boaz wondered if she had even heard him. After that he tried to get her to talk and tried to talk to her about things that she had shown some interest in prior to her media exposure, and was forced to conclude that she was sick of them, at which point he turned to her and said:

"What's the matter with you? What is this shit? They took your picture and showed you on television and put you in the newspaper, and that's it, you've forgotten where you came from? Because if you've forgotten, I'll tell you. You're from the slums of Ramle."

"So what," said Kati dismissively. "How many times do I have to hear you say that? You've forgotten where you came from. Every time we have an argument you bring that up. What are we, children? I haven't forgotten but I don't exactly remember either. Time rubs things out. You want to argue with time? Go ahead. Go to the loony bin and argue with time there. Let the doctors come and give you electric shocks at last."

"Electric shocks? Me?" Boaz flared up immediately. "What, *I'm* crazy? *You're* crazy. You deny your past, you behave, I don't know, like some movie star, looking down on me."

"I'm not crazy," said Kati. "I at least have done something for this family. The one who's crazy here is you. You don't care about me, you don't care about the children, you don't care about our future, you don't go to the National Insurance office, you don't look for work – just mix mincemeat all day and shut up. Play with the rice and shut up. Who's crazy here?" She mimicked the movements of his hands sorting the rice, and also the serious expression on his face.

The couple often argued. These arguments often concluded with the smashing of one or another object in the house. Mainly remote controls, telephones, videocassettes, windowpanes, kitchenware and so on. Many of their pots and pans looked as if they had been in traffic accidents. It was Boaz who converted his rage into this liberating kinetic activity.

To tell the truth, the question of who was crazy and who wasn't was a regular subject of debate between them. It was clear to both of them that somebody was crazy here, they only needed to prove it. It didn't occur to either of them that neither of them was crazy, or that they both were.

At the end of the week of the second or third of Shevat, Kati made sincere efforts to see the full half of the glass, and to get the most out of her few days of glory. She had learned that it was nicer to say "certainly" than "sure," and that it wasn't necessary to curse all the time. She had learned that there was a world outside Ramle-Lod.

But a few minutes after the end of the Sabbath, Kati underwent a jarring realization. She realized that her life wasn't anything to write home about, and that tomorrow morning she would have a very serious problem getting up for her dreary work, instead of what she had so quickly grown accustomed to: to wake up at five in the morning, to ride like a princess in a taxi to the television studios, and to sit in the limelight and recite the tale of her woes over and over again.

When it came home to Kati that she would never sit in the makeup room again, with the makeup artists talking to her in such close quarters, telling her that she had beautiful features, painting her lips mauve with a paintbrush, and concentrating on her face more than the beautician had on her wedding day, the ephemeral star sunk into profound melancholy, and the old, sickeningly familiar burden settled in her soul again.

The next day, when she reluctantly went back to cleaning the stairwells in Ganei-Aviv, nobody recognized her as the person who had appeared on television, because most of them watched the Russian television networks. Kati looked at the pails that were black with dirt – nobody had cleaned the stairs during the period of her fame and decline – and dripped salt tears into them. She remembered the phone calls from Moran and Michal and Sigal and Ronit who all talked so quickly and apparently without mistakes. "And Kati, remember, don't wear striped shirts," they would say a second before they hung up.

The tears flowed harder, when she remembered the long minutes she had spent in the makeup rooms, how nice they all were to her, asking her if she wanted anything to drink, and if she liked her coffee strong or weak. How the makeup girls had spoken to her with a patience and tenderness whose likes she had never encountered in all her life: "Look up – lovely – and now down – lovely, Kati. Now don't move, lovely, Kati. I'm putting on eyeliner, Kati my sweet, don't blink, darling, let it dry."

"Darling," "sweetie," they had called her there.

Only in the bank had someone once called her "sweetie." It was the head of the foreign currency department, who always stayed behind after everyone had gone home, and altogether she was under the impression that he was watching her to see if she was working properly, and sometimes she was so embarrassed that she dropped things, and he raised his eyes from his papers. Kati thought that he was too young for such a high-up position, but when she saw the bank manager she understood that the world had changed. Compared to the head of the foreign currency department, the bank manager looked like someone who had escaped from a nursery school.

ONLY FIVE PEOPLE ARRIVED at the cemetery to visit Liat's grave at the end of the shiva. Adir was so angry that he coughed and coughed, and an aunt asked him if he was having an asthma attack. Adir signalled that he was alright.

Ventura arrived without Danziger, who couldn't make it anyway. She already had enough money to fill her tank and take care of the oil and water and everything needed for her little car. All that remained was to hope that engine wouldn't fail her on the way. It was a sunny day, but very cold. Ventura looked around and took in the scene. There were empty graves waiting for new dead to arrive, and on the one hand she felt that the undertakers deserved praise for their foresight, but on the other hand she was shocked at the thought that there were people walking around in the world at this moment, healthy and whole, who were going to fill the empty places, and be covered with earth, which would be covered with flowers, which would wither, and after that everything would be covered with the gravestone.

On the way back to the parking lot, Adir, Tasaro, and Ventura walked together. There was a silence, which Iris broke by saying, "It's unbelievable, all these empty places waiting for the dead who are still alive amongst us."

"Yes," said Adir. "You can never know. Today I think undertaking must be the most profitable business. The most reliable. The whole economy's in a recession and here things are flourishing. I heard they've started burying people on top of each other."

"On top of each other?" said Iris. "That's terrible!"

"It's the same all over the world," said Adir. "After a few years, it all gets built over anyway."

Tasaro said, "You have to order a tombstone for her."

"Yes, what kind of tombstone are you going to get for Liat?" asked Iris. "What kind of marble? And what will you write on it? Are you going to write anything?"

"I haven't thought about it yet."

"Let's go and talk to the people who make tombstones on the way back," suggested Tasaro. "I saw some stonemasons at the entrance to the cemetery."

Iris found her car and she said, "Check it out, maybe you can get a deal."

"A deal?" Adir repeated in horror. "What are you talking about?"

Iris blushed in shame and got quickly into her car. When she started the engine, she looked in the mirror at Adir and Tasaro getting into his car. They were talking, and Iris was sure that Adir was saying to Tasaro, how stupid and tactless Iris is, she thinks there are deals in tombstones, two for the price of one, or stuff like that. But Adir was actually saying:

"Did you see, Tasaro? That degenerate Takdim, he didn't even come. It kills me, where Liat found her lovers. . . ."

"Let it go," said Tasaro. "Who needs him and his condolences?"

"You're right. But still, so few people came. I expected more."

"Look how sunny it is now. It's the end of the week, people are probably doing their shopping. Life goes on."

Tasaro was afraid that Adir would sink into a depression and lose interest in his surroundings, including her. During the seven days of mourning he had scarcely spoken to her, and she feared that he might withdraw into himself forever. As for her, she was already planning to get married to Adir and have his children, although she hadn't yet decided when to bring the subject up. Now she made up her mind to wait for another year. She noticed a tear gathering in the corner of Adir's eye, and she filled with compassion for him. She knew that she would make him an excellent wife. Simply excellent.

"I suppose that for the thirtieth-day memorial we'll be the only ones who come. *Sic transit gloria mundi.*"

He called Ventura's cell phone. She answered immediately. He thanked her for coming to the cemetery on such a nice sunny day.

"Don't mention it," said Iris in relief, because she thought he was nursing a grudge against her. "Of course I came."

"I want to let you have the rest of the money I owe you. Let's meet."

"Okay. When is convenient for you?"

"I want to get it over with now."

"No problem," said Iris and turned onto Trans-Samaria Road going west.

"So where should we meet?" she asked.

"Wait for me outside your building," said Adir. "I hope I'll be able to find parking, if not I'll honk and you can come down."

He hung up.

"What about the tombstone," said Tasaro. "Don't you want to go and choose one now?"

They were driving past a few stonemasons' workshops.

"Not today. I don't feel like it. Let's stop at an ATM. I don't like owing people money." He multiplied seven hundred dollars by the high representative rate of exchange and brought it down to round figures.

In Tel Aviv he stopped outside a bank, handed Tasaro his card and said, "I haven't got the energy to get out. 7740. Take out six thousand. I need a bit of cash."

➤   ➤   ➤

109

Iris stood on the sidewalk under her apartment, holding her daughter Herut by the hand. They waited. Although she recognized Adir's car from a distance, he honked loudly until she advanced right to the edge of the street. Tasaro handed her a bundle of banknotes, and smiled.

"Thank you," she said.

"You're welcome," said Iris.

"Thank you," said Adir leaning towards her from the driver's seat.

"You're welcome," said Iris.

"What's wrong with her?" said Tasaro and pointed at the little girl. "She must have a terrible cold. Look how her nose is running."

"It's like that all the time," said Iris. "I only hope it's not the Saudi flu. I give her things to boost her immune system all the time."

"Oy," said Tasaro. "Did you take her to the doctor?" she asked.

"Of course I took her to the doctor. What do you take me for?"

"And what did the doctor say?"

"To wait and give her aspirin."

"Be well," said Adir and drove off.

Iris put the money in her coat pocket and went inside. On the stairs she said to her daughter:

"Now Mommy and Heruti are rich. Mommy's going to go and buy a washing machine and Heruti will stay with Saraleh, right?"

"No," said the child.

"Darling, you know I'd take you with me, but it's cold and you're sick. You have a fever. I'm just going to buy a washing machine and coming right back."

Herut cried, "No, I don't want to. I want to come with you."

"You can't come with me. Not today. The sun's out, but it's very cold. Another day we'll go for a walk in Dizengoff Center, okay? I'll buy you toys. I haven't bought you a little present for a long time."

The little girl burst into tears. Iris said, "Stop crying. Don't you understand Hebrew?"

"I understand Hebrew," said the little girl in a tearful voice. "I want to come with you."

"I'll bet Sara's got candy. Today I'll allow you to have some."

Iris rang the bell of her neighbor's apartment, a widow of sixty who was very fond of Herut, and took care of her devotedly, for nothing. The door opened and Sara bent down almost immediately to Herut and said, "Come, sweetie, come to Grandma."

"I'm going to town. I'll be back in an hour or two. She's a little sick."

"I'm a little sick too, so together we'll be a lot sick," said Sara, and Iris thought that if she had any alternative she would have left her daughter with someone whose logic was a little less flawed. But now she had no choice. The older children weren't back from school yet, and afterwards they had afternoon activities. Osher had drama, and Oz had football. One activity each, she had agreed with Othniel at the beginning of the year.

"Go, go, it will be alright," said Sara when she saw Iris's worried face. "Go on, don't worry."

"Have you got enough baby aspirin syrup?" asked Iris.

"Yes, yes."

"Really, Sara, I don't know what I'd do without you.

Remember, fifteen cc's. I left you a measuring spoon last time."

"I know. You don't need to worry about a thing. Relax. I brought up children of my own," said Sara and closed the door.

Iris waited outside the door, until she heard her daughter say something to Sara about the candy Mommy said she could have. She went into her apartment, took the notes out of her coat pocket and put them in her wallet, and ordered a taxi. She didn't feel in the least like driving into town and looking for parking for an hour, and she also didn't know exactly where she was going.

In the taxi, the driver told her that at this very minute there was a heavy exchange of gunfire in the Jerusalem suburb of Gilo, and that the IDF had to go into Beit Jala and show them where they got off. The driver said that he was prepared to be isolated like the generation of the wilderness, and for his children to be isolated like the generation of the wilderness too, and for the whole world to hate Israel and the Jews, he didn't care, the main thing was to get it over already and kick the Arabs out of the country for good.

Iris had once had an opinion. A different one. Now she had no opinion. Actually she did have one, but she didn't say it out loud. Aloud she said, "You have to admire Israel for its restraint."

"Admire? What's to admire? Where do you want to go, lady?"

"Take me to a cheap, reliable electrical appliances store. My washing machine's broken down."

"Which store, lady? There's a few of them."

Iris adopted the air of an upper class lady, temporarily in need of assistance from the common man.

"Take me to the one you would go to yourself, if you had to buy a washing machine."

"I'm from Rishon Lezion, lady. You know how much you'd have to pay for delivery from Rishon?"

"Then take me to the store you would go to if you lived in Tel Aviv."

"Tell me, do I look crazy to you, to live in Tel Aviv?"

"Really, I can't believe that you don't know a single electrical appliances store."

"Okay, okay, I'll take you."

"Great," said Iris. "I really appreciate it."

He wanted to talk more and more, about politics, about what the Americans had done to the Indians, and how nobody talked about it anymore, except on the Indian reservations, or the National Geographic channel, but Ventura didn't cooperate.

In days gone by, when she was very poor, and counted the pennies so that she would have enough for the laundromat, and did the drying at home, Ventura would join in every conversation going, if only to assert the fact of her existence to herself and others. She needed to be answered in order to feel present. But now? She wanted people like this taxi driver, who was once more making that boring old comparison between the fate of the Palestinians and the American Indians, to know their place and be conscious of the gap between them. . . . She had worked very hard during Liat's shiva. For seven days she had experienced the humiliation of serving tasteless Jewish food and poppyseed and cinnamon cookies to Liat's and Adir's family and their friends. . . . And she had been very conscious of the patronizing way they had treated her, especially one couple, the woman had an MA in Akkadian and a ring in her nose. Iris would never forget the disgust with which she had held out her plate to her and said, "Haven't they discovered salt yet where you come from?"

How badly Ventura had wanted to throw the mashed potatoes in that Master of Akkadian's face. But she restrained herself and said, "Would you like me to add some?"

"Yes, please, a lot."

Iris took the plate to the kitchen, added salt, and brought it back, quiet and obedient as a geisha. All she wanted was to finish the week and get the money for the washing machine and other items on her list.

Her thoughts wandered and lost their balance. Suddenly she phoned Adir on her cell phone. Yesterday she had charged it with a new card. Adir answered, "What, Iris?"

"Hi, Adir," she said in the new mood that had crept up on her. "I'm sorry if I'm disturbing you. I only wanted to tell you that if you decide to rent Liat's apartment, I want the first option."

"Okay," he said.

"Thanks," she said.

Adir slammed the phone down and said, "She's off her rocker."

Tasaro didn't hear, because she was in the living room watching the fashion channel.

"You want secondhand or does it have to be new?" the taxi driver asked Ventura.

"What?" said Iris.

"The washing machine. Secondhand or new?"

"Brand new, with a guarantee. What a question."

"Then get off here," he said and showed her a building on Salameh Street. "They're having a sales promotion now, with installments. It's hard times for everybody now, lady."

Iris wanted to tell him that she didn't need installments, but when she remembered the real reason – she didn't have a checkbook or a credit card – she kept quiet, paid, and got out of the taxi.

"Just don't let there be a bomb here now," she thought and hurried to hand her bag to the security guard at the entrance of the store, where they were selling electrical appliances on installment plans with twenty-four, and even thirty-six payments.

"Can I help you, madam?" A thin sales assistant pounced on her. He looked very frail next to the crowded ranks of washing machines covering the floor. Iris thought that he probably didn't eat anything, maybe he was anorexic. Although she had never heard of men being anorexic.

When Ventura emerged from the electrical appliances store she saw that there was a parking lot for the customers, and she felt a pang of conscience at having taken a taxi when she had a car parked right under her apartment window, even though, on second thought, she had really needed that warm and comfortable taxi ride, and now she was prepared to take the bus. First she walked a way along Salameh Street, and although they had told her in the store, "Delivery within ten business days," she bought detergent in one of the stores she found there, as well as a softener that promised easy ironing, even though she didn't have an iron. She had forgotten it in Jerusalem, and when she asked for it, Othniel said he couldn't find it. She was furious with him and yelled, "How is it possible to lose an iron?"

The bus north arrived and she got on, paid, and went to sit down at the back, where she had always liked sitting in her youth. This way she was able to see both the road and the other passengers. In school, too, she always sat at the back, even though the classroom wasn't going anywhere.

Today, as a mature person, she could no longer afford the relaxed enjoyment of aimless observation. She was busy looking for suspicious characters on the bus. And indeed, sitting in the middle of the bus was a man of Middle-Eastern appearance, with a large canvas bag on the seat next to him. Ventura held back for a few minutes, and then she said to herself that if she wanted to prevent a catastrophe she had to act fast, and she got up and approached the driver and said quietly to him: "There's a suspicious character in the middle of the bus. The one in the checked coat. Look at the size of that bag."

"You're not kidding," said the driver, taking a quick look

into the mirror. He drew up at the side of the road, opened the doors and called out, "All passengers are requested to get off the bloodbath at once – the brakes aren't working."

He didn't mean to say bloodbath, he meant to say bus. The word "bloodbath" slipped out, and all the passengers immediately understood that this is what they would say about the bus on the evening news, and they stampeded, almost trampling each other as they made for the doors. Ventura too rushed out. In the street the passersby saw the panic and beat a hasty retreat from the explosion about to take place.

The driver followed the man of Middle-Eastern appearance, who was running with the rest, fell on him from behind, tackled him to the ground, and pushed the bag away with his foot. One of the passengers called the police, who arrived within seconds and cordoned off the area.

Ventura wanted to get away, but also to see. She took shelter behind a wall and watched. She had never been at the scene of a terrorist attack, and she was already imagining herself as an eyewitness suffering from shock, with a Band-Aid on her forehead. Curiosity got the better of her. It didn't even occur to her that she might be killed. The man with the Middle-Eastern appearance was surrounded by policemen. He spoke to them in ordinary Hebrew, without a trace of an Arabic accent, pleaded with them and said that he wasn't, he wasn't.

He shouted, he almost cried with fright and insult: "Stop it! I'm not a terrorist. Here's my identity card. Here, in my trouser pocket. Take it out." And one of the policemen took a blue ID card out of his pocket. Nevertheless, they continued to treat him suspiciously, until it was established beyond the shadow of a doubt that he simply possessed a Middle-Eastern appearance, like many of the policemen and the passersby, like Ventura herself, who had already realized, from her hiding place, that there was no bomb.

His bag contained clothes. His wife had thrown him out of the house. He came from a smallholders' farm next to Baer Sheba, and he was on his way to his brother's house in the northern part of the city, he explained.

Iris walked away and continued on foot to Allenby Street. There she got onto a minibus that let her off on the corner of Nordau and Ben Yehuda. She wasn't going to be on the five o'clock news as an eyewitness, or on the news flash that would have been organized on the spot if there really had been a bloodbath on the bus.

She decided to go on walking around for a bit before going home, because her heart was still pounding from the excitement of the incident, and she was not yet ready to fall into the demanding and intrusive responsibility of the hurly-burly of her life. She walked along Micah Street, crossed Micah Lane and Dizengoff Street, continued east along Malachi Street, reached Ezekiel Street, and after passing Obadiah, found herself completely by chance outside Adir's building.

The noise of a powerful vacuum cleaner came from his apartment. She knew that Adir had to vacuum because of his asthma, but she wondered who was doing the vacuuming. A maid? Him? Tasaro? Until the final clarification of this question, she stood there and thought that one day she too would have a powerful vacuum cleaner capable of sucking up every crumb and speck of dust in the house in ten minutes. Until then she would have to be satisfied with a broom.

Tasaro's profile appeared between the slats of the shutter, diligently plying the vacuum cleaner, and for one brief moment, one very very brief moment, Iris asked herself if it was wise of Tasaro to vacuum there – there were no window-panes on the porch, and perhaps the floor was still wet from the rain in the night, and she might be electrocuted. In fact, rain had collected there, but Tasaro had wiped it dry earlier, and now she was vacuuming the corner both diligently and safely.

"She really loves him," thought Iris, when she saw how hard she was working, and her heart contracted.

Tasaro was also talking to Adir, who was apparently sitting in the living room. In order to overcome the noise of the vacuum cleaner they were both shouting. Iris didn't understand a word, she only recognized their voices, and she continued in the direction of Jeremiah Street.

Just as she was turning onto her street her cell phone rang. It was her neighbor Sara. The little one had vomited, she said, and Ventura hastened her steps. She ran up the stairs, went into her apartment, threw the bag with the detergent and softener on the floor, and hurried to her neighbor's, who was waiting at the door with the child in her arms, drowsy and feverish. Ventura touched her daughter's forehead. She said, "Do me a favor, call a cab. I'm taking her to the emergency room," and Sara called a cab.

In the ER they gave Herut a comprehensive examination, and hospitalized her for observation. According to all the signs, there was no connection to the Saudi flu, the doctors told Iris, but to be on the safe side and to help the child feel better altogether, they were going to keep her in the hospital. Ventura called Othniel and told him that she was with Herut in the "Dana" hospital next to Ichilov, and there was nobody to look after the boys. He said that he was already on his way to Tel Aviv to fetch them and take them home with him.

"What about school tomorrow?" Iris asked her ex-husband.

"They won't go to school. No big deal. What department
is she in?"

"*No*, don't bring the boys here. The place is full of germs."

"They'll wait in the car. I'll come up to see her alone,
don't worry."

In the hours that followed, Iris felt very lonely. Herut's condition stabilized, her fever went down, and she received
Paramine for the vomiting, which had an immediate effect.
Iris said to herself all the time, be strong, keep calm, it's very
important for you to keep calm, and in order to give herself
something to look forward to, she phoned Dr. Danziger and
told him that she was calling from the children's hospital,
her daughter was there with the flu, evidently not the Saudi
strain, she wanted to begin dental treatment with him, next
week, if possible, in all probability by the following week it
would all be behind them.

Danziger made an appointment for her for the following
week, and asked her to notify him if she wanted to cancel.

After her conversation with the dentist, Ventura felt even
lonelier, she felt as if she was at the nadir of loneliness, a soli-
tary soul in a wasteland of herself, and she called Adir. Tasaro
answered. She asked for Adir, and told him what had happened, where she was, her ex-husband was on his way, tech-
nically everything was alright, but she was very frightened.

"You've got nothing to be afraid of," said Adir.

"Why haven't I got anything to be afraid of?" asked Iris.

"Because children don't die so easily."

"What?" said Iris in alarm, and added, "Anyone can see
that you haven't got children of your own. If you did, you

would never have said such a thing," and she hung up and buried her head in her hands.

A nurse walked past her and said, "What's the matter with you? Do you want a glass of water?"

"Yes, please."

They brought her a glass of water, and she felt better. By the time Othniel arrived to see Herut, she was already perfectly calm.

"What's the situation?" asked Othniel, who was dressed completely differently from when he was married to her. With her he had dressed in a casual, sporty style, and now he looked smart and tailored. It appeared as though his girlfriend starched his clothes. He gave off an unfamiliar smell, a combination of detergent and perfumed disinfectant.

"Better," she replied. "She's recovering. She's stopped vomiting."

He stayed for about ten minutes to play with the little one, who fawned all over him.

"Look how crazy she is about me," said Othniel.

"Absolutely Oedipus," said Ventura.

"I'll come to see you tomorrow, okay, Heruti?" said Grossman.

Herut cried when he left, but Iris said to him, "Go, go. The boys are in the car. I'll take care of her."

Othniel left.

"Never mind," she said to Herut. "Tomorrow Heruti will feel better, and Daddy will come to visit and everything will be fine.

For two days and nights Herut stayed in the hospital, until she had completely recovered. Othniel came to fetch her and her mother with the two little boys in the car, took them all home, and said goodbye downstairs, on Jeremiah Street. The three children watched him turn left onto Dizengoff and from there presumably onto the Ayalon South highway to Jerusalem.

"Let's go home, kids," said Iris. She was so happy that Herut was better and they were out of the hospital. "I forgot to tell you. I bought a washing machine. It'll be here in about a week."

"When are you going to buy a computer?" asked Oz.

"Soon. Just let me get back on my feet. I'll find a job, and then I'll be able to buy you a computer on credit."

ON THE EVENING OF THE 12th of Shevat the phone rang in Ventura's apartment, and a man's voice said, "Mrs. Ventura?"

"Yes?"

"Shalom. I'm supposed to deliver your washing machine. I'm here in my truck and don't ask, I can't make heads or tails of all these streets. So many prophets. Can you tell me how to get there?"

"Okay, where are you now?"

"Nahum Street."

"Okay, go back to the avenue, turn left and you'll come to the traffic light. At the traffic light turn left onto Ben Yehuda Street and go to the end, sorry not the end, to the crossing with Jeremiah Street. There's no right turn. Good, so you turn left onto Jeremiah and stop. I'll wait for you."

"Where?"

"Right after you turn left onto Jeremiah, I'll wait for you there."

"How will I know that it's you?"

"A red scarf, okay? I'll direct you from there, so you won't get even more confused. Most of the streets here are one-way."

"I'm going down to show the truck driver delivering the washing machine how to get here," Ventura called to her children. "Wait here. Oz! Osher! Herut! Mommy will be back right away."

She put on the red scarf that she had never worn, even though she had paid a fortune for it, and went downstairs.

Ventura and the truck driver found each other. She climbed in and sat beside him, and felt her spirits soar as she sat high up in the cabin of the truck, directing the driver, and chatting to him about the worsening political situation, and the policy of targeted interceptions that the Israelis had begun to adopt. Would it help or not, they asked themselves. Neither of them knew the answer.

At the same evening hour, when Ventura was so happy, Kati Beit-Halahmi was wallowing in the depths of despair.

After almost a year, Boaz had finally exerted himself and had gone to the phone company to get their line reopened for outgoing calls. He had congratulated himself on this achievement at least seven times in the course of the day. He said that they were in a one-month trial period, and joked that the siege closing them off from the world had been relieved for the time being, but neither the joke nor the actual freeing of the line were enough to improve the downcast spirits of his wife.

"Big deal, who am I going to call?" she said to herself. "My brothers again? Let them call me, if they've got anything to say. Anyway they're busy with their own lives and all the calls are the same. What's up? What's new? How's it going? How're you doing? How're the kids?"

Now she was cleaning the stairwell on Arba'a Onot Street. After one floor the water in the pail was already black, because she was sick of changing the water after every six stairs, as she had been in the habit of doing in the days when she had the will to work. In any case, the residents didn't give a damn about her or about the state of their stairwell. They went upstairs with their shoes full of mud – they never wiped them on the mat she took the trouble to place in the entryway. They didn't even spit in her direction and, in addition, one of the residents – Kolya, who always said "Shalom, how are you, Kati?" and for whom she felt a significant and frightening attraction – didn't say anything this time when he passed her on the stairs, or even look at her like he sometimes did.

She wanted to yell after him, "Kol-ya, Kol-ya," but who was she and why should anybody take any notice of her in the first place, she thought and kept quiet. She cleaned another half a flight, and then, on the second floor of the building, she gave the pail a hefty kick. The water poured down to the bottom of the stairs, and she followed it out of the building. As she was walking along the street parallel to the one she lived on, she felt dizzy and stopped. The street was dark and deserted, Kati felt that she couldn't take it any more and suddenly she screamed at the top of her voice. Luckily for her, there was a loud thunder clap over Lod at exactly the same moment, otherwise they would have heard her all over Ganei-Aviv and thought that she had gone completely off her rocker.

Kati arrived at home. There was nobody there. The children were at the community center getting ready for a show in honor of something or other, she didn't have a clue. Purim? Passover? Maybe Arbor Day? Boaz wasn't home either. Either he'd gone with them, or he'd gone to visit a friend.

"Thank the Lord," she muttered, opened the windows and took out a packet of cigarettes she kept hidden in the cupboard for when she wanted to smoke and Boaz wasn't at home. She lit a cigarette and inhaled deeply, and exhaled. Thus, enveloped in a thick cloud of the smoke that her husband hated so much, with the cigarette stuck in her mouth, as in the days of her youth, she went to the cupboard and took out the Yellow Pages.

Kati was looking for a way out. Perhaps she would have been wiser to open the Bible at those melancholy moments, when she felt that her life was a lie, and read a verse or two of Psalms. But she found the Bible too complicated to read, and she didn't feel the need for anything holy. She needed immediate, practical and efficient first aid.

The only edition of the Yellow Pages they had in the house was from 1993, and only for the region of Tel Aviv and the center of the country. She remembered when Boaz had brought it home, during the days when he was still a cab driver. Once they had used it to prop up a desk with a leg that had been broken when her husband had kicked it. Later on, they had thrown out the desk and kept the book.

She paged through it, and without knowing exactly what she was looking for, read about all kinds of plumbers and electricians who all seemed to her far better off than she was. Over the years Kati had taught herself to read, and the fact that Boaz called her illiterate only spurred her on to learn to read long words too, although she wasn't sure that she pronounced them right.

In the end she decided to look at the beginning of the thick volume, in the index. Suddenly her eye was caught by the entry "Makeup – schools" and her face lit up.

At the same time that she continued doing her hated cleaning work, she would learn to be a makeup artist! To tell the truth, she had already picked up quite a lot of the basics during the week when the girls in the makeup studios of the various television stations had worked on her face. In one of the makeup rooms she had even read an illustrated, framed chart hanging on the wall, with explanations of do's and don'ts regarding sunken eyes, long faces, big noses, sunken chins. And she even remembered the instructions written on it.

The name "Another Face – Angelica Gomeh's Makeup School" captured her attention. The school was in Tel Aviv, located in an apartment belonging to Adir Bergson, the only heir of Liat Dubnov's estate. On the last night of her life, when Liat was counting her and her brother's real estate in order to cling to something concrete, she didn't skip the apartment that had been occupied for many years by the sad widow Gomeh, who had lost her husband in a traffic accident exactly one year after their son, Hagai Gomeh, had been killed when two helicopters transporting troops to the front had crashed in mid-air over a village in the Galilee, on the 27th of Shevat, 1997.

Kati Beit-Halahmi was fully conscious when she got ready to dial a long distance number, something not to be contemplated in the impoverished household of the Beit-Halahmi family. She knew that the call would cost more, far more, than a call within area code 08. She vividly remembered the days when her husband Boaz would break something, usually the telephone itself, whenever the phone bill arrived. She knew and understood very well what she was doing, what she was thinking, and the implications for her situation and her family's situation. She had abandoned the stairwell in the middle of washing the floor, people could slip on the water she had spilled without wiping it dry, and break something, and blame her for it.

When she dialed 03 she finally realized that she was no longer capable of doing those cleaning jobs, not in the stairwells and not at the bank. She was simply incapable of wringing out any more cold floor cloths, and feeling the water almost freeze on her fingers when she scraped chewing gum off the floor.

Kati was the the family's only breadwinner. They lived on what she earned and the pittance that Boaz received from the National Insurance. She knew that if she gave up her cleaning jobs she was sentencing her family to even greater poverty, but she had to do something; if she didn't she would start to grow moldy herself. She could no longer stand the gap between what there was and what she wanted. Every day she watched the Spanish-speaking soap operas on the television. The people on these soap operas had so much time on their hands that they could afford to repeat the same things several times in different ways, while she didn't even have time to think.

No, no more, her mind was made up. If worst came to worst, she would go and get a disability allowance for something psychological, something in her soul, she didn't care. In this way she would also show that sucker Boaz how to work within the system. The main thing was to get *out*, *out* of this life that she was living and wanted to throw off – out into something that would take her even further out, and she called Angelica Gomeh's number on Nahum Street in Tel Aviv. Nine digits in all, and she waited. She didn't hang up.

"Hello?" said Gomeh.

Kati was very surprised that she said, "Hello," and not, "Another Face, good afternoon," or "Makeup School, good afternoon, how can I help you?" and she too said, "Hello?"

"Yes," said Gomeh, "who do you want to talk to?"

"Angelica Gomeh," said Beit-Halahmi, looking at the name again on the yellow page of the Yellow Pages, and hoping that she had pronounced it correctly.

"Speaking."

"Shalom, Mrs. Gomeh. I hope I'm not disturbing you in the middle of your work."

"No, you're not disturbing me. How can I help you?"

"Because if I'm disturbing you and you're busy with other students now, I can call another time, even though this is a long distance call."

"You're not disturbing me. I don't have any students here now."

"Oh, good, I'm so glad. I'm calling you from out of town."

"What?"

"From out of town, long distance."

"From outside the country?"

"No, from Lod."

"Lod," said Gomeh. "Do you want to sell me something? Because I don't. . . ."

"God forbid," said Kati. "I'm calling about your school."

"But you sound very young," said Angelica.

"Thank you. I'm forty."

"That's very young for my school. Don't you think?"

"Just a minute," said Kati. "What school?"

Outside somebody honked loudly. The noise was heard throughout Gomeh's apartment, coming through the closed window, through the gaps between the broken shutter slats, which the landlords had not yet mended, even though she had asked them several times, and it also reached the ears of Kati on the other end of the line.

"Someone's honking very loudly here. I can't hear. Just a minute," said Gomeh.

She put the phone down and Kati wondered how much more this wait was going to cost her, Boaz was really going to kill her. As long as he didn't come home now. She would hang up if he came in, and smile and say that she'd finished work early today, wasn't that nice. In the background she heard Gomeh shouting, and far in the distance somebody answering her.

"Listen, dear," said Gomeh into the receiver, "my car's blocking the street. It's a narrow street. Can you call back in a few minutes?"

"Sure, sure," said Kati.

Angelica hung up and went downstairs with the car keys.

"Is this car yours?" asked the truck driver.

"It is."

"What kind of parking job is that? Half a kilometer from the pavement?"

"Excuse me sir, but you're honking like a lunatic. What's all the hysteria about? So my parking job wasn't so great. I admit it. You're right."

"No, no, lady. You can't park like that, I don't care what you say. You can't call that parking. Who gave you a driver's license? I'm late as hell already. My boss is going to fire me. And these streets are driving me crazy. I had to deliver a washing machine to Jeremiah. I've got three more to go today, and my nephew's Bar Mitzvah. I won't have time to shower. I took the new one upstairs. I took her old one downstairs, and threw it away somewhere, in some garden there. I got into a proper mess on the way to her, a very nice woman. And now I can't get out again. I can't take any more of this. I'm not from here. Do me a favor," he said softly, "how do I get out of here onto the highway?"

Gomeh parked her car closer to the pavement and gave him directions, she even waited for him to repeat how many right turns, how many left, straight, and how many traffic lights to count before getting onto the expressway. Then she went back upstairs, and feeling that she had accomplished something, made herself coffee. While she drank, she waited for the woman from Lod to call, but she didn't. Gomeh thought that since times were so hard, she would take even a student of forty for lessons in drawing trees, tree trunks and tree rings. Due to the harshness of the winter her retirees – mostly women – were afraid to go out into Yarkon Park lest they catch cold, and they painted from pictures that she handed out to them. But because she didn't want too great a mess in her house she insisted that her "girls and boys" as she called them, take their paints and drawings home with them at the end of each lesson. She didn't want her home turned into a warehouse. They grumbled and took them. Only sometimes she relented and let them leave their things behind if, for example, one of them wasn't going straight home at the end of the lesson. But as a rule she insisted that they take everything away. What would she do if the woman from Lod refused to drag all her equipment from her hometown to Tel Aviv and back again? She would have to reach a compromise with her. Today every penny counts, thought Gomeh, and dialed *42, which connected her straight to the home of Kati Beit-Halahmi.

Kati answered and was very surprised that Gomeh called her back. She had intended to make the call herself, at a safer time, but now that it was at the expense of the other woman, what did she care? They arranged to meet in two days time at Gomeh's apartment. After the call from Tel Aviv, Kati called Boaz's friend, to find out how much time she had left. Boaz had fallen asleep at his friend's house, she was told, and she made eight phone calls one after the other, in which she informed the condo associations of Ganei-Aviv that she, Kati Beit-Halahmi, was giving them notice forthwith, for very personal reasons. She tried to sound secretive and mysterious. She didn't want them to start calling her at home, so that Boaz would find out and go berserk. She asked about severance pay and all the condo associations said that of course she was entitled to it, she had worked for them for all those years and there had almost never been any complaints.

After finishing these calls, she thought about her job at the bank and decided that for the time being she would keep it, and only when she finished the makeup course, would she tell the bank to go to hell as well, because then she would have other work, as a makeup artist. Where was she going to get the money for the course? She thought that the severance pay would be enough, and that Gomeh would meet her halfway.

THE 12TH OF SHEVAT was the coldest day in the history of the State of Israel: half a degree above zero on the coast, for example. The forecasters even spoke of a high probability of snow in low places, and explained how such a thing was possible, or, actually, explained that they didn't understand how such a thing was possible. On that day the news programs were extended, not only because of current terror attacks, but also because of the cold that was exceptional even in relation to the abnormal weather conditions that winter. On the special reports that ran after the news on the main television channels, military and political commentators sat side by side with members of the Knesset and cabinet ministers, but most of the screen time was taken up by the meteorologists, and after they had ceased to interest the public and their jokes were no longer found amusing, they were succeeded by experts on the physics of clouds and precipitation, on structural geology, planetary sciences, the physics of the earth, the dynamics of the atmosphere and climate change.

When the possibility came up again that a volcanic eruption had begun somewhere, perhaps in the depths of the Black Sea, and that it was this eruption that had led to the radical change in the nature of the winter in our country, a vehement public debate sprang up around the question of whether there had been a failure to foresee this exceptional winter, and if so, who was to blame, who should resign, and one man, who was actually an expert on comets, argued that all the weather teams in the State of Israel, whoever they were, should go on unpaid leave until a special committee could examine the matter.

Something interesting happened that winter. The worse the security situation became – the more people were killed in acts of revenge, or revenge for revenge, or were simply gunned down, or blown up – and the more Israeli forces went in and out of the towns under the control of the Palestinian Authority, in accordance with the security needs of the state, the more public debate began to turn away from the subject of what was going to happen from the point of view of the security situation, to questions about the weather. With the threat from the climate added to the threat from the terrorists, people preferred to talk about the terrible weather rather than the terrible security situation, or the recession that had taken hold in all branches of the economy.

That evening Ventura's children went to bed at about ten o'clock. The brand new washing machine, which had arrived the day before and was already working so well, put her into a good mood.

A pile of damp laundry lay in what used to be Herut's plastic bathtub, when she was a baby, waiting for its turn to be dried on the radiator. "My electricity bill's going to be out of sight," said Ventura to herself, and went into the children's room to tuck them in. There were damp garments drying on the radiator in their room too, and she turned them onto their other side.

The washing machine had reached the spin cycle, and Ventura thoroughly enjoyed listening to the efforts it was making on behalf of her laundry, and thus, feeling quite calm, she sat down on the living-room sofa, switched on the television, and fell straight into one of the piercing debates on the question: had there or had there not been a failure to predict this harsh winter, which, on top of everything else, was impeding the actions of the IDF in the territories of the Palestinian Authority.

A feeling of guilt ran her through with the speed of lightning, and seemed to split her in half lengthwise. Perhaps the children were right after all: perhaps in view of this terrible winter, and the difficulty of drying the laundry, and the skyrocketing electricity bill she could expect at the end of the month – she should have taken most of the money she had earned from Liat's shiva, and bought a new Pentium computer for the children, and not a washing machine, and gone on doing the washing at the laundromat until she found a job.

No, she convinced herself, but without much success, a washing machine and food were more important. Today, too, she had paid a few bills in red print, cable TV, electricity, telephone and water. Everything was about to be disconnected. If she had bought the computer, they wouldn't have had electricity in the apartment now. She had done the right thing when she bought the washing machine and paid the bills. No question about it. She asked herself if she should give Othniel a call and ask him to buy, on the side, as a dad, a computer for the children. No she shouldn't, she concluded, he would only say no, so why waste the money on a call to Jerusalem?

What she could do was suggest to her eldest son Osher tomorrow morning that when they were at Daddy's this coming weekend, when Daddy's girlfriend was there with them, he should ask him for a computer. Maybe in her presence he would want to make a generous impression and he would agree.

, , ,

She soon grew bored with the neckties and recriminations of the men on the television screen, and she switched channels rapidly until she came across the movie channel. It was showing a movie like hundreds she had already seen – pictures running past and people talking.

She felt hungry, and got up to go to the kitchen and get the item that had been on sale that day and that she had bought for the children, a packet of lemon flavored wafers. She nibbled a few, but she was careful, since she had a tendency to put on weight at an alarming rate. At the end of her military service she had weighed eighty-two kilos, and it had taken her a year and a half to get down to normal. After that, her parents died, and she put it all back on again. Before her wedding she had gone on a murderous diet, because she wanted to reach the finish line under the marriage canopy at sixty kilos.

The movie came to an end. One of the characters said something. Iris thought that just for the sake of this sentence it had been worth her while to sit there watching these people going through the motions of saying and doing the things that were written in their scripts. She repeated the sentence to herself in English and thought that she should write it down somewhere. She didn't have the energy to get up and look for a pen and paper. So she made an effort to remember, "Nothing is lost but everything is past." She felt that there was something to this sentence, something true, capable of explaining something about life to her, but then she was struck by the thought that it was a generalization, just a generalization. Only a generalization. Ventura suddenly felt the uneasiness resulting from an inner contradiction. And she tried to resolve it: So what if it's a generalization? Who says you can't make generalizations? Why not make generalizations? All blacks are blacks. There, I made a generalization. And it's obviously correct. I didn't examine every case on its merits. And I have no intention of checking every black person. And moreover – thought Ventura – isn't saying that you can't make generalizations a generalization? If it's so wrong to generalize why do generalizations exist? Why do most of the great sayings by wise men begin with the words "Everyone," "No one," "Always," or "Never"?

She turned to a local channel. Somebody was saying that, in his opinion, the cold that had attacked the country stemmed from an inexplicable deviation in the direction of the Atlantic Ocean's cold stream into the Mediterranean Sea. She thought of Adir. What was his opinion? Perhaps she should give him a call? On no account. He was with his exotic girlfriend now. Once she had gone into his laundromat, and before he noticed her she overheard him telling someone that the thing that had turned him on about Tasaro was that she hadn't changed her name to Aviva or Aliza or Ilana. She had stayed as she was.

And he had gone on to say that the officials in the Interior Ministry had automatically changed the first names of the immigrants who came with Operation Moshe, but with Operation Shlomo they had allowed them to decide for themselves.

That morning Ventura's children had worn their mother out. And the rest of the day had been quite badly behaved too, it was only now, in the evening, that she had found a bit of peace and quiet, in front of the television. She thought of the morning's traumatic events. "Traumatic events" was the right way to describe it, she thought. The children woke up and all three at once asked for the day off, "because it's cold." Iris wasn't built to spend the morning with the children, but only with herself, and with the smell of the laundry softener. She had reached her limit with the children, and if anyone needed a day off it was her. She planned, immediately after they left, taking Herut with them to her kindergarten on Amos Street, to shut the whole world out and be quiet. For at least a few hours, maybe even to sleep. Or to stare into space.

Once she had refused, point blank, to give the children the day off, Oz told her that his throat was sore, especially when he swallowed, and Osher asked for the thermometer and said that his head was pounding, he only hoped he hadn't caught the Saudi flu that people died from, and he began to cry from fear.

She left their room to get the thermometer and some aspirin, and when she returned she overheard them whispering and deciding what each of them would say next to convince their mother that they were sick, and what they would do after they had persuaded her to let them stay at home – play Monopoly or Find the Lunatic, their two favorite board games. Ventura burst into the room, tore the boys' duvets off them and threw them on the floor, she left Herut covered, she was still too little for such measures, and yelled, "I heard you, I heard you, get up and go to school, no more play-acting, no more excuses!"

Osher asked her suddenly, just like that, in a tone of resentful protest, why they didn't have a computer, why they didn't have anything, why he didn't have this brand of coat, and that brand of shoes, and why he didn't have any pocket money, all his friends had pocket money and brand-name coats and great computers. Iris wanted to give him a slap, but she stopped herself and mumbled, "You'll have a computer, you'll have pocket money – I'm working on it."

"Working on it..." said Oz scornfully. "You haven't got

138

a penny, Mother. Do you have a bank account at all?"

Now came the slap. Oz took it and shut up, and Iris, perhaps in order to create an effect of balance, then slapped Osher, who wasn't expecting it at all, and who was so insulted that he began to cry – something he hadn't done since she and Othniel had told them that they were getting a divorce.

Herut began to scream. Iris hurried to her and picked her up.

"Blood-sucking vampires," she yelled at the boys, and they got dressed, casting doubt on their mother's sanity as they did so. Let them cast a thousand doubts, thought Ventura, and in the meantime she dressed the screaming little girl and restrained herself forcefully from screaming back at her, "You shut up too!"

After Osher put gel on his hair and made it into spikes he kicked the door to his room and made a hole in it.

"This is a rented apartment," yelled Ventura, and he mimicked her words under his breath. She was still holding Herut who was already dressed, but whose sweater was inside out.

"What do I care if it's rented or not?" said Osher. "What's your case, slapping me like that? Are you crazy? Go to the loony bin!"

"What did you say?" said Iris, and looked at her watch. It was five to eight. They were going to be late for school. She was afraid for them.

"Sorry," she said. This seemed to her the quickest solution to the conflict. "I'm sorry," she repeated. "I'm afraid you're going to be late for school. You have to take Heruti to kindergarten."

"So we'll be late," said Osher, "what do I care. I hate that school."

"Mommy, Mommy," Oz now remembered, after looking at his school diary. "I need 120 shekels for the school trip."

"I haven't got it," screamed Ventura. "I haven't got it. Tell them next week."

"I told them that last week."

"When's the trip?"

"The day after tomorrow."

She hurried to her wallet and counted what was left. The time was two minutes to eight. She gave Oz 120 shekels.

"Suddenly you have got it?"

"Suddenly?" she almost lost her temper again. "I wanted to go to the supermarket."

She counted what she had left – thirty shekels, and decided to buy only milk and bread. She said goodbye to the children and they left. It was already after eight. She was afraid they would be punished, that they would be humiliated, and she felt very guilty, both for screaming and for slapping, and altogether for losing control.

Soon she found herself calculating whether she had enough gas to drive to the nearest mental hospital. It was quite probable that the children were right, and she had gone mad. She couldn't remember the last time she had an outburst like that. They were quite probably right. She tried to remember if she had enough gas to get there, in case they hospitalized her for a nervous breakdown, or else, if they let her go, she would use the thirty shekels to buy gas for the way back.

She was agitated and upset and she found it quite easy to convince herself that if she was a responsible person – and Ventura considered responsibility one of her virtues, the other being her self-control, in which she had just seen evidence of a crack – she should be examined by experts. She would drive to the psychiatric E R and they could get her to talk to them there. It was their job. They would let her talk, they would ask her her name, and for starters she would say that her name was Yael Dayan, that she was Yael Dayan, Moshe Dayan's daughter. That was sufficiently off the mark for them to keep her there for tests.

She got dressed. Yes, the same grey pants again, the same big black sweater. Ever since the birth of Herut, a little over five years ago, she had not succeeded in getting back to her original weight, and she weighed today what she had weighed when she was nine months pregnant with Oz. Seventy kilos. She covered herself with her biggest coat, it too black, and went downstairs.

When she got into her car and tried to start the engine, it responded with a polite cough and that was it. She tried a few more times, and then she stopped so as not to flood the engine.

Iris knew that she had to borrow those thick electric wires from some fellow citizen, the ones with that gadget at the end of them, she forgot what you called them – cables, jumper cables, that was it. She needed jumper cables, and to connect them to the battery of another car according to plus and minus guide marks.

She asked almost everyone driving past at that hour on Jeremiah Street, but they all said they couldn't help her. People were hurrying about their business. What ever happened to "Kol Yisrael Haverim – All of Israel are friends?" Throughout her childhood they had fed her that stuff about "all of Israel are friends," and she had believed it, and found it a great consolation.

"Are you leaving?" someone who coveted her parking spot asked.

"Only if you've got jumper cables. . ." she replied. "Do you have jumper cables?"

"Sorry."

She wasn't even capable of driving herself to the madhouse, fumed Iris, and she went home and made herself another cup of coffee. There wasn't any coffee left, except for one cup, and not even a heaped teaspoon the way she liked it. The coffee was quite tasteless. She threw it into the sink. Steam rose from the sink with a disgusting smell, Iris cried, "Yuk, gross," made a face and turned on the tap to clean the sink.

In the depths of the cabinet she found some tea, and made herself a cup. She decided to switch to tea, in view of the circumstances, and with her cup of tea and a cigarette she went out onto the balcony to smoke.

She hated smoking in the living room, because she didn't like the fact that she smoked at all, and hid the evidence from herself. Outside, an icy wind was blowing, and finally she succeeded, with difficulty, in lighting her cigarette. In the bathroom, the new washing machine was already furiously at work on a new load of laundry. Big hailstones were beating down on all the streets of the prophets. She tried to remember the names of all twelve prophets, and pretended that she had to answer the question in order to win half a million shekels on a television show. She tried to squeeze them out of her memory, but without success. She threw her cigarette over the balustrade, went into the children's room, and opened the Bible, and paged through it looking for the prophets, to see which ones she had forgotten.

Afterwards, she went into the living room and switched on the television, and what did she see? Yael Dayan speaking about the security situation in which Israel had become embroiled. Iris had once been a great admirer of Yael Dayan. When everyone criticized her for going to the beach on Yom Kippur, Ventura thought that it was her good right to do so, and she had even written a letter to the newspaper about it. But her letter had not been published; they had published other letters on the subject.

On the evening of the same crowded day, when the children were already sleeping and everything was quiet, she too felt calm, and she realized that she had been very lucky that her car had failed to start in the morning.

She could have been trapped there by the mental health authorities and not gotten out for years, and the children would have grown up with their father, and forgotten what she looked like, and she too ... in a month she would have looked like a ball, from the cocktail of medications and the food she would have eaten without any shame, and she too would have forgotten what she looked like. What luck that the car hadn't started, she thought again.

She stopped on the music channel. People were dancing to songs she didn't recognize. She was growing out-of-date, she reflected sadly. If she had been growing out-of-date and living with someone she loved, who was also growing out-of-date, she wouldn't have minded at all. She understood that growing out-of-date was inevitable, the question was how and with whom.

The phone rang. Iris didn't want to pick it up. Eleven o'clock at night. What did they want of her life? In the end she picked it up. It was Adir Bergson. He had another job for her.

"What do you mean another job?" asked Ventura.

"What do you mean what do I mean?"

"I mean what's the job?" He had succeeded in insulting her again.

"Look, I'll put it this way. I don't feel like going into Liat's apartment and clearing it out. I don't feel like it, I don't have the time, I don't have the inspiration, and it will also make me feel like shit, and I feel like shit with my asthma at the moment anyway. I don't want to upset myself unnecessarily, because what good will it do? In any case, she's already dead."

"You're right, I mean there's something to what you're saying."

"In short, Iris, I'm offering you the job of clearing out her apartment. Completely. I want to rent it or sell it. I haven't decided yet. Now's not a good time to sell. I'll rent it first and then sell it later. In any case, I need it empty. But absolutely empty, don't be sentimental. Do you understand?"

"Yes."

"Do it as quickly as you can, and truly, in all seriousness, with my hand on my heart – throw out whatever you feel like throwing out, and take whatever you feel like taking – I don't care. Have yourself a ball. I'll tell you what to do," he said. "Open the Yellow Pages. There are all kinds of listings there, 'Yossi buys everything,' or 'Motti buys everything.' Call one of those 'buys everything' characters. Work it out with him. Just tell me before you close the deal. Okay?"

"Why don't you ask Tasaro to clear the apartment out?" asked Ventura, amazed at the sentence that had come out of her mouth. And instead of stopping, she went on, "She isn't sentimental."

"She's really busy," he answered naturally. "They're photographing her now for an Ethiopian cookbook."

"Ah," said Ventura. "That's really important in order to give them a sense of equality."

"A sense of equality," repeated Adir. "So??? What do you say? Will you take the job?"

"Ah, how much will you pay me? And how? By the hour or for the lot?"

"I'll pay you for the lot."

"And what about cleaning up afterwards?" asked Iris. "Does it include cleaning up?"

"No. I'll get a cleaning firm in, just leave the place empty. And with regard to her calendar collection. . . ."

"What about it?"

"Give that to me. That I'll keep."

"Alright."

"So how much do you want?"

"I don't know . . . three thousand?" she said carefully.

"Three thousand," repeated Adir. "What can I tell you, the dollar's going through the roof. Okay, but according to today's rates."

"Okay, okay. No problem."

Iris had been talking about shekels, and she was in seventh heaven at getting the three thousand in dollars.

She was so happy that she called Danziger the next morning and made an appointment for the same day, and said that she would begin to pay him soon, five hundred shekels at a time.

THE NEXT DAY, Tuesday, the storm continued, and the terrifying hail continued to fall. Hailstones with a circumference of five to eight centimeters fell from the sky and lay for hours on the ground before they melted.

Scientists shut themselves in their laboratories, weighed the hailstones, and counted how many of them had fallen during a given time over a given area at different hours of the storm in different parts of the country. They also cut the cold stones into longitudinal sections, in order to examine the various kinds of ice of which they were composed, and thereby to discover the conditions in the clouds that had created these exceptionally large hailstones.

Kati went to meet Angelica Gomeh. That afternoon, she had to clean the bank, the only job to which she had not given notice. She hoped that the condo associations would keep their promise and give her severance pay, even though she had worked on the black market and had not filled in a single form during all the years of her employment. If they didn't come up with the money, she would not be able to pay for the makeup courses, and it would also be very difficult to hide the fact that she had stopped cleaning the stairwells from Boaz. But the frightened Beit-Halahmi told herself not to worry, she had an emergency plan inspired by the soap opera *Because of a Kiss*, which she would set in motion only "if and when." Kati liked the expression "if and when," and looked forward to having the opportunity to say to herself "if and when" about all kinds of things.

The enormous hailstones beat on the windows of the bus to Tel Aviv. If and when she had no other alternative, and the severance pay with which she intended to finance her course was delayed, or didn't arrive at all, she would put the idea into practice. But only "if and when," as she had often heard politicians say.

Now she was travelling on the bus to Tel Aviv. She looked out at the big hailstones and the cars coping with the conditions on the ground and those that had failed to cope with them and were stuck at the side of the road. She looked at the passengers too, who all looked boring to her, blank, uncared-for faces, dull women who had resigned themselves to their dreary lives. Not her. She was on her way to breaking through, rising up, founding, establishing. She was a pioneer.

At the new central bus station she asked at the information desk for the bus to Nahum Street. She was sure they would ask her Nahum who, and she felt embarrassed in advance, because she didn't know the answer. The person behind the glass window said, "That's in North Tel Aviv, bus number four," and pointed her to the appropriate platform.

Beit-Halahmi sat down behind the driver, and asked him to tell her when to get off when they came to Nahum Street. He too didn't ask her Nahum who, and said he would tell her.

Beit-Halahmi was half an hour early for her appointment with Gomeh. There was a lull in the hailstorm, and so she decided to walk around a bit and get to know the area, since it was, after all, the area in which her school was located. Apart from that, Kati wanted to see North Tel Aviv with her own eyes.

In her childhood, in the Ramle immigrant transit camp, "North Tel Aviv" was a very important place, where very very big bosses lived. Firstly, they're Ashkenazis, she was told, secondly, they're educated, they know Hebrew and at least six other languages, thirdly, they're not in the least shy, because they've got nothing to be shy about, and therefore

147

they're also taller, because they've got more money and they eat better.

In the Ramle camp, people talked a lot about North Tel Aviv. They said the North Tel Avivians had everything. Toilets, baths, showers – strong water pressure from all the taps, kitchens with fridges and gas stoves and ovens. And because they had fewer children there, in most cases every child had a room of his own, or at the most, they shared a room with their brother or sister. In any case, they had drawers of their own, where they kept things that were theirs, and nobody was allowed to touch them.

In the period after the Yom Kippur War, a woman from North Tel Aviv came all the way to Ramle, to Kati's mother, and brought her curtains and bed linen to sew, because she had heard that she was both cheap and skilled, and did quality work. The visitor would sit in their home for a few minutes, to agree on the price and chat a while, before returning to North Tel Aviv. One day Kati, who was then about fourteen, followed her when she left their house, in order to see the magnificent car taking her back to Tel Aviv. She was very surprised to see the lady getting onto the bus.

One day the North Tel Avivian came to have minor alterations made to all her trousers, because she had been on a diet and lost weight, and Kati heard her asking her mother why she left the front door open. Her mother replied, "To let some air in. It's hot."

"Aren't you afraid of burglars?" asked the guest.

"I'm at home all day, what have I got to be afraid of? And, besides, there's nothing to steal. . . ."

She heard her mother laughing, and she was even more ashamed. Was it anything to brag about that they had nothing to steal? thought Kati then.

, , ,

Now Kati Beit-Halahmi inspected the terrain. She looked at the buildings. The ones in Ganei-Aviv looked better and newer to her, although in relation to the transit camp there was no comparison, of course. Beit-Halahmi advanced into Micah Street and was very surprised. She herself lived in Micah Reiser Avenue, and here they called him only by his first name. It must be something to do with "protectzia," with having connections, she thought.

She nearly slipped on a puddle formed by the hail. She might have broken her leg, and what would she have told Boaz then? What was she doing on Micah Street without the Reiser, instead of on Halalei Egoz, cleaning three stair-wells in a row?

She went onto Malachi and from there to Ezekiel, and she thought what is this, all first names only? And by the time she reached Joel Street, she stopped thinking about it. Except to reflect that if she had a cell phone, and if she was on normal terms with her husband, she would have called him up and asked him what was going on over here in North Tel Aviv, what was the story with the first names? Because he had graduated from high school, and she had dropped out in grade school.

She had another twenty minutes to kill. The sky darkened again and threatened another heavy hailstorm. Ventura walked past her, hurrying on her way to Liat's apartment, to see what the situation there was. She still had a key from the shiva. Even though Liat had things that Iris coveted, she had decided in advance not to take anything. That was all she needed, for Adir to see her in his sister's shoes or boots. They wore the same size. Iris knew this from the days when they were best friends, in high school.

"Excuse me," Kati addressed Iris.

"Yes?" Ventura replied impatiently.

149

"Are you from around here?"

"Yes," said Ventura.

"So maybe you can tell me why all the streets here have only got first names?"

"What?" asked Ventura.

"Why have all the streets here only got first names without last names? Ezekiel, Micah, Nahum. What did they do, so that everybody knows them? Or is it protectzia?"

"'Protectzia'?" repeated Iris. It had been years since she had heard the word.

"Yes, protectzia, you know, special treatment."

"What special treatment?" asked Ventura in bewilderment.

"That they haven't got any last names . . . where I live it's only names with last names, or names of flowers, like in my neighborhood," said Kati. "And here, they get to be called by their first name only. Why?"

"Because they were prophets," said Ventura. "They get special treatment because they were prophets. It's from the Bible. In the Bible, there aren't any last names, or actually there are," she quickly corrected herself, "but not like now."

She gave Kati a long look, and wondered what she meant by her questions. She looked about her own age. She had evidently made an effort to dress well. Perhaps she was even wearing her best clothes: a tiger-striped blouse that fit her upper body too tightly, and black sequined trousers and on top of them a coat and gloves in a completely different style. Losing six or seven kilos wouldn't hurt her, mused Ventura, her thoughts straying, and then she came back to the weird questions again. At first she thought she was crazy, although she looked familiar to her from somewhere, she couldn't remember where. Suddenly she thought that she was being filmed for *Candid Camera* and she looked around for the hidden camera, but it was hidden, of course.

"Haven't you people got anything better to do?" she demanded angrily of Kati. "Stopping people in the street and asking them stupid questions? Why don't you make programs about something real? About poverty and unemployment, for example. Look what you waste money on. It's a shame and disgrace."

Ventura hurried away, to be on the safe side.

Beit-Halahmi stood still for a minute, trying to get to the bottom of these remarks, but it began hailing hard again and she opened her umbrella – one of those they had received in the wake of her first television appearance – and hurried to Nahum Street.

While Beit-Halahmi was standing outside Angelica Gomeh's door and ringing the bell, over and over again, the latter was in the shower, scrubbing her back with a brush that stimulated her blood circulation at the same time as it cleaned her skin. Kati stood behind the door, unable to understand why there was nothing written on it to indicate the presence of a professional makeup school, but only the name "Gomeh." She was angry, suspecting that the whole thing might be a con, and insulted because nobody opened the door, and nobody had notified her of a cancellation. After a few minutes Gomeh opened the door and all Kati's anger evaporated on the spot. It was the makeup teacher's appearance that took the air out of the balloon. Instead of being tall, as Kati had imagined, she was short, shorter than Kati, thin, and about fifty-five years old. Maybe more, maybe much more, maybe much less. Kati asked her where to hang her coat and exposed her colorful outfit.

Gomeh took the coat, umbrella, and gloves and put them on the rack in the hall. She, too, failed to comprehend the stylistic connection between Kati, the coat she had received thanks to the TV program *At Effi's on the Porch*, and the outfit she had on underneath it. Beit-Halahmi, for her part, was still busy inspecting Gomeh. Angelica was wearing a smock stained with different colors, and holding in her hand a thick blue brush, which she had picked up from the floor a second before opening the door.

Beit-Halahmi wondered, How can this be? This is how she applies eye makeup? With a brush that size?

"Are you Angelica Gomeh?" she asked.

"Yes. And you? Is your name Kati Beit-Halahmi?"

"Yes."

"Come in. Sit down. I'm just finishing a painting. Sorry I kept you waiting. I had to take a shower in boiling water to warm myself up. I hardly use the heater. It's very expensive, and boiling water keeps me warm for an hour."

"Very expensive," Beit-Halahmi agreed with her and thought to herself that Gomeh was a little strange. On the one hand she saved on the heater, and on the other she heated the water.

She stepped into the apartment, and this was the first time in her life that she saw a North Tel Aviv apartment from inside. This was not how she had imagined a North Tel Aviv apartment looking as a child in the immigrants' camp in Ramle: stuffy and stinking of cigarettes, every wall painted a different color, and sometimes the same wall painted a number of colors, as if they couldn't make up their minds what color to paint it.

"Am I in the way?" called Kati, without going into the room where Gomeh was busy with her painting. She noticed an old mirror and quickly fixed her makeup, so as not to, God forbid, make an ignorant impression.

"No, come in, sit down, I'm just fixing the sky above the cypress here for one of my retirees. It makes them very happy. Sit down," she pointed to a chair.

"What retirees?" asked Kati.

"After my son was killed in the helicopter disaster, actually. . ." she corrected herself, "since I was widowed, I started giving painting lessons to retirees. You know, trees, nature. In the summer, I take them to the park and they paint there. In the winter, they paint from pictures I cut out of magazines."

"Is it your hobby, like the walls?" asked Beit-Halahmi.

"Hobby? I suppose you could call it that. It may well be that the presence of my students makes me feel calm and relaxed, and that's why I do it. You know what else calms me and prevents me from sinking into a depression?" Gomeh said suddenly.

"What?" asked Beit-Halahmi. She was very confused. Where were all the cosmetics? Why did Gomeh herself look so neglected?

"Movies. I watch a lot of comedies. I belong to five video stores all over the neighborhood – I watch all their comedies over and over again. I began from the early days of the cinema. Silent films. Charlie Chaplin, Laurel and Hardy. Pies thrown in faces, people slipping and falling in the street, that's what makes me laugh the most. And now I'm watching a new movie with the guy from *The Mask*, what's his name? I forget. And Eddie Murphy, I like him a lot. And John Belushi, all his films. And that Englishman who doesn't talk, I like him too. Mister Bean. You know him?"

"My husband likes him a lot," said Kati.

"Aha. You're married."

"Plus four, bless them."

"Would you like something to drink?"

"Coffee."

"How do you like it?"

"Turkish. Black."

"Sorry, I don't have it. Only instant."

"Then without milk," said Kati.

"Sugar?"

"Two, please."

Gomeh dipped her brush into a glass of water and went into the kitchen. Unlike in Beit-Halahmi's place, the kitchen wasn't joined to the living room. There was even a door separating it from the rest of the apartment.

"Come along, come along," called Gomeh. "Come in, don't be shy."

"I'm not shy."

Beit-Halahmi went into the kitchen and sat at the formica table that had two matching chairs next to it.

"So tell me, my dear – what brings a girl like you to learn to paint trees with a bunch of old-age retirees? Hmm?"

"Oh no!" cried Beit-Halahmi in alarm. "What trees? I thought this was a makeup school. That's what it said in the Yellow Pages. . . ." She opened her bag and read out loud from the note she had copied down at home, "Another Face – Makeup School."

"Ahhhhh!" cried Gomeh. "It was a makeup school. But after my life lost its meaning, I closed the makeup school, even though . . . you should know, some of my ex-students are doing very well in the industry today, and they often phone me on holidays to wish me a happy holiday and to thank me and so on and so forth. I don't answer their calls anymore. I have a Caller-ID display. I haven't got the energy for them. I live in order to get life over."

"So this isn't a makeup school?"

"Not today. Drink your coffee, it will get cold. Isn't it good? I drink tea. I've got problems, don't ask."

Tears trickled down Beit-Halahmi's cheeks.

"My dear, you're crying! Why are you crying? Because it isn't a makeup school? You wanted to learn makeup? What is it?"

Beit-Halahmi told her her life history from the day she had met Boaz in Eilat, including the ostracism imposed on them by his family, the week of massive television exposure, and ending with this very minute.

She cried the whole time, and Angelica didn't have any tissues, so she brought her toilet paper, first a bit at a time, and then the whole roll.

Kati fell silent, and Gomeh said, "What are we going to do with you?"

"Teach me privately. I'll pay you as much as you like. I came all the way from Lod. And I went though so much to find the address. And I lied to my husband. I can't go home empty-handed."

"Let me think," said Angelica.

"What about?"

"If I've got any gear left. If it's still any good." She knitted her brow. "Yes, I have. If needs be, we can get some more. For one student, it won't be too much. I have only one question for you. How will you pay for the lessons? Did you quit your job cleaning the stairs without stopping to think? I don't give lessons for free, and I don't give discounts either. I don't do anything for nothing. Not anything."

"I didn't ask for charity," said Beit-Halahmi.

155

"So where are you going to get the money?" asked Gomeh again. "You said your husband doesn't know. I want four thousand shekels in advance, presumably I'll have to replenish my makeup case, check if the samples are okay. If not, I'll have to get new ones. And I suppose you'll want a make-up case of your own when you leave?"

"Sure," said Kati.

"And recommendations?"

"Yes. I really want to get into the business."

"And what do you want to focus on: television, movies or weddings?"

"Everything."

"Mmmm. Good. We'll begin and see what happens. In my opinion you'll need, for private tuition – in other words just you and me – seven, eight thousand shekels. Four thousand in advance and the rest. . . ."

"I'll get it and give it to you in one go. I don't want to walk around with so much money in cash. When can I come?"

"As soon as you have the money."

"I'll have it tomorrow."

"Then come on Sunday."

"No problem," said Kati.

PART THREE

PART THREE

"Welcome back to our show," said Ricki Lake to her viewers, and Tasaro Tasama read the Hebrew subtitles to herself and ordered Tusi "Down!" because the dog had grabbed her place on the sofa when she went to the kitchen to get a bite to eat.

Although she knew a little English, Tasaro preferred to read the subtitles. Once she had even asked Adir, and he told her that even though he knew English, his eyes went automatically to the bottom of the screen, to the Hebrew subtitles.

She was soon absorbed in her favorite television program, and this time girlfriends surprised girlfriends by bringing not only themselves to the show, but also their best friend, and the guy they knew their best friend had been in love with for a long time. The goal was for the best friend to be given a full makeover behind the scenes, including makeup and a new outfit at the expense of the *Ricki Lake Show*, and then, looking the best that she could possibly look, she would come out and have the courage to say to the guy in front of the studio audience and the millions of viewers at home, I love you, do you want me?

How Tasaro longed for the beloved to fall into the arms of the made-over best friend and say something like, "I'm crazy about you too, but I never had the guts to tell you," but nothing like this happened. In most cases the beloved didn't know how to repel the advances of the would-be lover, and one of them even said that he was dating someone else, but he was prepared to be a good friend to the woman who was in love with him.

The experienced Ricki Lake said to the disappointed women, "At least you've learned something here today,"

and, "You can carry on from here. Go for it!" While the credits rolled, Tasaro thought that it wasn't so terrible that she
didn't have any close girlfriends to worry about her – in any
case, she was already with the one she loved. Her only problem was figuring out how to make this situation permanent.
Tasaro couldn't bear it that everything in life was temporary.
Adir kept on saying this, and it hurt her. When she asked him
if they would stay together for many more years, he replied,
"Do I know what's going to happen in a year or two?"

She switched off the television and looked at the wall behind
which lay the bathroom, where Adir was shaving, and she
thought that she really was lucky to have met him, and she
should thank God for it. She didn't have to feel what the
women on Ricki Lake's show felt. The feeling that after they
had confessed their love and humiliated themselves in front
of the whole of the United States of America, and indeed,
the rest of the world too, nothing had come of it, and as if
that wasn't enough, they were exhorted to look ahead.
Tasaro hated being told all the time, especially now with all
the suicide bombings, to carry on, keep going and look
ahead. That's what they told them on the march to Sudan.
How good it was that the march was over. After her father
died, her mother said that her life wasn't worth living, and
sometimes her elder brothers had had to carry her. Tasaro
didn't like the way her mother behaved; she thought that
she was putting on an act, even though perhaps it wasn't an
act at all. Now she reflected that it was actually a good thing
that everything was temporary, and that the terrible journey was over.

She basked in Adir's love. He loved her – at least that's
what he had told her five times since they met, and he was
good to her too. He wouldn't have been good to her if

he didn't love her. It was true that she loved him more – she didn't know why she loved him more than he loved her, but that's the way things were.

Tasaro thought that Bergson was the angel that had come to save her. It was true that she had thought the same about Dido, who had saved her from the dangers of vagrancy, hanging around the new central bus station, but Bergson was younger, thinner, maybe too thin, and also handsomer. And another significant difference: Tasaro loved Bergson, while for Dido she felt affection and esteem. She was his friend, like the man said on the *Ricki Lake Show*.

If there was anyone in the world that Tasaro had to thank for her knowledge of Hebrew, which wasn't at all bad, it was Ricki Lake. Tasaro had an overwhelming desire to understand what they were all yelling about, both the studio audience and the guests on the show. A lot of blacks of all shades and features came to the *Ricki Lake Show*. Tasaro liked looking both at the whites and at the blacks, because it was only on this show that she had the opportunity to see such a wide range of colors and features in both races at once.

When Tasaro saw blacks and whites mixed up like this, she felt a great hope, with regard to her relationship with Adir as well. And when he told her, at her request, about Martin Luther King, she cried when he came to the assassination, and afterwards she made a special trip to the municipal library to read about him in the encyclopedia, and she even copied part of what she read into her diary.

Thanks to Ricki Lake, Tasaro had also mastered writing and spelling. Her Hebrew was the Hebrew of movie subtitles, to such an extent that sometimes when she was talking, even in the most trivial conversation, she would first see the white letters at the bottom of the screen, as if she were reading from a written text. Thus she was able to say the words in the right order, even if she didn't always get the pronunciation right.

Tasaro's dream was to get rid of all traces of a foreign accent, and to speak just like a regular Israeli, like Adir and Iris. After three years of vagrancy at the central bus station, and after seeing what had become of other Ethiopian girls who hung out there with her, she chose to apply herself to the study of Israeli culture. As a result, she would often use the same expression over and over again, *ad nauseam*. And, every time, a different expression. For example, for two months she kept on repeating "be that as it may..." and "without a doubt..." until one day Adir told her to stop it. To talk normally without saying "without a doubt" all the time....

"Nothing is so beyond doubt that you can say 'without a doubt' about it..." he said. She had almost completely stopped saying it.

In the many commercials in which she had appeared since she was discovered, they didn't let her say anything. They dubbed her voice with other girls' voices. When she first found out that this was what they were going to do, and that they were letting her mouth words so that her lip movements would be compatible with the words spoken by others, she was very insulted, because even though she was making good money modeling, she wanted to be a serious character actress in the movies.

People in the industry told her that she didn't have much of a chance. When anyone in Israel finally got hold of the funds necessary to make a movie, he filmed the script that had been lying in his drawer for years, and there weren't any Ethiopians in it, there simply weren't any. It wasn't a question of racism, but of facts, people wanted to film first and foremost what was close to their hearts – for example, their childhood – and there were no Jews from Ethiopia in Israel then. They explained to her that if an Ethiopian came along, and no doubt one would come along one day, with a script of his own, her chances of appearing in such a movie would be very good indeed. In the meantime, those were the facts of the situation.

Tasaro's agent insisted that it would be a bad move for her to start off as an extra, since according to her, this would cause irreparable damage to Tasaro's image, which was built on mystery.

"A lot of people think," the agent said to Tasaro in the cafe close to where she lived, during one of their recent meetings, "that if they start as extras, they're on the way to becoming actors, but this is one of the great illusions of the movies. It will ruin you as a model as well. Believe me," she said, "I've been working in the industry for years. It would be a disaster. You have to understand," she said and touched Tasaro's hand that was lying on the table, "I'm on your side. Absolutely. I don't want to exploit you and then throw you aside like other people do. I'm building your career long-term. You understand what long-term means, Tasaro?"

"Of course I do," said Tasaro.

"For many years to come," the agent explained anyway. "Many, many years to come. When you get a little older, you'll have money of your own to do other things with."

"Like what?" asked Tasaro.

"I don't know," said the agent. "Maybe you'll be a modeling agent yourself, like me. . . ." she laughed. Tasaro smiled too.

"Thank you," she said. "Thank you. I don't know what I would do without you."

"Yes," the agent agreed.

Thursday, the 15th of Shevat was the first dry day after a week of storms. Tasaro went to visit her mother and her brothers and sisters who lived close to their mother in Netanya. Once a month, she would make her way from her new Israeli life to her family in Netanya.

Whenever she went there she took something with her. Today it was the big microwave oven resting on her lap. The weather outside forced the driver to heat the bus, and Tasaro's lips were dry. On the way to Israel this never bothered her, but now she applied a transparent lip balm to them incessantly, so that she could highlight her amazing lips (all the makeup artists said the same thing to her, "You have amazing lips, you should model lipstick") with a light gloss, which was all that her amazing lips required. If the lips were dry, the makeup artists explained, the gloss quickly wore off, she had to constantly use lip balm to keep her lips moist. One of the makeup artists went so far as to remark to one of her colleagues in the room when she was making up Tasaro for the swimsuit catalog, "Maybe it happened to her because of that operation, what was it called, Moshe? What operation did you come to Israel on?" she turned to Tasaro.

"Shlomo," said Tasaro. "After Moshe."

Tasaro suffered from severe feelings of guilt for having succeeded in getting out of the ghetto, and therefore whenever she visited her family she wanted to get away as quickly as possible. None of her seven brothers and sisters – and certainly not her mother – none of them, apart from her, the eighth, the youngest of them all, had made enough of an effort in her opinion to fit into Israeli society, and this bothered her greatly. She was ashamed of them. She was angry with them. She forgot that she had been very lucky to meet Dido at the central bus station, and Adir later on. She rewrote her history in such a way that everything appeared to have been in her control.

Her mother, mused Tasaro as she sat on the bus with the microwave oven sitting on her lap, was a lost cause. She was still in mourning for her husband who had died on the journey to Israel, and she even blamed herself for coming to the country, even though of the two of them he was the one who was more enthusiastic to leave Ethiopia and emigrate to the Holy Land. Why didn't she turn over a new leaf? thought Tasaro and wrinkled her pretty face. Okay, she was lost. Her elder brothers were also lost, in her opinion. What good did it do them to have studied in that yeshiva high school? Now they were unemployed.

Only she, the youngest, had succeeded in getting out, she repeated to herself.

But her nieces and nephews? Tasaro suddenly thought, and her heart ached for them. The images of a few of them passed before her eyes. To Tasaro's disgust, they spoke Amharic peppered with Hebrew among themselves. And their Hebrew was full of jarring mistakes. How did they think they would ever succeed in this country? Tasaro was very worried about the future of her nieces and nephews, sixteen in number.

There were days when Tasaro would sit with her nieces and nephews and try to teach them Hebrew, or help them with their homework, but she would always get fed up after five minutes and recommend that they watch Spanish-speaking telenovelas on the television, and read the Hebrew subtitles.

➤   ➤   ➤

Now she sat in her mother's living room and tried to have a conversation with them. But it was impossible. There was so much noise. So many children. One of the nephews rummaged in her bag and pulled out the walkman that Tasaro had bought with the money she earned from a Tambur paint commercial. He put the earphones in his ears and listened to music. Tasaro yelled at him not to touch her bag, it was her bag, with her personal belongings in it.

Her older sister, Avivit, asked her to come into the kitchen for a minute. Standing next to the running water she had turned on to prevent their conversation from being overheard, she asked Tasaro for money. There wasn't any money. She needed money, for their mother, for herself, for the children. Tasaro asked her why her husband didn't have a job, and Avivit said bitterly, not everyone has a beautiful body.

Tasaro returned to the living room, to her handbag, and took out her wallet, so that her mother would see her taking it out, so she would see that she hadn't abandoned them and gone to live in sin with her Israeli boyfriend for nothing, some good had come of it too ... not only the end of the world. "My daughter is dead," she had been told that her mother had said about her once, in the days when she was living with Dido.

Tasaro went back to the kitchen and gave her sister five hundred shekels, leaving fifty for herself. In Tel Aviv she could withdraw more if necessary. She had a gold Visa card with the name Tasaro Tasama written on it in English letters. Adir had once told her that it was good in foreign countries too. He didn't like credit cards, but she did. A lot.

After giving her sister the money, she no longer felt any need or obligation to stay. Quickly, in Amharic, so they would understand, she explained how to work the microwave, and left them and their feelings of inferiority behind her. She felt them too, but no longer so powerfully, thank God.

On the bus trip back from the same visit that turned out so badly, she listened to Reggae music through her earphones. She wanted to forget and she absorbed herself in the music, and it therefore took several minutes for her to realize that her cell phone was ringing. She thought it was Adir. Sometimes he would surprise her and call for no reason. But it was her agent. She had an irritating voice, this agent, but she had done a lot for her.

"Hi," Tasaro said to her. "What's up?"

"Where are you?"

Tasaro said that she was on her way home, without saying where from. The agent didn't ask and came straight to the point, changing to a business-like tone.

"I've got something terrific for you, Tasaro."

"What?" said Tasaro. She was in dire need of something terrific that would make her spirits soar, after another visit to that depressing family of hers.

"As soon as you finish with the Ethiopian cookbook you've got a screen test, you hear me?"

"Yes, yes."

"You're testing for the girl who turns the wheel of fortune for the lottery, every Tuesday on television. It's not only a lot of money, it's also fantastic exposure. They want an Ethiopian. So am I a great agent or what?"

"Wow! Great, great," said Tasaro. "That's wonderful. Thank you, thank you."

The two of them agreed that the agent would "take the ball and run with it" and the conversation came to a close. Tasaro tried Adir, but he wasn't available. At home she got the answering machine with the recorded message in her voice, "You have reached Adir and Tasaro, please leave a message after the beep," and on his cell phone too she got the recording. She got it into her head that he was cheating on her with a white Israeli girl and a sharp pain pierced her stomach.

"Adir, please get in touch with me," she said and hung up. And then she was suddenly overwhelmed with relief, as she remembered that he had a doctor's appointment for a periodic checkup. She took a couple of deep breaths and brought her thoughts back to the good news she had just heard. Apart for Adir, she didn't have anyone else to call, and she called her mother and told her what was going to happen. She was so excited that she spoke to her in Amharic. Her mother said distantly, "Very nice, I wish you luck."

"Thank you, mother, thank you," said Tasaro and hung up.

All the way on the bus to Ezekiel Street and on foot from the bus stop home, Tasaro practiced silently, in her head, for the screen test. She imagined that she got the job and became famous throughout the land, and then her mother and the rest of her family would be proud of her, because she wasn't just exposing her body to make a living – but she had a real job on the television, speaking Hebrew.

She banished them from her thoughts again, and said to herself, So, ladies and gentlemen, what number has come up now? Let's see, dear viewers, what's the next lucky number? Fourteen, the number fourteen, and now nine, write down nine, and the extra number is eight. She practiced pronouncing the numbers correctly, with the stresses in the right places. And now let's repeat all the numbers together: fourteen, nine, twenty-seven, thirty-two, twelve, eleven, and the extra number – eight. Goodbye, ladies and gentlemen, until next week.... And if you didn't win this time it's not a big deal ... we have plenty of patience for you....

How badly Tasaro wanted this job!

She went inside. Adir wasn't at home. She was disappointed, even though it was expected. Whenever she came back from visiting her mother, Bergson would feel that she was putting a certain pressure on him, and he would disappear for a few hours to give her a chance to forget about her family. He didn't want to know what they thought about anything, and however much he tried to understand her, and where she came from, and however much he tried to understand himself – he didn't understand, and his frustration led to attacks of rage that sometimes ended in shortness of breath and the need to use his inhaler.

On a number of occasions, Tasaro had attempted to arrange for her boyfriend to meet her family. But it never worked out. Either the police had arrested her brother Tadesa again, or there was nobody home, even though for the past two weeks she had spoken to them of nothing but the meeting, or else it was Adir who backed out. "I'm tired," or, "I'm not emotionally ready," and the most annoying of all, "I want Liat to come with me," and Liat could never make it, because she had "something else going on."

As long as Liat was alive, Tasaro couldn't say anything, especially since she was convinced that it was his sister who was encouraging him not to set foot in her home, and once she had even asked her what she had against the meeting, and Liat said, "Why the formality? It's not as if you're getting married or anything...."

Once, when Liat was still around, they had almost, almost gone. It was the summer before the present exceptional winter, which had been hotter than usual, and the meteo-rologists had kept forecasting unseasonably high tempera-tures, great heat stress, and very little rainfall for the coming winter with worsening drought conditions.

Tasaro well remembered that 8th of Tamuz. At home in Netanya everything was ready. Even Tadesa was there, they informed her. Sleeping, but there. She had coordinated every detail with them, including the food they would serve, a combination of Ethiopian and Israeli, so that if Adir wanted to taste, he could, and if he wanted to eat, he would be able to do that too.

She had also implored them not to walk around in tra-ditional dress during the visit, but to wear regular clothes, and even discussed with them in advance what they should talk about, and what they were on no account to talk about, such as, God forbid, asking when are you getting married or anything like that.

In Netanya everyone was ready for the big moment. And also in Tel Aviv. Tasaro was dressed like a good girl, in a modest, flowing floral dress she had bought with the money from a tea commercial, especially for the historic meeting, and Adir was dressed as usual. Altogether there was a pleasant atmosphere, because Liat was in London, and there was nobody to put a spoke in the wheels.

This is how her plan failed: a few minutes after they got into his Golf, Adir switched on the air-conditioning. It started to work, and the sweat that had collected on their faces began to evaporate. Everything was fine, but just at the exit from Tel Aviv, at the right turn from the Paz bridge, Adir suffered a severe asthma attack. He couldn't speak, he made a whistling noise when he breathed, and his lips turned blue. He stopped at the side of the road and searched for his inhaler which, it turned out, had been forgotten at home.

Tasaro called for an ambulance. At the hospital they said that he had been "this close" to death.

He was in the hospital for a week until he recovered sufficiently to go home. Liat returned from London with an accusing face, and when he came home she stayed for an hour and forty minutes to see that he was alright. She sat down next to him in the living room, and Tasaro sat opposite them, not knowing where to turn. Tasaro thought that Liat was looking at her angrily, but the truth was that she wasn't looking at her at all. Liat had a very slight congenital squint, which had never been corrected.

Ever since that day, Tasaro had stopped trying to set up meetings with her family. She never again wanted to experience moments like those before the ambulance arrived. Now, with the opportunity for exposure to the public as the Lotto Girl knocking at her door, she felt confident enough to bring the subject up again.

It was a quarter past seven. Adir arrived. Outside, a strong, cold wind was blowing, but it was still dry. Tasaro said they could have hung the washing out to save on electricity, but she could hear the dryer working anyway. Then she told him about her day, with deletions and insertions, and also brought up the subject of visiting her family.

"You're starting with your mother again? Enough. I can't take all that melting-pot business. You're you, and I'm me. There's no need for ceremonies."

"I want us to get married," Tasaro said suddenly. "I can't stand the way they look at me anymore."

"I knew this was coming. You need their approval? You need a certificate from the rabbinate? I don't understand!"

"Yes," said Tasaro. "I need their approval and a certificate from the rabbinate."

"You can't wait to be Tasaro Bergson?" yelled Adir. "You can't wait to be Mrs. Bergson?"

"Yes," she said. "I can't wait. I'm making long-term plans for my life."

"I see," said Adir and sat down in the armchair, looking worried.

"What's the matter?" Tasaro asked with forced tenderness.

"Whenever you come back from visiting your family it's always something else. Now you want to get married."

"That's right," said Tasaro. "It's important to them. It's important to me."

"I knew that these differences of mentality would hurt us," he said.

"You're making them hurt us," said Tasaro. "If you love me. . ." she dared to say. "Do you love me?"

"I love you," he said and switched on the television. He flipped around a bit and stopped on the movie channel. A chase was on the screen. He escaped immediately into the chase. Two white Americans were running after two other white Americans and one Afro-American. The pursuers were the bad guys. The good guys, the cops, were being pursued. The overjoyed Tasaro looked at the screen and said confidently, "The black man will die first, you'll see."

"How do you know?" asked Adir in surprise.

"It's always the same in this kind of movie. I've noticed that the black guy dies first."

And indeed a few minutes later the Afro-American policeman got shot and died.

"You were right," said Adir. "I didn't know you paid attention to such things."

"I told you," said Tasaro, pleased with herself. "The black died first. What disgusting racists. You know something," she addressed him directly, as if she had completely lost interest in the movie, "you're a racist too."

"Me?"

"If you weren't a racist, you would marry me. If I was a pretty, cute white girl, with freckles. . . ."

"Okay, okay," said Adir sulkily. "I'm a racist. I'm a racist. Whatever you say. Now leave me alone and let me watch the movie.

She said, "In any case we live together like a married couple. So what's the problem?"

"So what's the problem?" retorted Adir.

"What's the problem with getting married, I mean," said Tasaro. "It will make my family happy. I can't get dirty looks from them both because you're not from our community, and because I'm living with you without being married."

"You want to reduce the reasons for your family's dirty looks?"

"Yes."

"Then stop visiting them. You're too dependent on them. That's your problem. You have to liberate yourself."

"You just don't want to marry me," Tasaro stated sadly.

"I just don't want to marry anyone. I like things the way they are now. I don't know how to be married. I'm afraid."

"What are you afraid of?"

"Of what I don't know. I know things the way they are. I don't want any experiments. Things were quiet up to now. Everything was fine. Why do you want to ruin everything? Hasn't enough already happened for one year? People get married because they want children. I don't want children."

"You don't want children with me?"

"I don't want children *at all*. I don't want to bring children into this world. Understand? It's dangerous. You know what I think," he said in a different tone. "I think that people get married so that the individual won't be a burden on society, but a husband on his wife and vice versa. I don't see myself as such a burden on Israeli society that I have to get married. I get along just fine. And so do you. Look at this offer you've just received from the National Lottery. A fantastic opportunity for you, if you pass the screen test. In any event, you make a living. You should be proud. Why add additional frameworks?"

"What makes you think that people get married in order to be a burden on each other and not on society?"

"Because I think so," Adir shouted, and added in a quieter tone: "And also as a result of trial and error. Take Ventura for example. She's a burden on society. As soon as I see her, I feel a heavy weight on my soul. Just seeing her is enough. And my late sister Liat too was a burden. I had to worry about her all the time – where she was, who she was with, so she wouldn't feel too lonely, that if anyone left her she wouldn't do anything foolish. From that point of view at least I can relax. I don't have to worry about her anymore. I don't like worrying about other people, because they don't know how to look after themselves. Apart from that, my sweet," he went on, "it would be a mixed marriage. You know what it means to be a mixed couple in Israel? Black and white? You know what they used to do here to women who married Arabs? And even Ashkenazis who married Sephardis? And they were all madly in love – Romeos and Juliets. And I'm telling you Tasaro, I'm serious, I don't want children. I don't like children. I don't want children. I haven't got the patience. I need my peace and quiet, not to produce another generation for catastrophe."

"What catastrophe?"

Adir didn't answer her. She said "It's racism."

"Nonsense. Okay, think what you like, I don't care," he said angrily. "I'm a practical racist. You're an impractical new immigrant. Okay? Even though you've been here for ten years. You're a new immigrant. I know the people here, I've had nearly forty years to get to know them. If by any chance, all of a sudden, we decide to have a baby, or you get pregnant by mistake and pretend that it's against your principles to have an abortion, the people here will eat our baby for brunch. Don't you understand? Our children will be exotic. A genetic phenomenon. Nobody will see them as individuals, on a one to one basis."

"You're wrong. I've seen lots of couples. . . ."

"No no no. Not in Tel Aviv you haven't. Maybe you saw them somewhere else. Not here, and I'm not prepared to move to anywhere else in the country. I don't possess a pioneering spirit. I possess the spirit of an asthma sufferer. That's it. And so, my dearest, if we have children, in order for them to turn out more or less normal, we'll have to send them to be educated abroad, and in that case we'll have to go with them. And I don't feel like making any more changes in my life. I don't want to leave. I've finished with changes in my life."

"I don't understand you," she said.

"So let me explain to you," he said. "They'll tear us to pieces. They'll turn us into a 'mixed couple.' They won't call us Tasaro and Adir, but the black woman and the white man. When we walk down the street they'll say: Here come the dominoes. Here come the chessmen. You don't realize where you are. I was born here, I'm telling you. Israeli society will snicker at our expense. Tasaro, be realistic." His voice softened as he said, "Listen to me, Tasaro," but the grim expression did not leave his face. "Contemporary Israeli society is undergoing a massive crisis because of the complicated

175

political situation with the Arabs. It's impossible to know what will happen tomorrow. It's impossible to know what's going to become of the State of Israel. Do you understand?"

"You can never know what's going to happen tomorrow. There are traffic accidents, too. Not only terrorist bombs," she said.

"I don't want to put myself in a situation where people turn their heads to look at me in the street! This is a small country, and I want to remain anonymous. I don't want people to know anything about me, and if I marry you they won't leave us alone. They won't leave us alone," he repeated.

"Who won't leave us alone?"

"Theaters will put on plays about us, journalists will come here every second day to interview us, everyone will want to get his own angle on us. No no no, I don't want to marry you. No. And it's not because I don't love you. I love you very much. I'm nuts about you, Tasaro. Marriage frightens me. Period."

"Coward," said Tasaro, and went to take a shower. Whenever she felt sad at heart, she took a shower.

CHAPTER TWO

For a week, Tasaro and Adir didn't speak to each other. It was Ventura, of all people, who broke the silence between them. She called, and Tasaro, who up to that day had avoided answering the phone in the house, and only taken calls on her private cell phone, which was the only number she gave to the people with whom she was in contact, suddenly picked up the phone. Judging by the tone of Tasaro's voice Ventura understood that she was in a lousy mood. Tasaro always answered the phone with "Good evening," "Good morning," or "Good afternoon." This time she said, "Hello?"

"What's going on?" asked Ventura.

"Nothing."

"Is Adir there?"

"Yes. It's for you," she said and threw the telephone onto the sofa next to him.

"Adir?" said Ventura. "Is everything alright?"

"Yes."

"Listen, I'll be finishing work on Liat's apartment soon. I just wanted to tell you that I found some Independence Day decorations, including quite a big Israeli flag, in the storage space under the ceiling. Do you want me to throw them out too?"

"Throw out the decorations," he said. "And hang the flag out on the porch. What do I care?"

"You want me to hang it out?"

"Yes."

"But it's not Independence Day now."

"I know. Hang it out because of the political situation. People are hanging out flags. Hang it out."

"Are you serious?" asked Ventura. She knew that Adir wasn't the kind of person who hung out flags, not even on

177

Independence Day. "Is everything alright with you, Adir?"

"Everything's fine with me," he said and hung up.

Ventura hung the flag on the balcony railing with clothes pegs, and the ice between Adir and Tasaro was broken.

"You spoke to me," said Adir.

"I said, 'It's for you.' Because the call was for you."

"But you answered the phone. And you're talking to me now too. Have you cooled down?"

"Yes. I've had enough. It makes me miserable when we're like this."

"Yes. . . ." said Adir. "To tell you the truth, I feel the same way. Let's forget about that matter for the time being. Okay?"

"Getting married?"

"Yes. Let me recover from my sister's death first. I have to digest it. What do you think?"

"It's alright. Forgive me if I put pressure on you."

"Applied pressure," Adir corrected her.

"Applied pressure," said Tasaro and she was glad that their relationship had returned to normal.

That same afternoon, Adir and Iris had arranged to meet at a cafe in the neighborhood where they both lived so that he could give her a check for the remainder of the sum he owed her for clearing out his sister's apartment. Ventura brought a large suitcase with her to the meeting, and some of the people in the cafe wondered where she was going – to a warmer country perhaps?

But the suitcase contained Dubnov's collection of antique calendars, separately wrapped in tissue paper. Adir didn't even want to go to Liat's apartment to pick them up, and he asked Iris to bring them to the cafe with her. He also asked her for the key, which he intended to hand over to the cleaning company, and then to the estate agent handling the rental.

Adir told Ventura that his girlfriend wanted to get married, and Iris asked, "To you?"

"Who else?" asked Adir.

"And. . . .?"

"And . . . no."

"And how did she take it? Another latte please. . ." she addressed the waitress passing their table.

"She took it. What alternative has she got?" said Adir. "Now she's going through auditions for the Lotto Girl, you know, the one who spins the wheel and reads out the numbers that come up. If she does well enough, she'll be on the air before you know it."

Iris said, "Great job."

"Are you being sarcastic?"

"A little. What can I say? To cross all those deserts in order to read out winning lottery numbers. . . ."

"You're awful," said Adir. "Liat was right."

"Liat said that I was awful?"

"Once. I have to go," said Adir and called the waitress.

"So do I," said Iris sulkily. She picked up the check and examined it. "I have to get to the bank before it closes. And I'm sorry if I offended you about Tasaro. I wish you well, in spite of everything. I apologize."

"I accept your apology. I wish you well too."

Iris put the check in her wallet and hurried away in the direction of the nearby branch of the Mizrahi Bank. While she was busy clearing out Liat's apartment, she had made up her mind to open an account at another bank and get a credit card there. She didn't want to show her face in her old bank again, because the people there had been quite nasty to her in her days of poverty, even though anyone

179

could see that she was a well-off woman experiencing a financial crisis and not someone poor from birth. She had manners, class, style. In Jerusalem she had employed a maid three times a week. She hadn't climbed out of the gutter. In short, she wanted a new bank, a new account, a new attitude. Today she had made inquiries and found that the restrictions placed on her were about to come to an end, and she was no longer on any credit company's black list.

She passed a book shop and for the first time in months she stopped to look in the shop window. She planned to buy a book or two. It was a long time since she had bought a book, a long time since she had read one. The biography of the Czarina Catherine, the last book she had bought, she had been unable to finish.

She glanced at her watch. The banks were about to close, and she hastened her steps.

Shortly after Ventura emerged with a spring in her step from the branch of the Mizrahi Bank where she had just opened an account, and the door shut behind her and was locked from inside, since she was the last customer, Kati Beit-Halahmi entered the branch of the bank in Lod where she was employed as a cleaner.

Over there, the last of the customers had already left, and also the last of the clerks, except for one – who always stayed behind after everyone else had left – the director of the foreign currency department, who looked so young for his position.

In the days that had passed since her meeting with Angelica Gomeh, Kati had not returned to her with the money, as she had promised; she had disappeared, and Gomeh had filed her away in her mind as another one of those people who came and went without an explanation.

Now Kati began to empty the wastepaper baskets into a big garbage bag. According to the leftovers, she could tell what each of the tellers had eaten for his mid-morning snack. From time to time she peeked at the diligent young man who was making calculations on a calculator.

Kati was very nervous, because at that moment she had decided to activate her plan inspired by Claudia Helena, the heroine of *Because of a Kiss*. The time has come for "if and when," she said to herself.

More than she feared the young clerk, Beit-Halahmi feared her husband. The clerk, at the most, could bring about her dismissal, which in any case she intended to do sooner or later herself. Her husband, on the other hand, could throw a temper tantrum and smash things in the house, because she had walked out of her job cleaning the stairs without consulting him first. It wouldn't be long before the family felt a significant shortage of money.

That morning she had dropped by one of the buildings whose stairwell she had, until recently, cleaned, in order to inquire about her severance pay. To her astonishment, she discovered that all the buildings where she had worked had incorporated themselves under a single association, whose sole purpose was to avoid paying her the money she had coming to her, on the grounds that she had never been registered as an employee of theirs, and she had no way of proving otherwise.

This was a real slap in the face, after she had worked in those buildings for a number of years and knew all the residents personally. She could testify to this herself. What, didn't her word count for anything? Kati was hurt to the quick when they told her that there was no proof of her having worked there all those years.

As she disinfected the mouthpiece of a telephone, according to her instructions ever since the outbreak of the Saudi flu, a tear trickled down her cheek. She knew if she didn't become Claudia Helena for a few minutes, she had no future. Kati was also very ashamed about her failure to contact Angelica and let her know that she was encountering difficulties in getting together the money for the course.

Angelica probably thought that she was just a liar, Kati said to herself, and felt even more humiliated.

"Sir," she addressed the man from the foreign currency department. Kati well remembered the trick that Claudia Helena had played on some villain in her favorite television series, and at this moment of madness and despair she stepped into the shoes of her heroine and cast the innocent bank clerk in the villain's role.

"You can call me Ido."

"My name's Kati."

"I'll be through in a moment," said Ido, without taking his eyes off the computer screen. "You want to clean here – in a minute, as soon as I get off the Internet."

Beit-Halahmi didn't know what the Internet was. She only knew that it was something very important, connected to telephones.

"No, I haven't reached you yet. I'll get to you in about ten minutes. I have to do Stocks and Shares first."

"Ah."

"It's something else entirely."

"What is it?" he raised his eyes from the screen.

"I know everything."

"What?!"

"I know everything. You think I'm blind? I'm a cleaning worker. If I see dirt – I know it's dirt."

"What are you talking about?"

"So. . ." she leaned on the handle of the vacuum cleaner,

and placed her foot on the base. "What am I talking about? You want to play games with me? You think I'm deaf? I've heard a lot of talk."

"What talk?"

"I heard the girls saying that the manager was having you watched."

Ido's face fell, just like the villain's on the soap opera.

"Who said so?" he said.

"Who said so . . . who said so . . . what does it matter who said so? They've been keeping tabs on you for two months already."

"Keeping tabs on me?"

"And how. I know that they deal with these things internally. That's what I've heard. But sometimes they go to the police. If there's a lot of money involved, for example, it can get into the newspapers too. . . ."

She switched on the vacuum cleaner and began vacuuming "Current accounts."

Ido stood up and came towards her. She switched off the vacuum cleaner.

"There are some people here who want to go to 'Gotcha!' or maybe they've already gone. People talk next to me, you know, as if I don't exist, and I hear everything."

"Did you say 'Gotcha!'?" he asked.

"That TV show. . . ."

"I know it. Good God! They want. . . ."

"To catch you red-handed," continued Kati. "To film you and record you and show you cheating on television. They want to screw you, but for justice, not like on *Candid Camera* where they do it for laughs."

Ido asked, "What do they know, tell me?" Beads of sweat formed on his forehead and nose. "What do you know?" he asked again, looking terrified. Kati felt sorry for him.

"What's your problem? Is it the mortgage?" she asked.

"The mortgage. Yes."

"It's eating everybody up. But not everybody steals."

"No, but listen, listen, you have to listen. I'm having a psychological crisis. After my parents died, I went into a severe depression. My wife and I sold the apartment we had in Rishon LeZion, and we bought a house in a small community. Everything was fine and dandy except that now it turns out that we're on the green-line, you understand? My wife and I thought that there was peace and the children would have a garden to play in. Now we live in terror. There's an Arab village next door. Sometimes there are shootings. My wife and I want to go back to Rishon but we can't afford it, because our house today is worth nothing. Why should anyone be crazy enough to come and live there? That's what my wife says and she's right. We've got two children. It's terrifying. We moved their rooms out of the range of fire. Nobody's been killed yet. But they will be, I'm telling you, it's just a question of time. Tell me what you heard, and I'll give you money."

"How much money?" asked Kati.

"Ten thousand shekels. That's all I can get together. I have to put a stop to it. To speak to the manager and tell him to call off the investigation. Don't let them show me on television, for God's sake. Afterwards we won't be able to show our faces in the street, we'll be so ashamed ... just think of the children. I have to stop it. I'll resign. Anything. Just make them call off the cameras."

Kati wanted to know what, exactly, he was doing, but of course she didn't dare ask him. She asked, "When will you give me the money?" She felt dizzy – it all seemed like a dream, but it was actually happening, and she couldn't switch channels.

184

"Within a week," said Ido. "Let me get organized. Tell me, what did you hear? I have to put a stop to it. Talk to the manager, confess, and let them fire me. What do I care. I can hardly breathe anyway."

"Why can't you breathe?"

"From fear. And I'm passing my fear on to the children. Now my children wake up at night and come to our bed. Every little noise and they think we're being shot at. Life has become a nightmare."

"Within the week I'll tell you what I heard," mumbled Kati. "I have to get it organized in my head. Write your cell phone number on a piece of paper. I'll give you a ring."

"Fine," said Ido. "Fine. I have to stop it. That's it. To get a hold of myself and stop. To breathe."

He sat down on a chair, put his head in his hands, and breathed heavily as he wrote down his cell phone number.

Kati sat down on an unoccupied chair and phoned Angelica Gomeh. She remembered her phone number by heart. She told her that she would come at the beginning of the next week with the money, and that she wanted to have lessons every other day. Angelica agreed and said that she would buy her a makeup case as soon as she received the money, and Kati couldn't believe that it was happening to her, that she would have a makeup case, that she was going to leave cleaning work for the open market.

Afterwards, riding on the same mysterious impulse instilled in her by Claudia Helena, she wrote a note to say that she was giving notice, and asked Ido to pass it on the person in charge of human resources.

When she had concluded her business she went outside. The cold air seemed to reproach her, but she took no notice. The burden of twenty years dropped off her back. She had broken out – apparently. She had succeeded – apparently.

She even walked taller. For a moment only she thought of returning to Ido and telling him that it wasn't true, she had make it all up, he needn't worry. She remembered how he had broken out into a sweat and she had felt sorry for him, buying a house on the green-line, driving his kids crazy. But her pity didn't last for more than a second or two. She eradicated it from her heart, thinking that an opportunity like this came once in a million years. Besides, life had been cruel to her too.

CHAPTER THREE

WHEN SHE CAME HOME, her cheeks red with the cold and the excitement, still high from the confrontation with Ido, Kati saw her husband preparing a vegetable omelet for the family, according to the recipe given to him by his mother Fanya Beit-Halahmi, the grandmother of her children who was growing old and senile on the farm, where she had even forgotten the fact that she had rejected her son, her daughter-in-law and her grandchildren.

Boaz asked Kati if she had brought bread.

"I forgot," she said. "It was too cold outside. I couldn't go to Sergei's. We owe him too much money."

"You could have bought bread somewhere else," said Boaz.

"I forgot."

"Well," said Boaz, "let's hope the kids don't leave the table hungry."

"Add pasta."

"To a vegetable omelet? Are you crazy?"

"Why not? Cook it first, and add it to the pan."

"What nonsense," said Boaz.

"If you're hungry you eat anything." Kati took off her coat and switched on the television. There had been a terrorist attack in Afula. Boaz found a quarter of a loaf of bread left over from two days before, cut it into slices and put them in the oven for a few minutes. His eyes too were caught by the images on the television screen. A terrorist had shot at people sitting in their car when they stopped for a red light. The security forces had succeeded in killing him only after a two hundred meter chase. They showed the terrorist's body. It always seemed to Boaz that it was the same terrorist.

187

"I want to give up all my jobs," said Kati.

"Don't you dare," said Boaz and removed the crusty slices from the oven. "This is a shitty time. People take any job they can get."

"Except for you."

"You're right," he said suddenly, to her surprise. "I thought about it. I'm getting ready to go to the employment office, take a course, and get whatever job's available."

"Sure."

"No, no," said Boaz firmly. "Don't mock me, Kati, don't mock me. This time I'm serious. I want to get my act together and take control. I've been thinking about it a lot lately."

The children came in and switched to the telenovela channel. They asked their father for permission to eat supper in front of the television, and promised not to get the sofas dirty. Boaz told them to switch back to the news immediately, and to eat wherever they felt like it. He took his supper, and with a slice of bread in one hand and a plate with some of the vegetable omelet in the other, sat down in front of the television. Kati dished out food for the children. She wasn't hungry. Boaz said ceremoniously, "Soon it will be Purim. Next Friday is the first of Adar. This year," he turned to the children, "I want you to take first prize in the costume competition at school."

"Why this year of all years?" asked Kati.

"That's what I want. I've already got everything planned. Children, you're going to dress up as the four musketeers."

Adi and Topaz looked sulky.

Topaz said, "I don't want to dress up as a boy."

"I'll dress you two up as musketeeresses," said Kati.

"Excellent idea," said Boaz. "Your mother will sew your costumes, the hats we'll buy. Right, Kati? That way it will both look good and also be cheap. Right, Kati?"

"Right," she said quietly.

"These eggs are really disgusting, what do you say, Moshe?" he turned to his son.

"They're normal," said Moshe.

"I say these eggs are disgusting. Disgusting eggs."

"So what now," asked Kati indifferently, "throw them all out?"

"Kids, you can do what you like. As far as I'm concerned, I won't eat eggs like this."

"Give me your omelet, Daddy," said Topaz.

"Here, sweetheart, you can have it with pleasure," said Boaz.

"Give me half," Adi asked her sister.

"No," said Topaz.

"Just remember. . . ."

"I don't understand how people aren't ashamed to sell them," exclaimed Boaz and rose to his feet. "The eggs on our farm. . . ."

"Oho," said Kati, "now come the fairytales. . . . Eat up, children, those eggs are very good. The whole country eats them."

"You call that very good? I'm not making any more dishes that call for eggs," stated Boaz. "I'm not prepared to poison the children. I'm not prepared to poison anybody."

"Don't. I'll make them fried eggs. Sunny side up. Adi, bring us your paints every day and we'll paint the yoke orange to satisfy your father."

She giggled. Moshe and Adi joined in the laughter. Boaz went into the bedroom and slammed the door, which was already broken anyway, from many previous slammings. He pushed a rack full of clothes against the door and lay down in the dark across the width of the double mattress.

Boaz made supreme but unavailing efforts to wipe out his memories and the bitter fact that he had not inherited the poultry farm and the land that had been promised to him throughout his childhood and youth. If his parents had kept their promise, his life would have continued rising on a moderately upward gradient, instead of sliding downhill in a relentless decline.

There was a time when Boaz couldn't bear to look at an egg, and the family had been on an eggless diet. And if Kati bought eggs, he would throw them down the drain. Egg after egg.

It was a full-scale production.

Later on, when he calmed down a little, and allowed eggs into the house, he always had something to say about every single egg. Something derogatory. He would also force the children, he had already given up on his wife, to listen to long lectures on the quality of the eggs. He wanted to pass on his heritage, in spite of everything, and he explained, just as his beloved grandfather, his father's father, Noah Beit-Halahmi, had explained to him, an egg with droppings on its shell, or with a cracked shell – was not fit to eat. And his grandfather, who was sure that Boaz was going to be a poultry farmer, had also taught him to recognize poultry diseases, and to take pity on the broody hens, who donated calcium from their own bones to the eggshells, and sometimes collapsed and died.

There was a period around the time of his Bar Mitzvah, when Boaz had wanted to be, apart from the owner of the poultry and the land, a veterinary surgeon specializing in birds. He had told his grandfather this while he was teaching him the chapter from Prophets he would have to recite in synagogue. Boaz would have given a million dollars for his marvelous grandfather to be alive, he, in his greatness, would never have allowed his family to deny him for such specious reasons, to disinherit his beloved grandson, he would have moved heaven and earth to see justice done and logic triumph in the Beit-Halahmi family. He had invested so much in him, and taught him everything, what hadn't he taught him: marketing the eggs according to public health regulations, the difference between retail and wholesale packaging, storage methods. The differences between basic flocks, breeding flocks and distribution flocks. Together, they would exterminate pests and disinfect the poultry houses. Together, they would remove the diseased birds, identify their diseases, and get rid of the carcasses. Boaz would bury them in mass graves.

Noah Beit-Halahmi was a combination of a religious Jew and a stubborn pioneer, who wore khaki clothes and a yarmulke under his cloth hat. He never lived to see his grandson complete his veterinary studies in Italy, or anywhere else in the world. Nor did he live to see him begin such studies either. The last spring rain was falling – Boaz remembered it like yesterday, he was already a soldier home on leave. His grandfather went to bed and he didn't get up in the morning. The evening before, sitting with Boaz in their garden, which Boaz's mother cultivated with an artist's hand, he had remarked to the soldier doing his basic training in boot camp, "The first rain in the month of Kislev and the last rain in the month of Nisan means rain between the two."

On Tuesday, the 27th of Shevat, in the morning, Kati phoned Ido at the bank to find out how matters were proceeding. They were proceeding excellently, said Ido, he already had nine thousand out of the ten. Kati said that she would take the nine thousand today and the rest at the end of the week. They agreed to meet at the entrance to Ganei-Aviv at ten o'clock. Ido would bring her the money in an envelope. For a moment Kati was afraid that he was laying a trap for her, in his turn, and she even asked him if he was setting her up. Ido said, "Have you become paranoid too?" He swore on his children's lives that he wasn't playing a trick on her, and the conversation came to an end.

At ten o'clock, Kati went downstairs and saw Boaz filling in the Lotto slip at the neighborhood store. There was a long line before and behind him, because the lottery prize was very large that week, a prize of thirteen million shekels. Kati calculated that by the time his turn came, she would already be back at home with the money, after talking to Angelica Gomeh on the phone. She wanted so badly to learn a profession.

At ten o'clock the bank clerk arrived. He handed her the envelope from the window of his car. She checked to see if the money was inside and asked him if she should count it. He said that there was nine thousand exactly, and she put the envelope in her bag. At home she quickly counted the money, and called Angelica Gomeh to set up her first lesson for the next day, Wednesday morning.

That whole day, Kati was on cloud nine, and in the evening, when the Lotto drawing was being shown on television, she remained in the kitchen, washing dishes, and she didn't even turn around to listen to the winning numbers, as she always did, whenever Boaz filled in a lottery ticket.

She knew that he wouldn't win. He never won. Her husband had no luck.

Boaz sat in front of the television, holding his lottery ticket, and listened for the results in great suspense. At the beginning he was surprised and muttered, "Who's she?" at the sight of the new presenter, and then he called, "Look,

Kati, they've brought in an Ethiopian girl. Nice." But after a moment he got used to her too, and wrote down the winning numbers and compared them with his ticket. He had two numbers – all the rest another time. The Ethiopian too, who had such white teeth and shining eyes, smiled and said, "If you didn't win this time, maybe next time. . . ."

Boaz tore up his ticket, and Kati, who was in an excellent mood, said, "Never mind, Boaz, it will be alright, don't worry."

"You know what I planned to do with the money, Kati? You know what I'm going to do with the money if and when I win?"

"What, bless you, what?"

Suddenly she had patience for him, and he opened up and said, "I'll take you all away from here, we'll leave everything and go up to the Galilee. And I'll start a farm there, just for us. We'll breed flocks of laying hens. We'll live a good life, and our children, Kati, will not only take first place in the Purim costume competition of the Upper Galilee local council, but when the time comes they'll also inherit the farm from us. You won't have to work at all. You'll grow fruit and vegetables on our land. All organic. If you want to. You won't have to. I'll have a room with a pool table. I'll have new friends from the Galilee. Farmers like me. They'll come and play with me once or twice a week. You want to see a sketch of the farm?" he asked enthusiastically.

"A sketch?"

"Yes. I drew it." He stood up and opened a drawer in their shaky sideboard. He spread a large sheet of paper in front of his wife and said:

"You see, here are the hen houses, here's the house, here's the garden ... and maybe we'll have a horse, and a few dogs. . . . And as long as I live, you know what, Kati, as long as I live I'll never disinherit any of my children, not even if Adi marries an Arab. . . ."

"God forbid," said Kati.

"That's only an example, so you'll understand. Even if, she'll get what she's entitled to. I won't do to them what was done to me. Understand? For me, children are sacred."

"Yes," said Kati, and her thoughts strayed to her makeup course and to the fact that she would have to find a safe place to hide the makeup case that Gomeh was going to give her.

UNTIL FRIDAY MORNING, the 30th of Shevat, Adir Bergson succeeded in maintaining the unity and integrity of his personality, relative to the traumatic events that had assailed his life. The unveiling of Liat's tombstone had already passed. He and Tasaro were the only ones there. The dwindling in the number of mourners from the funeral to the thirtieth day memorial service is a well known fact. Tasaro chose the basalt stone – and he chose the Spartan inscription in black letters: *Here lies Liat Dubnov, From ... To ..., R. I. P.*

It was only on that Friday that the meaning of his sister's death sank in; it meant that he, Adir, had been left in the chaos of life in Israel in particular, and the world in general, alone, without a single close relative. Although his father, as far as he knew, was still living in New York, he had never played any role in his life. His mother had taught him as a child to regard him as a complete stranger.

As a result of this realization, Adir was filled with fear that his illness would overcome him, and he too would be wiped out and turn into a tombstone. Over the course of the years he had learned to recognize the signs of an impending asthma attack, and he usually managed to nip it in the bud. His experience had taught him that his illness was averse to states of extreme emotion, such as the one he felt this morning. He felt loneliness of a type more searing that anything he had ever known before.

Bergson tried to reconstruct in his head everything he had been through since the day she died. Although he had performed all the rites and rituals of mourning in a reasonably proper way, he nevertheless felt that he had been remiss, because he didn't have nightmares that woke him up in the middle of the night, he didn't call out her name at two o'clock in the morning, he didn't think of her very much, but of himself and his recovery from her loss. He felt wrong carrying on side by side with his beautiful girlfriend, who was making such good progress in climbing the ladder of Israeli success, but what else could he do? She was already gone, he was the one who was still around, he was the one who was alive. He was very sorry. He had no explanation for the fact that he, who had always excelled at coming within a hair's breadth of death, was still alive, as opposed to his healthy mother and sister.

He thought about Tasaro. He was proud of her for passing the screen test with flying colors and becoming the weekly national lottery drawing presenter on television. She passed the screen test with flying colors, he repeated to himself, trying to relive the satisfaction he had felt when he heard her telling him that they had snatched her up. How flattered he had felt when he heard how the judges had dismissed all the candidates following her, and sat down immediately with his girlfriend's agent to work out the details of the contract and sign her up.

Suddenly Adir understood why Tasaro wanted to marry him. She wanted to fight against her feelings of uncertainty, and why shouldn't she? She too was isolated from the rest of her family, sitting in Netanya and living a completely different life. She too was actually an orphan, he decided.

Women, he went on thinking, wanted to tick off the things that society expected of them, and the more conventions they ticked off, the more internal freedom they could achieve for themselves, without nagging and interference from outside. Tasaro wanted to marry him because her

196

family was nagging her and putting pressure on her, and she wanted to be left alone to do her work in peace. He understood her very well, but, at the same time, he was unable to fulfill her wish.

"Married life – something else to cope with," he thought and sighed, "what do I need that for now?"

He called, "Tasaro!" but there was no reply. He got up to look for her. She wasn't there. Adir was surprised. She hadn't left a note. The dog had already been out, which meant that Tasaro had taken her out, brought her back, and gone out again, without him hearing anything.

What was the meaning of this silence? As a rule, her movements were noisier. He could always hear her making coffee, and when she made popcorn for the two of them, it sounded as if there were a shooting going on in the street.

Adir didn't like what was happening to him. It was frightening to be shot out of the rest of the world like a rocket, into the isolation people called "splendid" only in order to make the dismay of the individual left on his own easier to bear.

"Carbon dioxide – that's what I need now," he thought and deepened the pauses between inhaling and exhaling and vice versa.

He had always tried to avoid developing a stifling dependency on Tasaro, but it now appeared that it was no longer up to him. He was becoming dependent on her, and he had better face up to it. For the first time, he was flooded by a pleasant feeling of resignation to the new situation, which was immediately followed by a wave of profound desire to cut himself off from his fellow man. Adir sensed the strength of these contradictory emotions and he felt pressured. He hated it when parts of his personality gained control over the rest and for a few seconds he became "like this" or "like that." He demanded of himself to remain harmonious, and to keep in balance. Only in this way could he feel all the components of his personality moving inside him without threatening each other. Adir was always careful to maintain this balance, and everything he did in his life was aimed at preserving his peace of mind. His atmospheric studies, his work at the Weizmann Institute, and finally his early retirement at the age of thirty-three in favor of home and its comforts, had created an inner equilibrium, which he liked to cuddle up with, but now he couldn't find it. Had it collapsed?

He became confused. His soul yearned to unite with his pleasant self, and not with this weakling, whose appearance repelled him, and whom he usually succeeded in banishing to the melancholy margins of his existence. The appearance of the weakling reminded him of himself in the vile days when all kinds of complexes had taken over his personality, especially one:

At the beginning of his twenties, Bergson suffered from a complex that almost killed him before he got rid of it. He felt guilty and oppressed because he was well off from an economic point of view, whereas others whom he encountered along the way were not. This was the period when the asthma, which had lain dormant throughout his childhood and youth, attacked him every second day. At that time he behaved like Robin Hood. He stole from himself and gave to the poor. In this way, he silenced his conscience, albeit for a limited time, until the next check. He became so involved in his need to compensate his surroundings, and kept on widening their definition, until they took on cosmic dimensions, that he began, like a lunatic, giving donations to all kinds of human rights and aid organizations in far-flung corners of the world.

He managed to get hold of the telephone numbers of all these different organizations, however elusive, and sent them money, and they made him a member of this and that organization and he had membership cards from charitable societies all over the world, and he was very proud of them and showed them to people without even being asked.

During these accursed years, Adir turned his friends into his life project. He felt an obligation to help everyone he had ever known since he was a child who was finding life a heavy burden to bear. He fixed people up with jobs and loans, signed guarantees and held heart-to-heart conversations, after which he rushed for his inhaler. The number of his friends grew apace. One of them, who he had known since grade school, had set up a chain of pizzerias that failed. Adir pumped money into his business. Another, who was a good friend of his in high school, had lost everything due to a badly managed divorce. Adir made the first payment on an apartment in Holon for him. A third, somebody or other's cousin, needed a kidney transplant. Adir put his hand in his pocket and sped up the process. A fourth, he couldn't remember where he knew him from, needed three hundred thousand shekels to pay loan sharks who were pursuing him, threatening his life and the lives of his children. Adir saved him.

Liat said to him then, "You're fucked in the head. What do you think, that you're some sort of saint? These people don't come to you, they come to your money." He didn't care, on the contrary. All that mattered was that they came, and he helped them. Bergson asked his sister not to say anything to their mother, who was against philanthropy, volunteering, and helping the weak, on principle. Not because she was mean, but because she herself was a self-made woman, and she believed that if she had succeeded in making money and bringing up two children on her own, everybody else could too. Kosta didn't believe in luck, but in hard work. Apart from that, she had been so emotionally devastated by the abandonment of Shimon Bergson, Adir's father, and Reuven Dubnov, Liat's father, that as far as the troubles of others were concerned, her heart, in her own words, had turned to stone.

"You think that you're God. But you're just a compulsive altruist," Liat yelled at him on his twenty-fourth birthday, after everyone had left. "Instead of rebelling against our mother at age sixteen, you danced attendance on her all day long, and look what you're doing with her money now! It's her money! Aren't you ashamed?"

But Adir wasn't ashamed. A whole year passed, during which vast sums of money flew out of Adir's pockets, until his bank accounts dwindled to nothing. His bank manager called him in and read him the riot act, and even though Bergson knew that as long as his mother was around he would never be thrown into the street, he experienced enlightenment, but in reverse – in other words, his world darkened, and he was thrown into a panic when he contemplated what he had been doing to himself over the past few years.

The bank manager also said to him, "What makes you so sure that when you're in trouble, somebody will come to your aid?" And even though he had already heard this argument dozens of times before, without being persuaded to stop throwing his money away, when it came out of the mouth of an authority like the bank manager, who Adir had known ever since he was a little boy going to the bank with his mother, he pulled himself together and disappeared from the scene as completely as someone in the witness protection program.

➤   ➤   ➤

He changed his telephone numbers, and also the front door lock to his apartment, since he had given the keys to more than a few people so they could use the apartment whenever he went abroad. In the end, he also transferred his accounts to another bank, outside Tel Aviv, locked up the house and went to London to recuperate and also for a "cooling-off period," as his accountant had advised. He stayed there for three months. Liat came to visit him almost every month, and they went on wonderful trips together.

After London he went to distant South Africa. He wanted so badly to cut himself off from his past, more and more, and indeed Liat didn't even offer to come and visit him there.

He arrived in South Africa a week before Mandela's release from prison, and entered into the celebrations of the blacks. He stayed in an excellent location in Johannesburg, but he liked wandering around in the black townships and said that he was a journalist.

Adir became a great admirer of Nelson Mandela and he still had a big framed poster of him from the days when he was running for President hanging in his living room. He was eager to know all he could about Mandela's life, and he read about him, studied his speeches and his ideas about racism, and acquainted himself with the details of his daily routine in prison, which he continued to follow, more or less, after his release as well.

Bergson would never forget what Mandela replied to a British journalist, also a black man, when the latter asked him how he felt about his imprisonment, right after he came out after spending nearly thirty years in jail. Bergson sat in his house and watched Mandela on television answering without a trace of bitterness, "You have to look ahead, and that is what I do." Mandela's words made a profound impression on Bergson.

For three years, Adir remained in South Africa, until shortly after Mandela received the Nobel Prize. These were the happiest years of his life. He well remembered the healthy detachment he felt then from Israeli reality, and now, in this bitter winter, he missed that detachment and longed for it.

For the first time since returning to Israel, which he had not left since, Adir felt like packing everything up and getting out. This time he wanted to merge with Canadian peace and quiet. He didn't want any more violence or upheavals. Life in Israel seemed unbearable to him. He couldn't stand to see all this death around him anymore. He saw Israel as a big graveyard with enclaves of settlements in which people were still living, but they too would probably be dead soon. Every day, more people were killed. Every day, there were funerals. Suicide bombings. Shootings, rockets, explosive belts – and where was the solution?

He asked himself if the country was going to hell, and made up his mind that even if Tasaro dragged him to the altar, a lot more time would have to pass before they had a child to let loose in this mess.

At eleven o'clock in the morning his girlfriend called and said that she was at a rehearsal at the National Lottery building, she hadn't wanted to wake him when she left. He wanted to take her with him to Canada. Why couldn't she be a model there? The body was cosmopolitan, and besides, Tasaro had already experienced a lot in her life. Anyone who had crossed deserts and survived the Tel Aviv central bus station deserved a prize, and he was going to see that she got it by taking her away from here.

As soon as Tasaro came back from her rehearsal, he would give her the good news: they were going to Canada.

He made his plans, and at the same time he watched a commentator on Arab affairs explaining the implications of

202

the latest escalation. His commentary was interrupted by a news flash: a stunned newscaster reported a terrorist attack at Mount Hermon. The initial estimate – ten dead. Here are the first pictures from our reporters in the North, he said, and the television showed pictures of bodies in ski clothes lying on the reddening snow.

This was too much for Adir. He switched off the television, as if by doing so he was banishing this event from his house, and got up to make himself a cup of hot chocolate, as only he knew how to prepare. But before he reached the gleaming kitchen, which Tasaro always kept spotlessly clean, he was overcome by a great weakness. He tried to get air into his lungs, to reach the emergency button he had had installed in the house, but before he could get there he collapsed on the parquet floor, hit his head, and lost consciousness. The only word he heard himself soundlessly cry was, "Liat!"

At the end of her rehearsal in the National Lottery building, Tasaro called Adir on her cell phone. She had heard about the suicide bombing at Mount Hermon, and she wanted to know if Adir had also heard the news. When she couldn't get him on his cell phone, and he didn't answer the telephone at home either, she hailed a cab. The driver tried to get her to talk, like the cab drivers always did, to tell him about the long march, and how she found life in Israel. Is this what she had dreamed of – blood on Mount Hermon?

She usually answered, but now, what could she say? The driver turned up the volume of the radio and they listened to the reports from the North.

"Stop here, please," she said, and ran upstairs, where she called an ambulance and knelt on the floor and stroked his head, until the paramedics came and saved her darling Adir.

All weekend and another day and a half Adir stayed in the hospital for observation and tests. Tasaro was at his side whenever she had a spare moment. Ventura dropped in for a ten-minute visit after meeting Tasaro in the street on Sunday morning and learning from her that Adir was in the hospital.

On her way to the hospital Iris stopped at a flower shop on Ibn Gvirol Street and bought him a fifty-shekel bouquet, thinking as she did so how temporary her poverty had been. Yesterday, at long last, she had ordered a computer for the children on the shopping channel, to be paid for in thirty installments. The computer was supposed to arrive within ten working days. She had room to breathe, but she knew that it wouldn't last – she had to find a steady job.

The florist shop where she bought the bouquet needed a sales assistant. Iris made a mental note to return there the next day. She owed Danziger three thousand shekels too, although perhaps she would marry him and that would settle things. Ventura was sick to death of being frightened, she wanted to go to bed without being afraid of bad dreams, and with someone by her side.

More than once, during her dental treatments, lying with her eyes closed under Danziger, his face above her covered by a green mask, Iris thought that if she opened her eyes and the sight that greeted them wasn't too ghastly, she might consider marrying the dentist and saving herself from the ambushes of poverty and the fear of the future.

But when, on the 2nd of Adar, she saw Adir lying in the hospital, so thin and miserable, she knew that there was no substitute in her heart for this man. Since she didn't have too much to say, she asked him every few minutes, "How do you like the flowers? Isn't the color combination fantastic?" and Adir said, "Yes it is."

, , ,

Early in the morning Tasaro woke up in a panic. She had dreamt that the people she was working with on the lottery drawing rang her up from the hospital and told her that Adir had died, and she hadn't even managed to tell him that she was pregnant, and she gave birth to a baby called Tadesa, and straight after the birth she had to give him up for adoption, because she wasn't married. Tasaro immediately took steps to distinguish reality from imagination, she called the hospital ward, and there they told her that Adir was sleeping the sleep of a guiltless mind.

After hanging up, she took a home pregnancy test, the kind that gives results even before the due menstruation date. It came out positive. She couldn't believe it, even though it was perfectly logical. The screen test and TV appearances had distracted her from the pill, and she had forgotten to take it on a number of occasions. Tasaro wondered when to tell her beloved that she was pregnant, should she tell him as soon as he returned from the hospital and settled down at home, or perhaps it would be better to tell him while he was still in the hospital, so that in case he had another attack there would be professional help at hand.

She told him when he was sitting on his bed almost dressed and ready to leave, fifteen minutes before he was discharged from the hospital.

Adir actually reacted quite calmly to the news that his girlfriend was pregnant. He didn't understand, however, why she had chosen to tell him in the hospital, and when she explained he burst out laughing and then grew serious and asked, "But how did it happen? Aren't you on the pill?" and she confessed, "There were a couple of times when it slipped my mind. Because of the catalog and the screen test and the pressure. I'm sorry. Are you angry with me?" And he said, "No, just a little stunned."

He fell silent, and Tasaro said, "I can have an abortion. I'm single, it wouldn't be a problem. I'm thinking about it. Being pregnant could screw up my new job with the Lotto too. I've only just gotten into it, and my agent says. . . ."

"*No*, why should you have an abortion? Let your agent have an abortion," said Adir, planning a little ahead, which he didn't usually dare to do: an heir for the real-estate, an heir for the laundromat, or an heiress. Why not marry Tasaro? Why not? Let the pundits pretend to understand what was going on here, he had never pretended to understand it, so why should he deny himself fatherhood? Let him bring someone else into the world to try to understand the riddle of existence.

In any case, after this last attack he had realized that nothing was in his hands, and as for Canada – why on earth should he go to Canada?

He looked for his other sock.

"There it is." Tasaro pointed to the grey sock that had rolled under the bed and bent down to pick it up.

"Tell me," she said, sitting up and looking at the terminal patient in the bed next to Adir, "do you think it will be a problem for me to be pregnant and do the Lotto drawing? I'm worried . . . after they took me so quickly and everything. . . ."

"Not at all! I'd like to see them try to touch your job. We'll fight for your rights. We'll say that pregnancy could even be sexy on the screen."

Tasaro smiled. She planned how she would tell her agent how being pregnant could look sexy on the screen. Suddenly her face fell. And what if the agent said, "Out of the question," and looked for someone to replace her? Would her career be ruined? When she reached somewhere quiet, Tasaro decided, trying to find an anchor for her thoughts, she would call up her agent and tell her that pregnancy was sexy. But not today. When it began to show.

At the same time Adir was imagining himself holding a little baby in his arms. He thought that if it was a boy, he would call him Nelson Absalom Bergson, and if it was a girl he would leave it to his wife to decide, maybe she would want an Ethiopian name.

Iris Ventura started work at the flower shop on Ibn Gvirol Street during the week of the Purim holiday. The owner, Mira Brodski, gave her a little test to perform before she hired her: to compose a romantic floral arrangement of tulips, crocuses and foliage – and Iris passed the test with flying colors, she was a graphic artist after all.

Brodski taught Ventura that in her shop they didn't go straight up to customers the moment they walked in with questions like: "How can I help you?" or: "What can I do for you today?" because in her experience this put them off, since most people didn't like it when sales people tried to push them into things, or to exercise hegemony over their independence.

"Most people like to look around first. To absorb the atmosphere of the shop. To take in what we have to offer them. All you have to do is say quietly, "Shalom," and go on with what you were doing."

As far as the cash register was concerned, Brodski said that at this stage she would take care of that side of things herself, since she had to sit down, and indeed, she stressed, if not for the fact that her knees were killing her, she would not have needed an assistant at all, but would have continued doing everything herself, as she had up to now. But what could she do – when she was only twelve years old the doctors had told her that if she didn't do something about her knees they would go to hell when she was fifty. She didn't do anything, and they really had gone to hell. Brodski told Ventura about an operation she could have had that had a fifty percent chance of success.

Iris didn't like hearing about operations and illnesses, because it reminded her of death, and even though the weather was grim, and death had become a commonplace daily affair, and Israel was one of the most depressing places in the world today – "When the month of Adar comes in, rejoicing abounds," she said.

"Don't make me laugh," sighed Mira Brodski. "You can't imagine how much pain I'm in. It's terrible. And no pills help. . . ."

Four thousand shekels net is the sum that Ventura earned at the flower shop. She worked full-time, from nine to one and from four to seven. Her salary did not make her new bank account jump sky high, but banks like to see a steady income, and she had two: one from Othniel's alimony, and the second from herself. These, plus the child allowance from the National Insurance, would enable Iris to drag herself and her children through their childhood, she thought.

"What are your children dressing up as for Purim this year?" the owner of the flower shop inquired the day before the holiday.

"My children?"

"How many do you have?"

"Three. Osher, Oz and Herut."

"Bless them."

"Thank you."

"So what are they dressing up as?"

"I'm dressing the little girl up as a clown. The boys aren't interested in Purim this year. You understand, their new computer came yesterday, I was sure it wouldn't arrive till after Purim, and suddenly it came and they're stuck to it like glue."

"Do me a favor, Iris, bring the narcissi in a bit. Yes . . . that's right. . . ."

"Okay?" called Iris from outside, bending over the pail full of narcissi.

"Yes, once somebody walked past here and pinched a bunch of narcissi. Dressed like a gypsy and stealing narcissi. I was really revolted."

"Last year my kids dressed up, don't ask, it was really something. The oldest dressed up as a knight, with all the armor. The middle one as a pilot. And the baby as a rabbit. You can't imagine how cute they looked. I really love the classic costumes. Not like today, all the same things from TV shows. Just let's hope there aren't any bombs, that they don't ruin Purim...."

She fell silent, because she saw that Brodski was looking for a phone number in her address book and she wasn't listening to a thing she said. Ventura understood the rules of the game. When Brodski felt like talking, they talked, and when she felt like it and Brodski not that much, she, Ventura, could internalize what she wanted to say. She had no audience.

At the home of the Beit-Halahmis in Lod, Purim was celebrated this year as it had never been celebrated before. For almost two weeks, Kati had been studying to be a professional makeup artist at Angelica Gomeh's, and she enjoyed it so much that she turned up in the streets of the prophets almost every day. At her second lesson she received the makeup case, and when she came home she hid it under her coat and hurried to the bedroom to bury it inside the closet among the surplus items of clothing they had received during their days of media attention, which she was keeping for the future.

During the days before the holiday, Kati successfully navigated her way between truth and falsehood, and in the evening, when she came home tired from Nahum Street in Tel Aviv, instead of supposedly from her back-breaking cleaning work, she would sit up until late at night, sewing the children's Purim costumes according to Boaz's sketches. Boaz liked knowing that she was sewing next to him in the living room while he watched television, and sometimes he even abandoned the small screen to look at her lovingly, and feel a deep satisfaction, as if he had managed to produce some little moments of happiness for himself and his family, in spite of their situation. For his wife, however, this domesticity was repellent. She wanted Purim to be over, so that she could get a decent night's sleep again and arrive at her lessons refreshed. Altogether she wanted the house to be empty, or for everyone to be asleep, so that she could practice on her own face with Gomeh's makeup in front of the old bathroom mirror.

Once when Boaz was out and the children were sleeping she was making herself up using the techniques she had learned from her teacher. Suddenly she heard her husband climbing the stairs, and at the very last minute she managed to hide the case and run to the bathroom to wash her face.

Kati too wanted to buy her children a computer, and she planned to do so with her severance pay from the condo association, if and when she received it, because as things stood now it was her word against theirs. What was left of the money she had obtained from Ido she hid deep in an empty box of condoms, for a first payment on the computer. As she sat and sewed the costumes, a feeling of pleasure crept into Kati's boredom and annoyance at the thought of how soon her children would be able to say that their mother was a professional makeup artist in the movie industry, and they would no longer be so short of money, even though Angelica had warned her that times were hard, there wasn't any work, she would need a lot of patience and luck, but if worst came to worst she could always go to the employment office with her diploma and get something through them.

Kati preferred to think that her diploma would enable her to find work in her new profession. She dreamt of the day when she would be able to show her diploma to her husband, and go to work in the studios she had come to know at the beginning of winter. One day she would bring home money that was first quoted in dollars, and her children would be able to be proud of her and say, "My mother makes up movie stars. . . . My mother works in a beauty salon for brides. . . . My mother. . . ."

This year, Kati planned to prepare rich Purim treats for Adi and Topaz and Moshe and Aaron to hand out, not like in previous years, when the children on the receiving end of the Beit-Halahmi children's treats felt they were left with the short end of the stick. This year she would buy lots of goodies, she would even take a little money from the first payment for the computer hidden in the closet, and the sun would shine on the face of anyone lucky enough to get a treat from one of her children.

The day before the holiday Kati took fifty shekels from the money left over from Ido, and at the new central bus station, on her way home from her studies, she bought the traditional Purim hamantaschen cookies, lots of other sweets, and cellophane paper in two different colors, so that one would shine through the other.

Ventura, by the way, forgot all about it, and on the morning of Purim itself she ran to the supermarket and bought three ready packaged treats for an extortionate price.

⸙ ⸙ ⸙

On the morning of the holiday, Kati took her makeup case out of its hiding place, and told her husband and children that she had borrowed it from a woman who worked in a bridal beauty salon, who lived in one of the buildings where she cleaned the stairs.

"Her name's Olga," said Kati. "Her children don't dress up anymore. They're grown up."

Using the brushes, sponges and powders in the makeup case, whose contents fascinated the whole family, Kati transformed her four children with the hand of an artist into two musketeers and two musketeeresses, all gorgeous.

First she made up the boys, and then the girls. The whole family watched admiringly as the mother made up her children's faces with all the tools and materials of her trade.

Boaz looked at the delicate, professional movements of her hands. After years of wringing out floor cloths he was sure that her hands would be rough and coarse, and he never dared to look at them. Now he couldn't take his eyes off her long fingers, and he thought that although years had passed and she was no longer twenty years old, she still had beautiful hands.

Kati refused to let any of them look in the mirror until she had finished making them all up. As soon as she was through with one of them, he tried to peek at his reflection in the mirror in the hall, but both Boaz and Kati shouted, "No!"

Finally Boaz got up and took the mirror off the wall and turned it round.

These were very happy moments in the Beit-Halahmi family, moments such as they had never known before. When Kati had completed her work, the parents allowed the children to see the results and their joy knew no bounds. The boys fingered the moustaches she had painted on their upper lips, and the girls asked their mother if their lipstick would come off.

"Don't eat until the competition," she advised them, and Boaz stood up and kissed his wife on the cheek. He was aiming at her mouth, but she moved at the last minute.

"Great work, Kati," he said. "You've got golden hands. Golden."

He kissed the back of her hand too. She pulled her hand away and said, "Thanks, honey."

The children ran outside. Boaz peeked out of the window and saw them walking down the street. He was very happy.

"Is it raining?" Kati asked anxiously.

"No," said Boaz.

"Thank goodness, their makeup won't get smudged."

"You did a wonderful job."

"Thank you."

"The kids will come in first this year, you'll see."

He called the school to find out when the contest was taking place.

"What did they say?" asked Kati when he put the phone down.

"When it clears up. Doesn't it look clear enough to you? Look what donkeys they are. Don't they know it's winter outside?"

"They can have it in the school hall."

He called the school again and asked they why they didn't hold the contest in the hall.

They told him that the contest would be held in the hall in an hour's time.

Boaz tensed.

"Do you want to go?" asked Kati.

"I want to go, but I won't."

"I won't go either. We'll wait here."

"You want coffee?" asked Boaz. "It'll pass the time. Do you have to go to work?"

"Me?"

"Yes."

"No, not today. You know what, make me coffee. Black, you know, the way you make it."

"Coming right up," said Boaz, very pleased and flattered, and limped to the kitchen.

"I'll make you real coffee," he said to her, all smiles, and filled the coffee pot with water.

How Kati wished that her husband would get a normal job, and that he would stop feeling like a nothing, but some things, she knew, were beyond her capacities. She didn't want to spoil the moment and she said nothing, except that the coffee was excellent.

The children came home at one o'clock. They had come in second in the competition. They were all so happy that they refused to take off their costumes when they sat down to eat the lunch that Boaz had prepared. At the end of the meal Kati got up and said that she had to go to work. Boaz said, "But honey you said before. . . . Never mind, it doesn't matter. Work is work. You go, sweetheart, I'll tidy up here."

"I'm taking the makeup case to return it to Olga."

"No, no," shouted Topaz. "Leave it here."

"I can't. I have to take it back to her, but I'll ask her if I can borrow it again. I promise."

"Phone her now," said Boaz.

"I don't know her last name. It's one of those complicated ones."

"Ah."

215

"I'll ask her, and I'll call you from the street to tell you what she said."

"You can call collect," said Boaz. "Just this once."

"Okay," she said. She took the makeup case and left the house. Outside she breathed a sigh of relief.

THAT EVENING BOAZ BEIT-HALAHMI went to play pool with his regular gang. They hardly spoke to each other, just played the game and smoked cigarettes. Boaz, who only smoked when he played pool, liked the tense silence during the game; it gave him a special kind of excitement. During a break, one of the regular players told him that he had recently gone to a certain psychic in Jerusalem and that this psychic was hot stuff. At first Boaz just listened without paying much attention, but then something the player said made him prick up his ears. The man told him that this Jerusalem psychic gave you a picture of the present and the future according to numerology, astrology and coffee grinds. And he went on to say that the Jerusalem psychic was so good that he was able to help people in all kinds of areas: marriage counseling, career guidance and communication with the inner self and even previous incarnations.

Before Boaz went home he got the psychic's telephone number, which he saved in his cell phone's phone book.

Boaz asked how much the psychic charged, and the man replied that he didn't take a fee, you left as much as you felt like, as much as you could afford, on the plate resting on his secretary's desk.

Boaz decided that he wouldn't give too much. Why should he? Let the psychic exercise a bit of charity on his behalf. In any case, previous incarnations didn't interest him. So he would tell the psychic in advance not to bother with previous incarnations. He only wanted to know about this incarnation.

On Sunday morning, after Kati had left, Beit-Halahmi called Jerusalem. A woman answered and made an appointment for him on the 20th of Adar, at three o'clock, on Haniviim Street in the capital. Boaz asked if it was an office or a residence, and the woman replied that it was an office, and that payment was made after the meeting, to her. She said that the fee was two hundred shekels minimum. If he wanted to give more, he was at liberty to do so.

On the Sunday and Monday of that week the weather was normal for the season, and for a change it didn't rain either. On Tuesday a very cold front, this time from Scandinavia, entered the area, and strong, icy winds began to blow again. In the hilly regions it snowed heavily, with roofs caving in and trees falling down from the weight. There were many casualties due to the cold. In addition, the routine terror attacks continued, at a rate of two or three a day. Before the rescue teams had finished evacuating the wounded from one bombing, another bomb exploded. The media went from one attack to the next, the television screen was split between the reports from the different sites, and at the bottom of the screen information hotline numbers ran past. At the same time the warnings, too, became a matter of routine. There were constant warnings about impending terror attacks and terrorist infiltrations, focusing on one, or more than one, area at a time. General alerts concerning the country as a whole were by now commonplace, and the security forces found it necessary to warn people not to become apathetic, but to remain alert and on the lookout for every suspicious movement, vehicle, man or woman. Because during this period women, too, were given religious authorization to carry out suicide bombings, and up to then, in the month of Adar, three suicide bombings by women had taken place, causing terrible devastation.

, , ,

The evening before his visit to the psychic in Jerusalem, Boaz tried to draw 400 shekels from the ATM. After entering his secret number he was about to request 200, but after the various sums it was possible to withdraw appeared on the display, he was tempted to draw out 400. The display announced, "Your bank balance does not allow for the withdrawal of the sum in question," and Boaz pressed "Another sum" and requested 280. This time the machine responded affirmatively, and ejected the money in a number of bills, which he tucked into the secret back compartment of his wallet with a feeling of great satisfaction.

"I'll manage with this too," he thought as he did so. "Two hundred for the psychic and eighty for the gas, and if there isn't any oil, which there definitely isn't, either motor oil or brake oil, then there isn't, what can I do about it."

On the 20th of Adar, his wife could have told him that she was flying to Mars for a vacation with the children, or that the children weren't even his, but some other Tom, Dick, or Harry's, like on one of those soap operas she was always watching – Boaz Beit-Halahmi was in such a state of suspense that he was deaf to everything but what was happening in his own mind.

When they all finally left the house, he muttered a hasty goodbye, dressed as warmly as he could, including a parka, a muffler, a hat and a pair of gloves donated by the nation to the Beit-Halahmi family, and set out for Jerusalem.

No more than six, maybe seven, times in his life had Boaz visited the city holy to three religions. Mainly during his military service. Twenty years had passed since then, and he had not become better informed about the streets of the city in the meantime. In the pouch in the door of his car he had an old book of road maps covering the whole country, and including street maps of the big towns. In bygone days, when Beit-Halahmi was a taxi driver picking people up at Ben Gurion Airport and taking them to destinations all over the country, this book had given him a sense of security, but now he was afraid. He listened to the radio. Apart from updates on traffic jams, on the snow, the movement of the clouds and the wind, they kept on repeating, over and over again: six targeted red alerts concerning terror strikes in Jerusalem.

Beit-Halahmi, who wanted very much to start a new life, and was very keen to know how to bury his old life deep in the ground, the way they buried radioactive waste (he had seen this on the Discovery channel, with concrete and earth and more concrete and earth), set out on the expressway to the capital in his brown Ford Cortina, feeling anxious about the future. His pulse was racing, he had a pain in his stomach and pressure in his chest. He looked at the other cars driving on the highway to Jerusalem and imitated the confident expressions on the faces of the drivers. He thought that the complacent expression would have a calming effect on his inner turmoil and panic.

As he overtook a truck, he made up his mind not to go to any crowded places, not to sit in any cafes, and he was glad that he had brought a thermos of black coffee with him from home. He returned to the right lane, slowed down, carefully poured some coffee into a cup and sipped it, doing everything skillfully and without spilling a drop. He had done the same thing hundreds of times when he worked as a taxi driver.

And then he remembered that once, when he took his car in for repairs to a garage in Yavneh, someone had given him a tape of the singer Zohar Argov. The guy that gave him the tape, a mechanic who had become religious, told Boaz

220

that he was related to the dead singer, and that he recommended with all his heart that he listen to the tape on the road to Jerusalem. Boaz remembered the conversation vividly. It took place on the day that another popular singer, Ofra Haza, had died, and everybody in the garage was talking about all the Sephardi singers who had already died.

From that day until now, Beit-Halahmi had not listened to the tape, because he hadn't had any occasion to travel to Jerusalem. But now it all came back to him, the mechanic's insistence, and the connection he had made between the tape and the journey to Jerusalem, and he pulled over for a moment, at the safest place he could find, rummaged through the glove compartment, which was full of old papers, until he came across the cassette, which was the only one he possessed, hiding behind the automobile registration and insurance papers. Boaz didn't want to know, it seemed to him that all the documents were out of date, but he counted on the police being busy with security and not having the manpower to worry about fining him for stopping on the side of the expressway and for his vehicle registration being out of date.

He inserted the cassette into his old tape deck, and got back into the traffic going east. The music filled the cold interior of the brown Ford Cortina, which was cold because its heater didn't work.

At first, Beit-Halahmi couldn't understand what the newly religious mechanic was getting at. He knew the songs – who didn't know them? – they were all famous old hits, and he stopped the tape player, filling the car with a stream of news reports. The newscaster stressed that there were red alerts from the Islamic Jihad, the Tanzim, the military wing of Hamas, the regular wing of the Fatah, the Izzul Deen Al Qassam Brigades and the Al-Aqsa Martyrs Brigades, and she repeated that Jerusalem was the target, and that the police and the border police were out in force, and the forces who weren't already present in the capital were on their way there, and Boaz, who was also on his way there, switched back to the tape.

After listening to two or three songs, Boaz classified the cassette as the best of Argov's depression-songs, and he came to the conclusion that the aim of the mechanic was to make him feel so lonely that he would have to believe in God. Boaz Beit-Halahim believed in God all the way to Jerusalem. Usually he didn't think about it. He didn't think that God needed people to believe in him in order to feel that he existed. It seemed to him a little un-Godlike. But who was he? God? How did he know what God needed?

He went back to the beginning of the tape and listened to it again. After that, he listened to the song "Alone" over and over again, and he grew sad, because he could identify with the singer.

The song "Hidden Things" found him already singing along.... "We'll never understand, we'll never know...." and he felt better, because there were hidden things that he didn't understand, and here he was on his way to a psychic in order to get a few of those hidden things clarified.

Not far from the Jerusalem city limits there was a road-block. Armed policemen in flak jackets were checking all the cars and looking in their trunks. Boaz didn't know whether to be afraid of the policemen or to be glad that they were there. On the one hand, if they asked for his papers, he was in trouble; on the other hand, it was a good thing there was somebody doing this serious work. He stood in the winding line with all the other cars, and looked at the snow piled up outside and on Jerusalem in the distance. Suddenly he felt very moved by the beauty greeting his eyes, and he was immediately sorry that he wasn't experiencing this beauty with his wife and his children. At that moment no snow was falling, but all around the mountains were white. He wanted to bring back some snow for the children, but he didn't have anything to put it in, and he thought to himself that later on, after he was through with the psychic, he would get hold of a plastic bag and fill it with snow. He would say that a friend of his had gone to Jerusalem and brought back a huge bagful of snow for all the children, and he had given him some too.

A border guard inspected his car, and a policeman examined his face. After the border guard had searched the trunk he nodded at the policeman, who said, "Go," with the same guttural pronunciation as his wife, which gave him a tremendous feeling of legitimization for this trip of his. Even though his papers were apparently not in order, Beit-Halahmi felt that he was on the side of the good guys.

At the entrance to Jerusalem he didn't have a clue whether to go right or left. He took a right and stopped at a red light. Next to him was a man of secular appearance, whose car was plastered with stickers saying, "The Holy One Blessed be He, we love you."

Boaz stuck his head out of the window and asked him the way to Haniviyim Street, the man gave him directions, and when the lights changed he called out to him, "And when you get there, ask...." and drove away. His breath remained hanging in the air behind him for two or three seconds, until it disappeared.

Boaz drove into a white Jerusalem. For a minute he listened to a Hassidic song on a religious radio station, but after they started talking he looked for the stations he usually listened to, but he didn't know what frequencies they were on in the Jerusalem area, and instead his radio started playing Arab music. Boaz turned it off. The silence that fell in the car made him uneasy, and he turned it on again, and fiddled with the knob until he found a local, Hebrew-speaking station, where they were explaining how snow was formed. He listened, learning the subject as he advanced, according to the instructions of the passers-by, into the city center. On the radio they explained how the nucleus of a snowflake grows and grows and grows until it forms a big ice crystal. The big ice crystal combines with other crystals like itself, and because of its weight. . . .

"What do you think you're doing?" someone yelled at him from a car coming in the opposite direction, just as he was trying to remember the instructions of the last person who had given him directions. "This is a one-way street. . . ."

Boaz muted the radio, stopped at the side of the road, took out his map book and found the Jerusalem street map. He identified his location on the map and with a pen that had been warped by the heat of the previous summer plotted his route to Haniviyim Street. From the moment that he had the route marked, he felt calm.

A suspicious object had been discovered on Jeremiah Street. Boaz waited with everyone else for the road to be opened to traffic. The suspicious object turned out not to be a bomb, and he continued on his way.

A few minutes later he found himself on Haniviyim Street, and almost immediately located the tall office building that housed the office of the psychic. In the parking lot next to the building there were ten parking spots laid out, with a sign saying: Parking reserved exclusively for clients of the Pure Light Institute. Other vehicles will be towed away.

Boaz felt important, as a client of Pure Light himself, and parked his car in one of the reserved spots next to a Toyota, which he said to himself must belong to the owner of Pure Light – in other words to the psychic himself.

It was freezing cold outside. He couldn't believe how cold it was. He quickly wrapped himself in his scarf, put on his gloves, and looked around for the entrance to the building.

THERE WERE THREE PEOPLE WAITING in the waiting room. Two men and a woman. One of the men had a Jerusalem Beitar soccer team scarf round his neck. They were talking to each other when Boaz came in, and he asked, "Are you together?"

"No," they replied. And the owner of the Beitar scarf added, "Everyone has his own troubles."

Boaz sat down, but before doing so he looked out of the window at the magnificent white view. On a clear day, he said to himself, perhaps you can see Masada from here, the Dead Sea, Jordan.

He sat down and looked at the characters waiting for their turn. He wondered where their cars were, the only car in the parking space was that Toyota, but after a second it occurred to him that just because he had come by car, it didn't necessarily mean that the other people in the waiting room had arrived at the psychic's door by the same means.

A woman who looked as if she belonged in the place came out of one of the rooms.

"Who are you?" she asked Boaz.

"Boaz Beit-Halahmi. I have an appointment at three o'clock."

"You'll have to wait," she said. "There's a delay."

"Delay?" repeated Boaz, unfamiliar with the English word.

"We're running late. You'll have to be patient."

"Okay. As long as I don't have to drive back in the dark."

"No chance of that," she said confidently. "You can take off your hat and gloves. The heater is on."

"You're right," said Boaz in embarrassment, and did as she suggested.

> , , ,

At twenty to four he opened a door which bore the name plate: *Doctor Amihud Shilo – Specialist, Fortune Teller, and Problem Solver.*

Boaz thought that as soon as the inside of the room was revealed to him, he would see all kinds of crystal balls, curtains, a lot of soft fabrics, and there would be a smell of incense and aromatic oils in the air. It was even possible, thought Boaz, that the psychic himself would be hiding behind a screen or curtain of some kind, and only his arms and hands, smeared with the oil that was the source of the strong smell, would emerge from time to time from behind the screen. However, Dr. Amihud Shilo's office was furnished with a shiny black desk, a tall chair smelling of leather for the psychic, another chair on the other side of the desk for the client, and on the desk, facing the owner, a computer with a thin screen, a keyboard shaped like a wave, and a mouse not connected to the computer by any visible means.

Shilo said to Boaz, "Good afternoon, sir. Sit down."

Boaz sat down and inspected the man on the other side of the desk. He felt quite disappointed. The psychic looked like a high-up official in the local council, one of those whom Boaz was always imploring to divide his debt up into as many payments as possible, and maybe let him off a few of them. As a result of this association, Boaz felt slightly repulsed by the man sitting opposite him.

Shilo asked Boaz for his personal details. His first and last name, date of birth according to the Hebrew calendar, date of birth according to the Gregorian calendar, hour of birth, family status, house number, vehicle license number and what floor he lived on.

"You work with a computer?" asked Boaz, disappointed.

"I work with calculations that the computer can make in

a minute, and that would take me quarter of an hour. So all that remains for me is to use my intuition. I interpret the data. This the computer can't do. Your numerological number is five."

"Five," Boaz echoed.

The secretary came in with black coffee.

"Drink it, we'll turn the glass over and see what comes up."

"Listen," Boaz suddenly remembered. "I don't want to hear about previous incarnations."

"What do you mean?"

"Previous incarnations. I was told that you give information about previous incarnations. I don't want to know about previous incarnations."

"So how will you do the Tikkun and put things right?"

"I'll do it, believe me. I really want to put my life in order. All I need is a push in the right direction – I don't care where it comes from."

Shilo looked at the screen, and wrote down numbers on a sheet of paper. Boaz drank the coffee and turned the glass over. After a while Shilo looked at the empty glass, typed, and said nothing. Boaz felt tense.

"Are you involved with racing cars?" asked Shilo.

"No, but I was once a taxi driver."

"Did you have an accident?"

"Right! You can see that?"

"I can see that you limp. I'm not blind."

"Sorry."

Shilo returned to the screen. His face was illuminated by a faint light from an unclear source, but Boaz was sure that it came from some light switched on by the psychic himself, by means of one of the keys on his computer, even. And thus illuminated, the psychic said:

"You're young in spirit. There is a big stain on your past. Perhaps a great abandonment. You're very disappointed in the human race, but in order to go on living you have to regain your faith. You love children. You love cooking. Your wife is undergoing a crisis, she's fed up. She works at some menial job that she hates. You don't work. She hates you because of it. Not a lot, but enough to produce a lot of negative energy that she spreads around."

"There's something to what you say," said Boaz.

For a long time Shilo went on inspecting Beit-Halahmi's coffee grounds. Boaz was bored and looked outside at the snowy roofs of the city that was the cause of so much strife, and he wondered how much longer people would go on fighting in it and over it. Shilo said, "Did you come here by car?"

"Yes."

"Your own car?"

"Yes."

"Is it new?"

"No, an '87."

"An antique. You know that you have a problem with your nerves? You're very, very nervous. Sometimes violent. You should see a neurologist. Have you ever seen a neurologist?"

"Yes, he gave me pills, but they impaired my motor skills, and I've got enough problems with them as it is."

"So that's it, you stopped taking them?"

"Yes."

"You sometimes break things, right? I can see a lot of frustration here."

"I admit that I have broken things. But I won't do it anymore."

"You need work. That's the long and the short of it. Go and work, or hang on – what's your disability rating?"

"Nineteen percent."

"Go see a doctor. I'm telling you that you can get fifty percent. You have a problem with your peripheral nervous system, it's quite clear. I can't say whether it's a consequence of the accident or not. Go to a doctor and get yourself screened."

"Never mind about the disability allowance – I want to work. I'm going crazy at home."

"Tell me," said Shilo, with a hesitant look, "were you ever a fisherman?"

"No."

"Then what's this?" Shilo stared at the coffee grounds. "What is this? Turkeys? Geese?"

"Chickens."

"Capons?"

"Eggs, slaughtered afterwards. But we didn't do the slaughtering ourselves."

"Mmmmm . . . and now it's all gone."

"Right. It's gone. I should have been a poultry farmer . . . but. . . ."

And he told Shilo the story in brief. Boaz was already sick and tired of hearing himself tell the story of his disinheritance. He felt so bored by it all that he interrupted himself in the middle and said, "But how long can I go on crying over spilt milk? Enough is enough."

"Quite right. And the sooner the better, because otherwise I see here the destruction of a family in Israel. Divorce. Pain and suffering."

"Oh my God!" cried Boaz. "Okay, from now on I'm going to take things seriously in hand. I have to pull myself together."

"That's the spirit," said Shilo. "I wish you luck. And

remember, Amihud Shilo told you that you can save your life from ruin. It all depends on you."

"Thanks," said Beit-Halahmi.

He left the room, and put a two hundred shekel note into a big glass bowl in the waiting room. In less than a second the secretary fished it out, and said to Boaz, "Good luck. Will we be seeing you again?"

"Yes."

He walked out of the door, more determined that ever to pull himself out of the mud into which his life had sunk.

The Ford Cortina was covered with snow. Boaz looked at it, not knowing whether to remove it or leave it to melt. He didn't know what people were supposed to do with snow. Shilo's words troubled him. How did he know those things? And what crisis, destruction and divorce were that man and his state-of-the-art computer talking about? He felt a sense of anticlimax, and with it guilt at having wasted two hundred shekels, with which he could have done a lot of shopping on the weekend. He wanted to hit his fellow pool player for praising the psychic. His wife was angry with him – he knew that without the help of Pure Light.

He got into the car and turned on the wipers to clean the snow that had collected on the windshield. Then he switched on the radio. While he had been in Pure Light there had been a bombing in Hadera. Boaz heard the Prime Minister's spokesman saying, "From now on nothing will be as it was. There's a before and there's an after."

Boaz switched off the radio. How many times had he heard government spokesmen say there was a before and after. Enough. Why didn't they do something? But what? He asked himself again, and then he put the subject out of his mind altogether, he scolded himself for being sucked into worries about the fate of the State of Israel again, instead of worrying about the fate of his family and his children. He made up his mind: first thing tomorrow morning he would go to the Ramle employment office, be first in line, at the most second, and take any job they offered him.

Then he would go to the HMO clinic and get a referral to a neurologist to get himself examined. Maybe there was something chemically wrong with him that made him nervous. Chemical medicine was very advanced today. He had heard there were pills that fixed everything.

The pleasant streets of a neighborhood he had driven into while his mind was occupied with these thoughts led Boaz to think that perhaps he should move the whole family to Jerusalem. Then he dismissed the thought immediately as completely illogical. Who would leave Ganei Aviv for Jerusalem today? The children were getting along in school, they had come in second in the costume competition, they were satisfactory students, good kids. Why move them? And in general, how much did an apartment cost in Jerusalem? And where was the employment office here? He didn't want to live in a place that three religions were fighting over.

Many thoughts that he had not yet pinned down were running around in his head. He would have to identify and deal with them, otherwise they would bother him all the way to Lod and perhaps after that as well. Boaz was not yet ready to go home, and anyway, he had always liked driving and thinking. When he was a taxi driver, he had not been one of those who never shut their mouths, but one of those who never open it. The fare would give him an address. He would mark out the route in his head, or look up the address in his map book, memorize the way there with his photographic memory, and the rest was plain sailing.

If the passenger tried to start up a conversation, he would get the kind of curt replies from Beit-Halahmi that discouraged any desire on his part to go on talking. If the fare spoke to him in English, Boaz said he didn't understand, even though he understood and spoke English fairly well.

Now Beit-Halahmi drove around Jerusalem, trying to figure it out. It seemed a very complicated place to him. So many streets were named after famous people – like Maimonides, for example.

Boaz decided to cruise the streets a little longer. As he did so he would no doubt come across a blue or green road sign indicating the way to Tel Aviv. He glanced at the seat next to him, sure he would find the map book there, but all he saw was the Zohar Argov cassette. He didn't want to stop and ask people, excuse me, please . . . he didn't want to come into contact with others lest their words dilute the determination mobilized by his willpower in the wake of Amihud Shilo's words. And also he was ashamed to open the window and ask all kinds of Jerusalemites, "Excuse me, how do I get to Tel Aviv?"

He felt there was some kind of sin here, as if every Jew was obliged to know how to find his way in the labyrinths of Jerusalem. As opposed to a Jerusalemite, who you were obligated to help if he lost his way in Tel Aviv or some other town.

The number of policemen and border guards he saw was really impressive, and Boaz envied the Jerusalemites for being at the center of attention of most of the security forces in the country.

⁊ ⁊ ⁊

He drove along Haniviyim Street, turned down a little street, and from there into another street, and found himself back on Haniviyim Street again. He drove further and arrived at a street named Ki'ah. It was an acronym. Boaz was an expert at acronyms. At home he solved crossword puzzles. The children always came to him with their questions. Who else could they go to? Kati? Then he turned onto Agrippas Street and asked himself who Agrippas was? When he got home he would open the *One Thousand Famous People* encyclopedia he had bought secondhand. He was always hearing about Agrippas Street on the news. It was high time he found out who he was.

So he drove down Agrippas, and some other street, until he reached Ben Yehuda, and from there straight down Bezalel Street, until he came to Yizhak Rabin Avenue. Ah, Rabin, he murmured, and he felt at home, because he knew Rabin, after all, and he had cried when he was assassinated.

He felt hungry and regretted not having brought something to eat from home. His sandwiches were renowned in their house. He was the one who made the kids their sandwiches for school, layer upon layer, perfect, precise, and now here he was without a sandwich for himself.

He went on driving until he came to Museums Avenue, and he wondered how many museums there were on Museums Avenue. Boaz knew that this was an excellent question for *Who Wants to Be a Millionaire*, even if it wasn't fair to contestants who didn't live in Jerusalem.

At a deli on Yehuda Burla Street there were sandwiches for sale. Beit-Halahmi stopped the car and went to buy a sandwich. The sandwich cost him fifteen shekels, so he didn't get anything to drink. When he got back into the car he was already planning the deli he was going to open in Ganei-Aviv, which would sell sandwiches of all kinds at affordable prices. He was busy thinking of a catchy name for the deli when he remembered that he didn't have a penny to invest, and with an uneasy feeling in his stomach he went on driving, hoping that he would soon find a way out and onto the Tel Aviv road.

Now Boaz turned north, he had a feeling that this would take him to a road leading out of the city. He stopped at the side of the road to seriously search for his map book. Before he had put it down on the seat next to him, so where was it now? There was such a mess in the car, it would take him an hour to find it. A bus behind him honked, because his car was blocking the road, and he got back into the driver's seat and went on driving up the road. He was dying to be on his way back already, to work on what the psychic had said, and to come to meaningful conclusions that would lead directly to action.

In North Jerusalem, Boaz planned to take a left, in other words go west. This would put him in the right direction for Tel Aviv. He understood this from the position of the sun, and he was also sure that he would find a blue or green road sign there – never mind which – all he wanted now was to go home and he didn't care how he got there.

On the way north he passed streets that he had passed before, and this gave him a feeling of familiarity and also of satisfaction, since he was beginning to get the way the streets were organized here mapped out in his head. All the streets he was passing now – Boaz knew the people they were named after, albeit not personally. Rabin Avenue again, then Shazar Avenue, he remembered President Shazar very well, then Jeremiah Street, which reminded him of his matriculation exams in Bible Studies. He didn't get the question on Jeremiah – he just remembered that there was one. And then Harel Brigade, Levi Eshkol, Chaim Bar Lev, and Yekutiel Adam.

On Yekutiel Adam Street he stopped and left the engine idling. Suddenly he remembered the circumstances of the major general's death. He himself had been quite young. He remembered how sad it had made him. Boaz remembered the moment he had heard about his death on the radio and grown sad. And thus, in a melancholy mood, he removed the cling-film wrapping from the sandwich and bit into it. After he finished eating the sandwich he went on sitting in the car, watching the snowflakes pile up on the windshield, and running the windshield wipers from time to time.

A strange, deep, fateful mood came over Beit-Halahmi as he started the car and turned west, taking good care not to enter Beit Hanina or any other Arab suburb, especially as darkness was about to fall. When he had no alternative and thought he was lost, he turned back into Moshe Dayan Avenue again – and there he gave up and asked for directions. Someone explained that he had to get to Yigael Yadin, right into Golda Meir, and in Yigael Alon – or better, make a U-turn. . . .

He had been trying to get out of Jerusalem for nearly a hour. A cold sweat broke out on his back. He opened the window to feel the cold wind. The sun had already gone down. Boaz wanted to be home as early as possible, so that Kati wouldn't be annoyed with him and start asking questions, lest the consequent yelling and fighting lead to the breakup that Shilo had spoken about.

Now he asked every third person how to get onto the Tel Aviv road, and people helped him. They did their best, and to tell the truth they explained it to him nicely and slowly, it was just that he was tired and confused. When he finally got onto Road 443 and saw the green sign saying Tel Aviv, he stepped on the gas as hard as he could and raced ahead, listening to the radio and news flashes. The further west he drove the clearer the reception became.

Precisely at the moment the radio began to play David Bowie's song about the man who got lost in space, Boaz Beit-Halahmi suddenly heard hailstones hitting his car, very loudly and decisively, and he automatically turned on the windshield wipers.

But it wasn't hail. It was a terrorist ambush. The gunmen had hidden behind a snowdrift and fired forty bullets at him. Boaz died instantly. On the radio the song went on playing to the end. The shooters escaped. The driver in the car behind him alerted the security forces on his cell phone, while he himself stepped on the gas and drove away at 160 kilometers an hour.

The security forces arrived a few minutes later with an ambulance. A doctor pronounced Boaz dead. A policeman from the border patrol turned off the windshield wipers.

"I don't hold the popular belief that we come into this world in order to learn," said Angelica Gomeh to her student Kati Beit-Halahmi, who was busy making up the life-sized head of doll with particularly problematic features, which Angelica had sculpted herself.

"Do you know what we're doing here?" Angelica gave her student a questioning look, and continued, "I don't know what we're doing here. You have to apply concealer under the eyes before putting on the makeup. Don't forget. It takes off years."

"Sorry. You're right," said Kati.

"Not like that! With the tips of your fingers. Pat it in. Here, let me show you. Don't smear, pat. So it looks natural, not painted. The cream is very important too. If you work in television, and someone arrives made-up from home, tell her first that what she did is great, but for television you need a completely different concept. You know what concept means?"

"I've heard the word."

"Approach."

"Aha."

"Because of the lighting, you have to exaggerate. You know why? Because everything on the screen looks seven times greater than it is. So we have to conceal or emphasize. Do you understand?"

"Yes."

"Why aren't you taking notes today? Didn't you bring your notebook?"

"I forgot it at home," said Beit-Halahmi, shamefaced.

"Never mind. I'll give you a sheet of paper. You can copy it into your notebook at home."

She brought her a blank sheet of paper.

"Have you got lines to put underneath?"

"What?" asked Gomeh.

"Lines. So it won't come out crooked."

"Concentrate, and it won't come out crooked," said Gomeh firmly.

"Okay."

"Write: Sequence of operations. We'll expand upon each one later. Some we've already learned. But I want you to have it down pat, exact as a Swiss clock. One: Cleaning previous makeup from the subject's face. Two: A new line for two, okay?

"Application of non-greasy moisturizer. To be gently patted in. Three: New line. Concealer. Four: Makeup. Some people reverse the order. I recommend patting in the concealer, then the makeup on top of it, and if corrections are required – then a drop of concealer in addition. Five...."

Beit-Halahmi wrote down fifteen articles before saying, "My hand hurts."

"Remind me to teach you how to relax your hands. It's very important for the fingers to be loose."

While the two of them were busy with the fifteen articles, two messengers on behalf of the state, wearing army uniforms, arrived at Micah Reiser Street in Lod. The children were alone at home.

The two men rang the bell.

"Who is it?" called Adi from behind the door.

"We've come to see your mother."

"Our mother's not at home and we're not allowed to open the door."

"Where is your mother?" one of the men asked through the door and Topaz answered, "At work."

"Where does she work?"

"In buildings. In the stairwells."

"Do you know where exactly?" They both hated their work.

"No. Daddy knows. You have to wait for Daddy. Daddy's not here either. We can't open the door. Mommy and Daddy won't let us."

"It's getting complicated," said the taller of the two.

"Yes," his colleague agreed.

They rang the neighbors' bell. Russian immigrants, a couple in their fifties.

"Come in, come in," said the neighbors. "How can we help you?"

For two hours the messengers sat in silence in the neighbors' living room. Their hosts offered them coffee, cookies, but the two soldiers declined their offers. One of them, the shorter, asked how many children the Beit-Halahmis had and was told four. He whispered to his companion, "At least they'll get 'Victims of Hostile Actions' benefits now. Economically they're fixed up."

"How can you talk like that?" demanded his colleague. "What kind of a sick way is that to think? It's disgusting. That's what you're thinking about? Think about the children. About their shock. Their father's dead."

"He's dead and gone, there's nothing to be done. As for their shock, they'll get over it. But what about later on? What's wrong with thinking about later on?"

"Me you and the God by my side one day we'll win the fight. . ." Kati Beit-Halahmi sang along with the driver's radio on the direct bus to Lod. She was thinking about what she was going to say to her husband about getting home so late, but before she found the answer she began reviewing various articles from the fifteen stages of makeup application that Angelica Gomeh had taught her that day. She had them all written down on a sheet of paper folded up in her bag, but Kati enjoyed the satisfaction of knowing that she already remembered most of them by heart. "Me you and the God by my side one day we'll win the fight," she sang again. "Not by might but because of the wind blowing at my back. . . . Not by might. . . ."

She was in high spirits. She sang relatively loudly, too, so that the people in front of her and behind her would hear, she had a nice voice, so why not?

Outside, the rain was coming down in floods. Kati looked out of the window at all the drops advancing towards her face and bursting on the glass. It was a good thing she had this windowpane in front of her, she mused. And then she sat up, struck by a thought – all the ground is soaking wet now, wet to its depths. We won't hear about drought for a good few years now, they'll shut up at last with all those advertisements of theirs about not using water. She was sick and tired of them already. Now they could all shut up.

There was a news flash. The driver increased the volume, the rain was interfering with the reception besides making it hard to hear. They heard: "In a shooting incident on Road 443, an Israeli citizen of about forty from the center of the country was killed a short while ago. His family has not yet been notified. Forty bullets were fired at the victim from an ambush set by terrorists behind a snow drift. He was pronounced dead by a doctor who arrived on the scene with the ambulance. In another shooting on the Wadi Ara Road, Varda Bar-On, aged sixty, from Afula was mortally wounded.

241

We are now going directly to the Emek Hospital in Afula, to talk to Professor Aaron Yitzhak, head of the trauma unit. Shalom, Professor Yitzhak, we're on the air."

"Shalom."

"What can you tell us about the wounded woman's condition?"

"At the moment, her condition is severe to critical. Resuscitation was performed. We succeeded in obtaining a pulse and sent the patient to undergo a CAT scan in order to assess the extent of her injuries. There is extensive damage to the inner organs as well as damage to the cervical vertebrae. We are doing everything we can. . . ."

After the interview with the doctor the broadcast was returned to the studio, where they began to play a song. In the past, the not very distant past, when there was a terrorist strike, the tone of the broadcasters would change, to something slower and sadder, and the songs they played were quieter, and usually in Hebrew. But when bombs and death became a matter of routine, a kind of convention came into being where, after up to five deaths, the broadcasts would continue as usual, and only from five and up would they go into a lower gear and play quiet songs, in English too, preferably about human destiny, such as "Dust in the Wind."

From ten dead and up, the radio networks switched to a far more serious mode, confined to Hebrew songs only, such as Corin Alal's "I Have No Other Country," or a new song, grim and realistic, composed in those terrible days and sung by Yehuda Poliker, "Who's Next in Line?"

From twenty dead and up, they changed the format to Plan B, like hospitals on high alert, and broadcast frequent news flashes interspersed with "Friendship" performed by the IDF Nahal Troupe or Esther Ofarim, "For a Man Is Like a Tree in the Field" sung by Shalom Hanoch and "When Angels Cry" sung by Yehudit Ravitz or Mati Caspi.

Now, with only one man dead and one wounded woman fighting for her life, the radio stations went on broadcasting ordinary songs, with an occasional reminder to their listeners that they and their country were facing a severe crisis that had to be overcome. The reminder and the motivation were conveyed to the Hebrew listener through the song "Our Road" sung by Sarit Vino-Elad and Roni Furstenberg, especially by the well-known line, "No it isn't easy, our road is not an easy one. . . ."

Kati's thoughts turned from the news to her personal affairs. She thought that when she got home, even before Boaz, who was probably furious with her by now for being so late, could take out his nerves on her, she would tell him the truth. The whole truth. She would also tell him how the condo association had united to cheat her out of her severance pay, and how she had been obliged to blackmail one of the employees at the bank. Luckily for her, she had hit on someone by chance who was really up to no good with the bank's money, and was also a nutcase who thought that everybody was out to get him. She would tell Boaz all about it. He was her husband after all. He would be angry at first, but afterwards he would be happy that she had broken out, she hoped.

Kati didn't like lying to her husband. She felt guilty enough as it was that his family had cast him out because of her. She had even cut herself off from a large part of her own family, in order to even things out somehow.

Deep in her heart, Kati really appreciated the fact that her husband had never even tried to renew his ties with anyone from his horrible, sick family, not even in secret, and she gave him a lot of credit for it. They sometimes talked about it. On more than a few occasions she had said to Boaz that she felt like going to that farm of theirs and killing them one by one, all his two-faced brothers and sisters and brothers-in-law and sisters-in-law, because of what they had done to him, and she also felt like slitting the throat of every single Beit-Halahmi there. She was quite capable of doing it right now, with their kitchen knife, all he had to do was say the word, and Boaz silenced her and said, "Shhhhh ... what kind of a way is that to talk? You're spoiling our children's good name."

All in all, Kati Beit-Halahmi knew why she had fallen in love with him and why in fact she was still turned on by him. It was because of the respect he showed for people, because they were human beings just like him, and that's why he forgave them, or almost forgave them. Like he always said to her when she wanted to go to the farm with the knife. He would calm her down and say, "Let it go, let it go, it doesn't matter. Let it go. Don't upset yourself, my eyes."

"I understand him even when he breaks things," said Kati to herself. "He's a human being too and they hurt him terribly, especially his parents. They hurt his manhood, my poor man."

Half an hour later, she rang her doorbell.

"Who is it?" her children asked from inside and she just had time to say, "Your mother."

And then the door of the neighbors' apartment opened. Two soldiers were standing in the doorway, facing her. Behind them the neighbor woman called her name, very timidly.

"Ka-ti."

She sensed immediately that something was wrong. It

244

was the same feeling she had felt when they told her that he was lying wounded in the Asaf Harofeh Medical Center, after his accident. There was no taxi now, but there was a car, only Boaz hardly ever drove anywhere in it. What could have happened?

The two soldiers introduced themselves. She invited them in, the neighbor hesitated outside for a moment, and then she joined them.

"Children go to your room!" said Kati. The children refused, but she yelled, "To your room!" and then she turned around, her eyes full of dread, and sat down on the sofa that they had bought in Bidya before the war broke out.

"What happened?"

"We regret to have to inform you that your husband, Boaz Beit-Halahmi, was killed in a shooting on Road 443. He was shot at close range. He didn't suffer at all."

Kati bowed her head.

"Maminka," cried the neighbor woman, and advanced towards her.

"No, no, no, no. . . ." murmured Kati, her head bowed and her hand hiding her eyes. The neighbor embraced her. The children came running out of their room.

"Mommy, what happened?"

"Daddy's dead," she said. "He's dead. They shot him. There was a terrorist attack. Daddy was in it and he died. We have to let the sons of bitches know," she said sullenly. "Oho," she flared up, "now I'll show them. Now I'll show them."

"Who?" asked the neighbor anxiously. "The Arabs?"

"The Arabs? How can I show the Arabs? His family. I'll show them. I'll give them a good taste of the pain Boaz kept inside him all these years."

She opened a cupboard and took out the Lod-Ramle telephone directory, which included all the agricultural settlements in the vicinity. The directory fell open in one place, as if it had been opened there many times before. And yes – it was Boaz's family's listing. He had pored over that page himself on numerous occasions, and so had she. How often she had wanted to phone them up and curse them. Now she would show them what was what. He must have gone to Jerusalem to put a note in the Western Wall, asking for them to make up with him, and died on the way back. My poor Boaz....

On the midnight news they showed a picture of Boaz Beit-Halahmi. Kati chose the picture from a pile of snapshots that had been waiting to be put into order for years. How often she and her husband had argued over who should do it and when. On television they said that the family of the deceased had been informed. Kati sat in front of the television and wept. The children fell asleep in the living room, next to her on the sofa. She too fell asleep there, at about two in the morning, with the television on.

On hearing the morning news, Angelica Gomeh made the connection between the dead man's name and her student, and she called her to verify her suspicions. As soon as she discovered that Kati was alone in the house with the children, with nobody to help her, Gomeh called for a taxi and went to Ganei-Aviv. During the time between her ordering the taxi and her arrival in Lod, the President of Israel received a text message on his cell phone to say that today, the 21st of Adar, he had to attend the funeral of the victim of a shooting attack in Lod. The funeral procession would set out at one o'clock in the afternoon. The mourners would assemble at the gate of the new cemetery. Further details would be supplied later.

About five minutes later, Kati received a phone call from the President's bureau, to inform her that Tekoa would attend the funeral, and for some reason this information calmed her greatly. When Angelica entered the Beit-Halahmi house, the first thing Kati said to her was, "The President is coming to the funeral," and Gomeh replied, "That's nice."

Angelica stayed by her student's side and listened to her. After that she taught her everything she knew about being in mourning, and the various stages she would pass through, and explained why it wasn't a good idea to rant and rave at the funeral and denounce her husband's family, out of respect for the dead man, may he rest in peace, and out of respect for the President of Israel, long may he live. In any case, said Gomeh, even if she wanted to kill Boaz's family with her own hands, they were going to die anyway, what were they, something special? Immortal? And Gomeh also spoke to her about the comedies she should watch during the seven day mourning period, and especially after it was over, when everyone disappeared back into their own lives and she, Kati, was left to cope with the new situation in her life, and she had to keep going, if only for the sake of her fatherless children.

A little after noon, on his way to the funeral, President Reuven Tekoa noticed a gray crane sitting on a treetop, and thought to himself that the crane probably didn't understand what had happened to the winter in this place to which he and his friends migrated every year. The President, who was an amateur ornithologist, saw from a distance that it was a gray crane. He knew that the cranes made life very difficult for the farmers who grew peanuts and chickpeas in the Huleh Valley and the western Negev. The Minister of Agriculture had once told him that the farmers complained to him about it. His conversation with the Agriculture Minister had taken place in other days – very different days, thought the President.

What was going to happen now? he asked himself. What would the gray crane do? What were the cranes going to eat this year? All the harvests had gone down the drain because of the cold. Israel was in a state of emergency.

"Look, a gray crane," said the President to his driver.

"Where?" asked the latter.

"High on the right, on the third pine tree from the left."

The driver asked what the bird's wing span was. Every bird the President showed him, the first thing the driver wanted to know was its wing span. Not if it was sedentary or migratory, vegetarian or carnivorous. Only the wing span.

"Two meters, two and a half meters."

"Wow," said the driver.

"If it hasn't missed the boat, it will probably fly on with its flock to Africa. There's nothing for it here."

"There's nothing here even for the birds," said the driver.

"Nice, very nice. So who is there something for here?"

The President didn't answer. The driver turned on the radio. They heard Kati Beit-Halahmi being interviewed before the funeral on a current affairs program on the Voice of Israel. She said, "I want to say something to the people of Israel."

"Yes?" the program presenter said encouragingly.

"They have to carry on and keep going. We have no other country."

"Thank you very much, Kati Beit-Halahmi," said the presenter enthusiastically. "Be brave."

"And I want to say something to the Prime Minister. . ." continued Kati Beit-Halahmi.

"Switch to another station," said the President. "I've had it up to here with all this talk."

"Once you didn't want anything but talk. What am I talking about, once? Only two days ago I put on music, and you said it wasn't nice to sing when people were dying."

"Quiet, all I want is quiet. No music and no talking. Just quiet."

Silence descended on the limousine. All they heard was the rain falling, and as they grew closer to Lod, the rain too subsided. The President opened the window and a cold wind blew onto his face. He touched his cheeks. They were colder than they had ever been. Colder than they were when he had gone with his wife Pua to visit their daughter in Boston, last autumn, and he had walked down JFK Street with the two of them, on a very rainy day, to buy her notebooks and pens for her second year at Harvard. She was studying history. For two weeks they had stayed there, to help her find an apartment not far from the university. They couldn't make up their minds whether to rent or buy. Tekoa and his wife said that they couldn't afford to buy. Their daughter said the investment would be worth it in the long run. Tekoa remembered that his daughter had been carrying a book entitled *The Burden of Southern History* and that the title had aroused his curiosity, but before he could ask her to hand him the book so that he could page through it, they reached the tall building where the apartment she wanted them to see was situated. His daughter rang the bell at the building's entrance and said, "Wait until you see the amazing view."

A NOTE ON THE TYPE

HUMAN PARTS has been set in Minion, a type designed by Robert Slimbach in 1990. An offshoot of the designer's researches during the development of Adobe Garamond, Minion hybridized the characteristics of numerous Renaissance sources into a single calligraphic hand. Unlike many faces developed exclusively for digital typesetting, drawings for Minion were transferred to the computer early in the design phase, preserving much of the freshness of the original concept. Conceived with an eye toward overall harmony, its capitals, lower case, and numerals were carefully balanced to maintain a well-groomed "family" resemblance – both between roman and italic and across the full range of weights. A decidedly contemporary face, Minion makes free use of the qualities the designer found most appealing in the types of the fifteenth and sixteenth centuries. Crisp drawing and a narrow set width make Minion an economical and easy going book type, and even its name reinforces its adaptable, affable, and almost self-effacing nature, referring as it does to a small size of type, a faithful or favored servant, and a kind of peach.

Design and composition by Carl W. Scarbrough